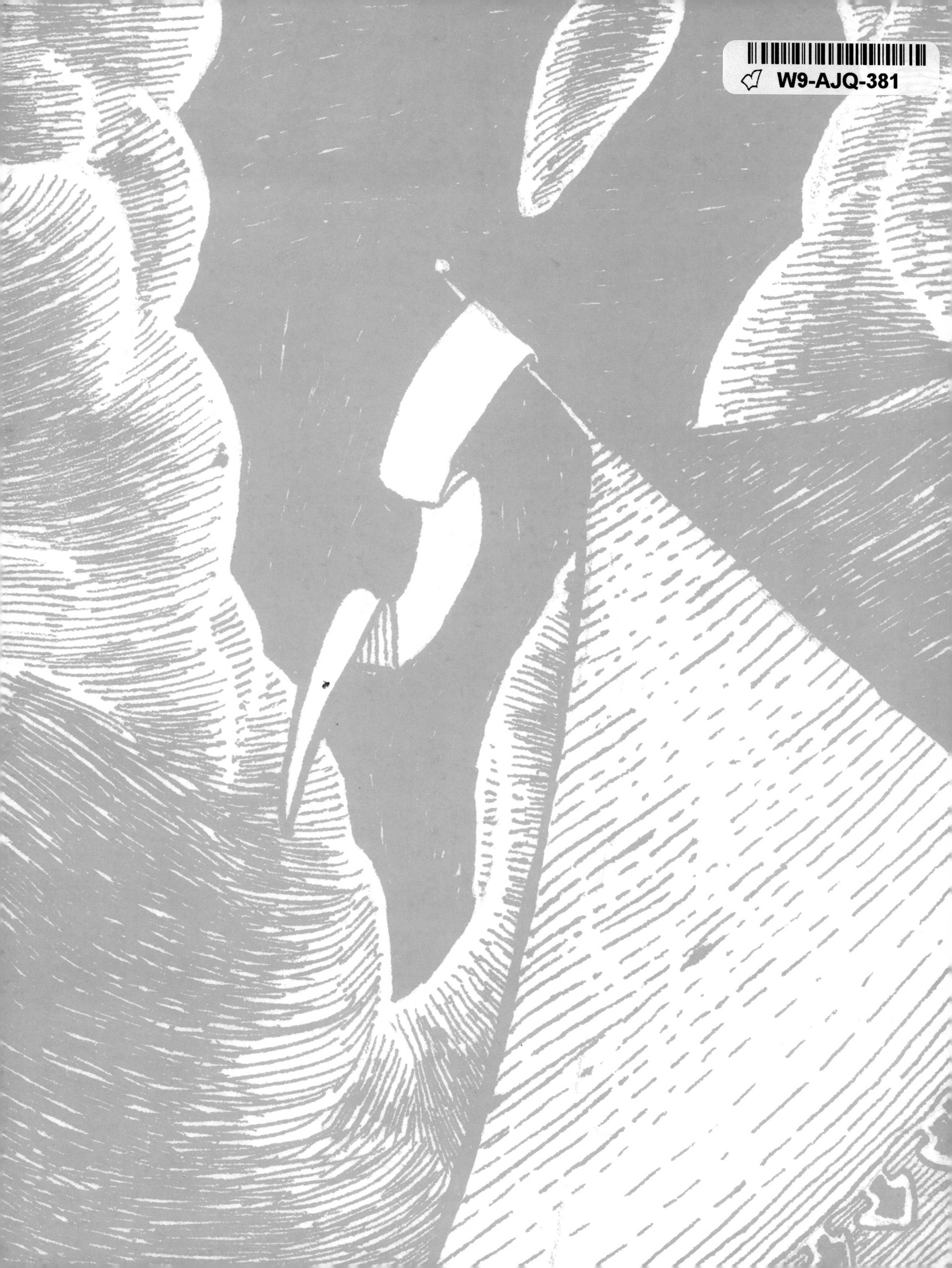

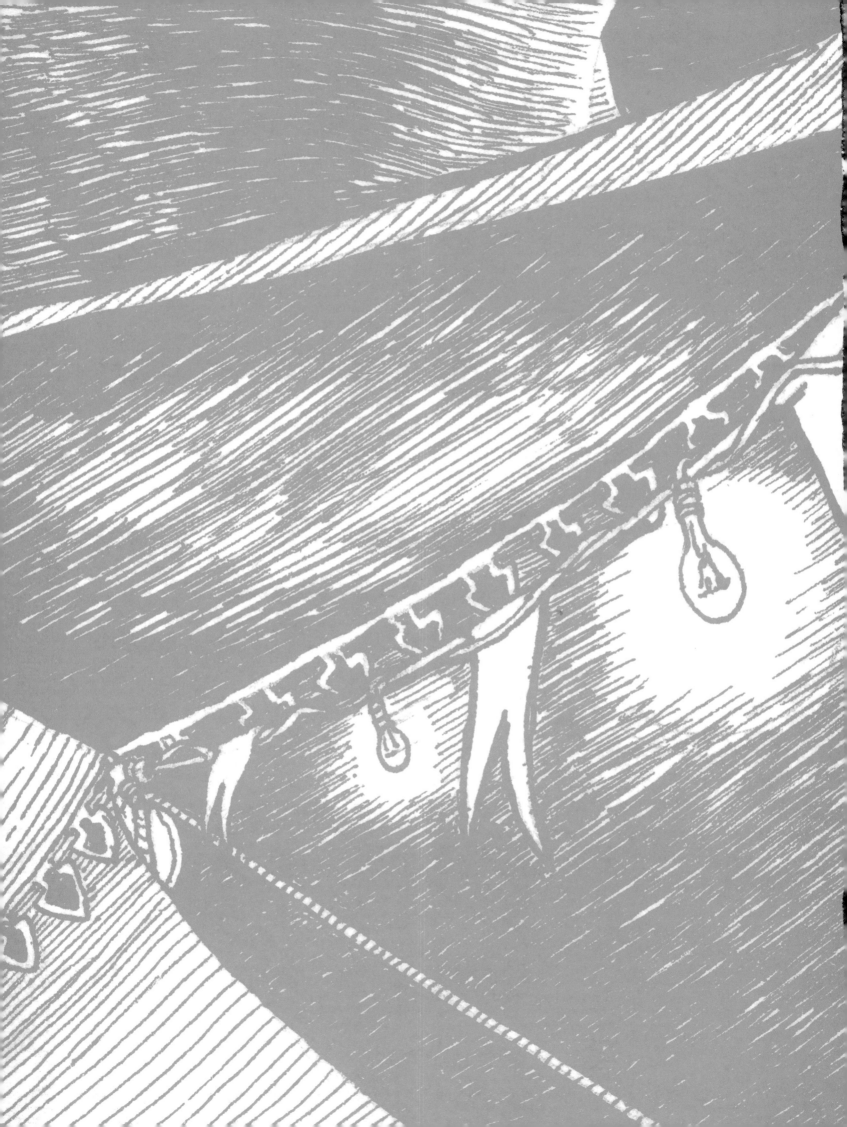

Salem Brownstone

ALL ALONG THE WATCHTOWERS

by John Harris Dunning
& Nikhil Singh

CANDLEWICK PRESS

"A wonderfully imaginative and stylish piece of work and a perfect example of the adventurous new directions that comic books should be taking in the future."
—**Alan Moore**, author of *Watchmen* and *V for Vendetta*

"*Salem Brownstone* is a hypnotically beautiful gothic fantasy."
—**Jefferson Hack**, *Dazed & Confused* Magazine

"*Salem Brownstone* kicked my ass and made me believe in the beautiful darkness of the world again."
—**Harmony Korine**, screenplay writer of *Kids* and director of *Gummo*

"*Salem Brownstone* is a graphic novel that is both original and compelling. There's a seamless relationship between the images and the text, and the characters linger in the mind."
—**Anthony Minghella**, director of *The Talented Mr. Ripley* and *The English Patient*

"Our new century demands a new charismatic comic-book magician to weave his spells on us. Updating classic conjurors like Mandrake and Doctor Strange with a twist of Oscar Wilde and Aubrey Beardsley, John Harris Dunning and Nikhil Singh have crafted a haunting, hypnotizing master of the mystic arts in *Salem Brownstone*. Their sharp, surprising storytelling and intense, imaginative illustration combine to create real magic on the page."
—**Paul Gravett**, author of *Graphic Novels: Everything You Need to Know* and director of London's Comica Festival

There are those who love the rum and unusual, the uncanny, the macabre. Perhaps they wish for thrilling horrors in their own seemingly mundane lives. . . . But they should beware what they wish for.

Take Salem Brownstone, for instance. For many years he ran the Sit & Spin Laundromat and was content with his lot. The laundromat was his own fiefdom, and the customers presented him with a never-ending cavalcade of variety. And yet, somewhere deep down, Salem believed he was destined for greater things—stranger things. Then one day they came to him in the unlikely form of a simple telegram. . . .

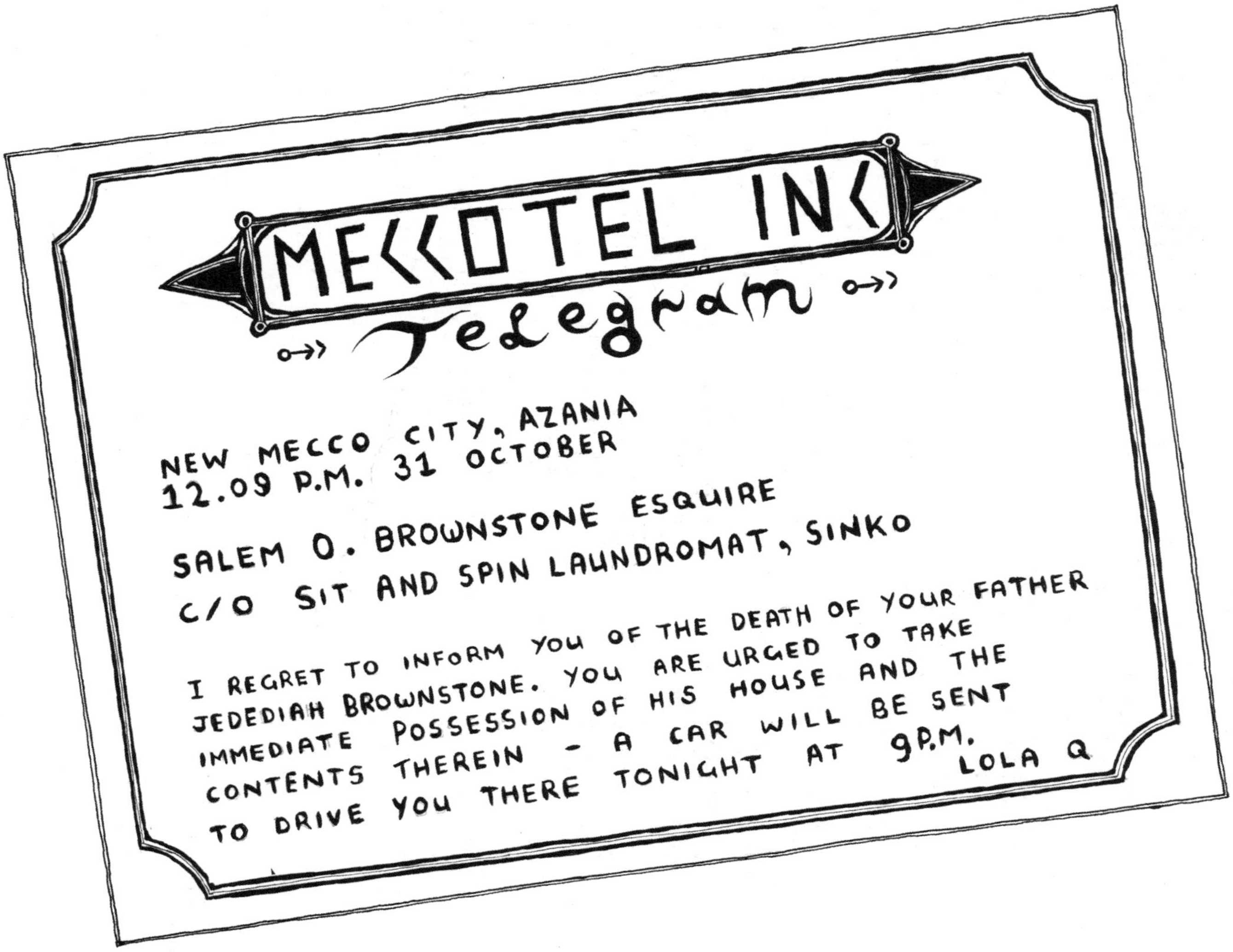

MECCOTEL INC

Telegram ◦→》 ◦→》

NEW MECCO CITY, AZANIA
12.09 P.M. 31 OCTOBER

SALEM O. BROWNSTONE ESQUIRE
C/O SIT AND SPIN LAUNDROMAT, SINKO

I REGRET TO INFORM YOU OF THE DEATH OF YOUR FATHER JEDEDIAH BROWNSTONE. YOU ARE URGED TO TAKE IMMEDIATE POSSESSION OF HIS HOUSE AND THE CONTENTS THEREIN - A CAR WILL BE SENT TO DRIVE YOU THERE TONIGHT AT 9 P.M.
LOLA Q

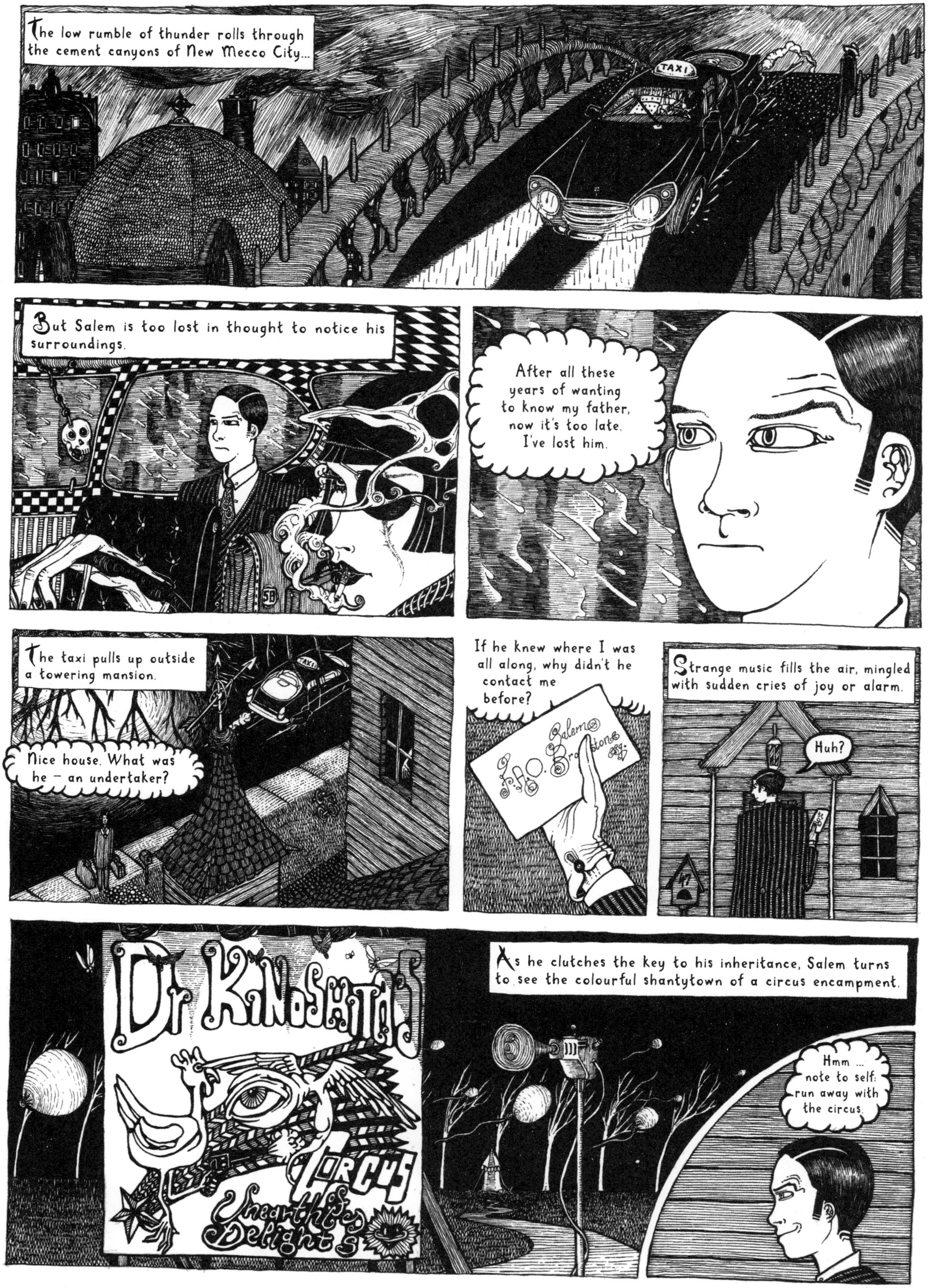
The low rumble of thunder rolls through the cement canyons of New Mecco City...
TAXI
But Salem is too lost in thought to notice his surroundings.
After all these years of wanting to know my father, now it's too late. I've lost him.
The taxi pulls up outside a towering mansion.
Nice house. What was he – an undertaker?
If he knew where I was all along, why didn't he contact me before?
Strange music fills the air, mingled with sudden cries of joy or alarm.
Huh?
Dr Kinoshita's Circus of Unearthliest Delights
As he clutches the key to his inheritance, Salem turns to see the colourful shantytown of a circus encampment.
Hmm ... note to self: run away with the circus.

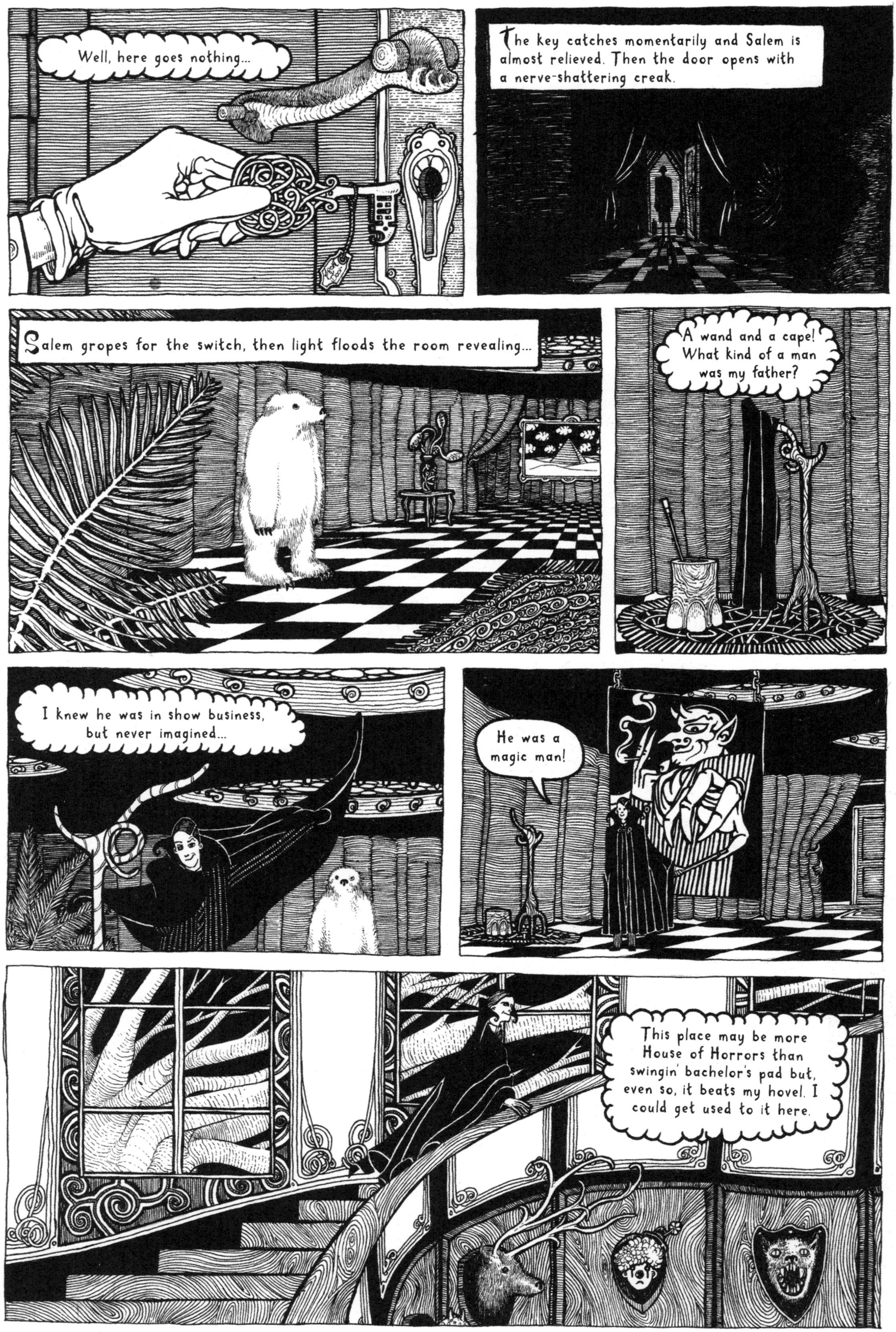
Well, here goes nothing...
The key catches momentarily and Salem is almost relieved. Then the door opens with a nerve-shattering creak.
Salem gropes for the switch, then light floods the room revealing...
A wand and a cape! What kind of a man was my father?
I knew he was in show business, but never imagined...
He was a magic man!
This place may be more House of Horrors than swingin' bachelor's pad but, even so, it beats my hovel. I could get used to it here.

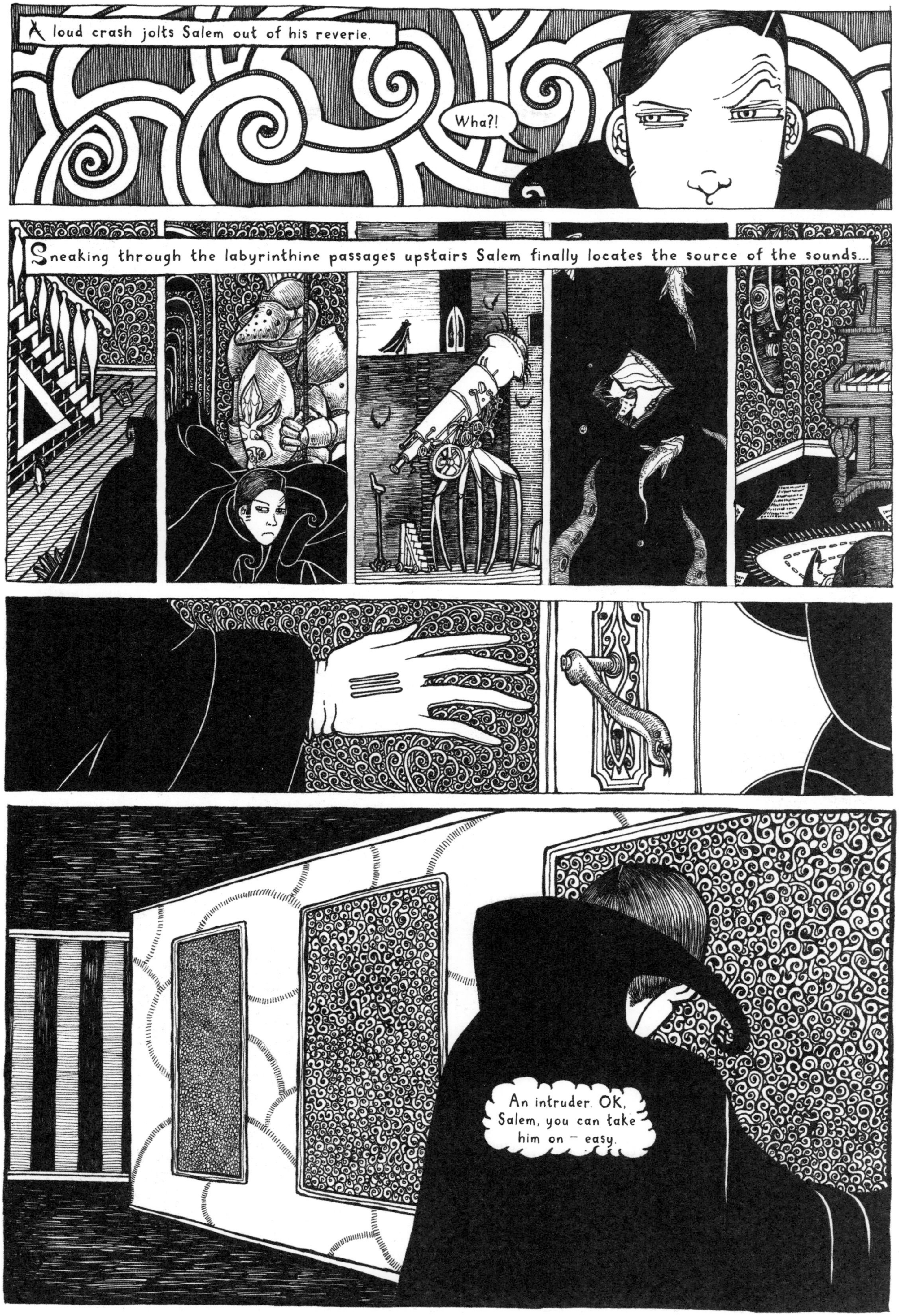
A loud crash jolts Salem out of his reverie.
Wha?!
Sneaking through the labyrinthine passages upstairs Salem finally locates the source of the sounds...
An intruder. OK, Salem, you can take him on – easy.

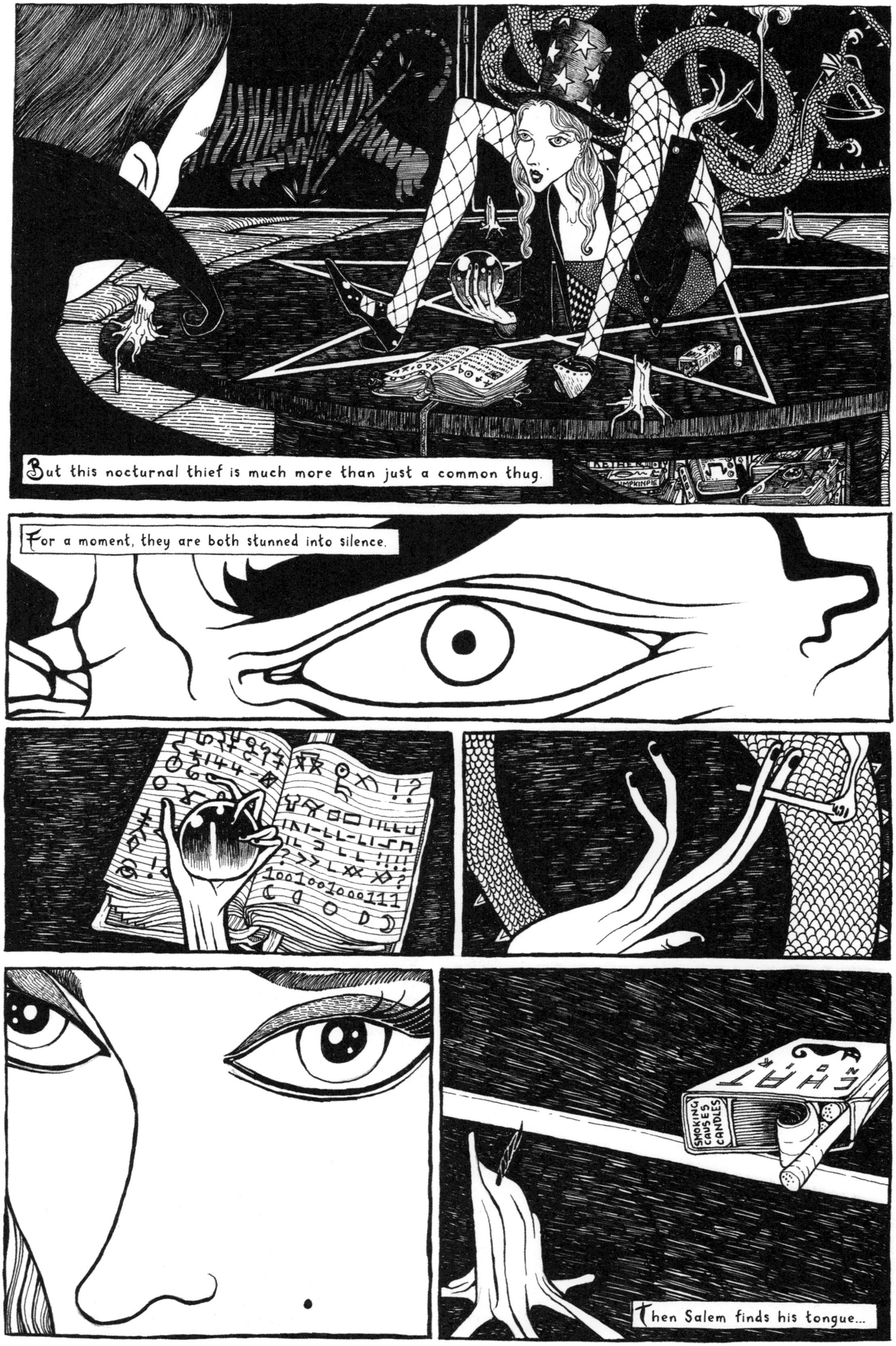
But this nocturnal thief is much more than just a common thug.
For a moment, they are both stunned into silence.
SMOKING CAUSES CANDLES
Then Salem finds his tongue...

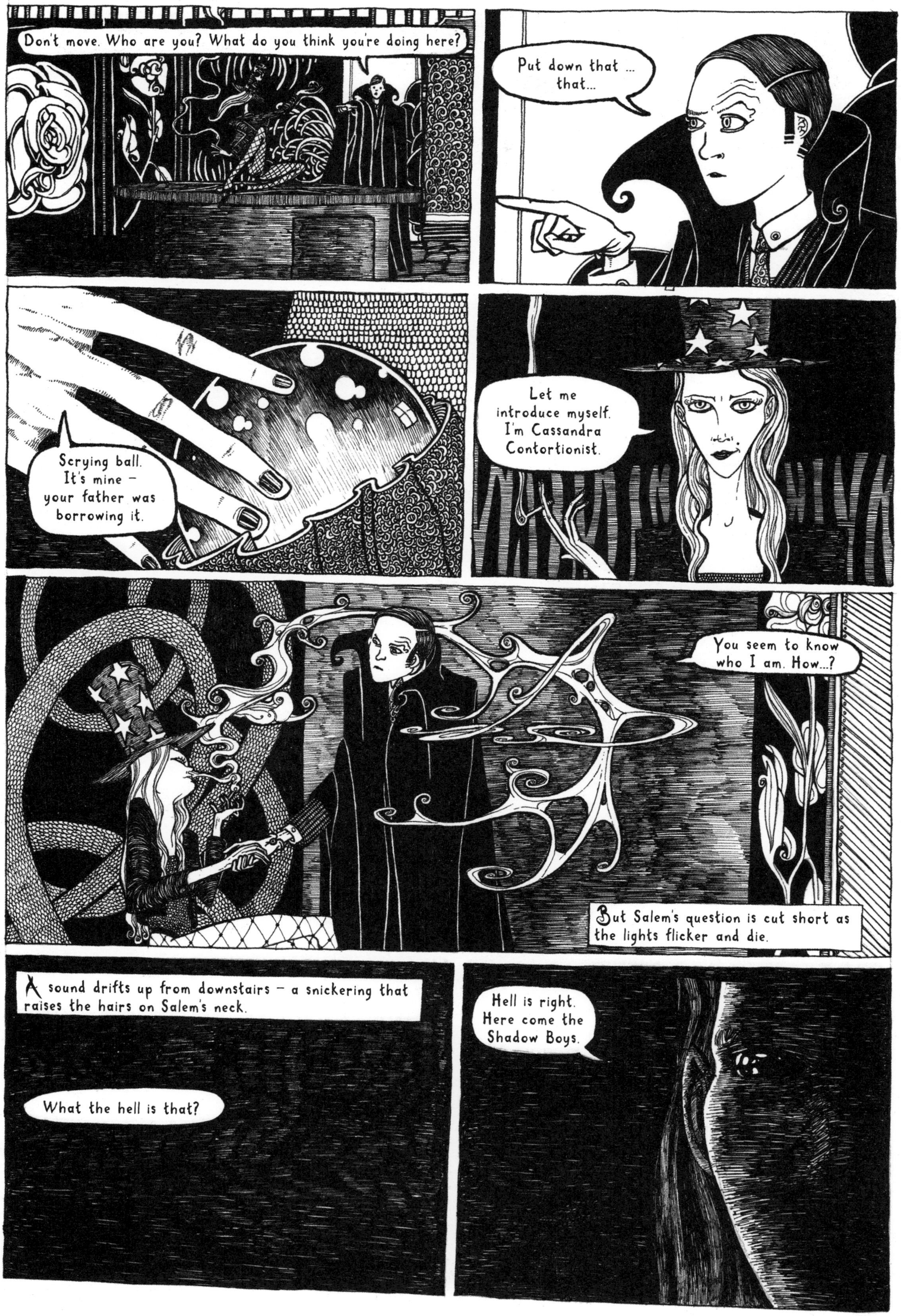
Don't move. Who are you? What do you think you're doing here?
Put down that ... that...
Scrying ball. It's mine — your father was borrowing it.
Let me introduce myself. I'm Cassandra Contortionist.
You seem to know who I am. How...?
But Salem's question is cut short as the lights flicker and die.
A sound drifts up from downstairs — a snickering that raises the hairs on Salem's neck.
What the hell is that?
Hell is right. Here come the Shadow Boys.

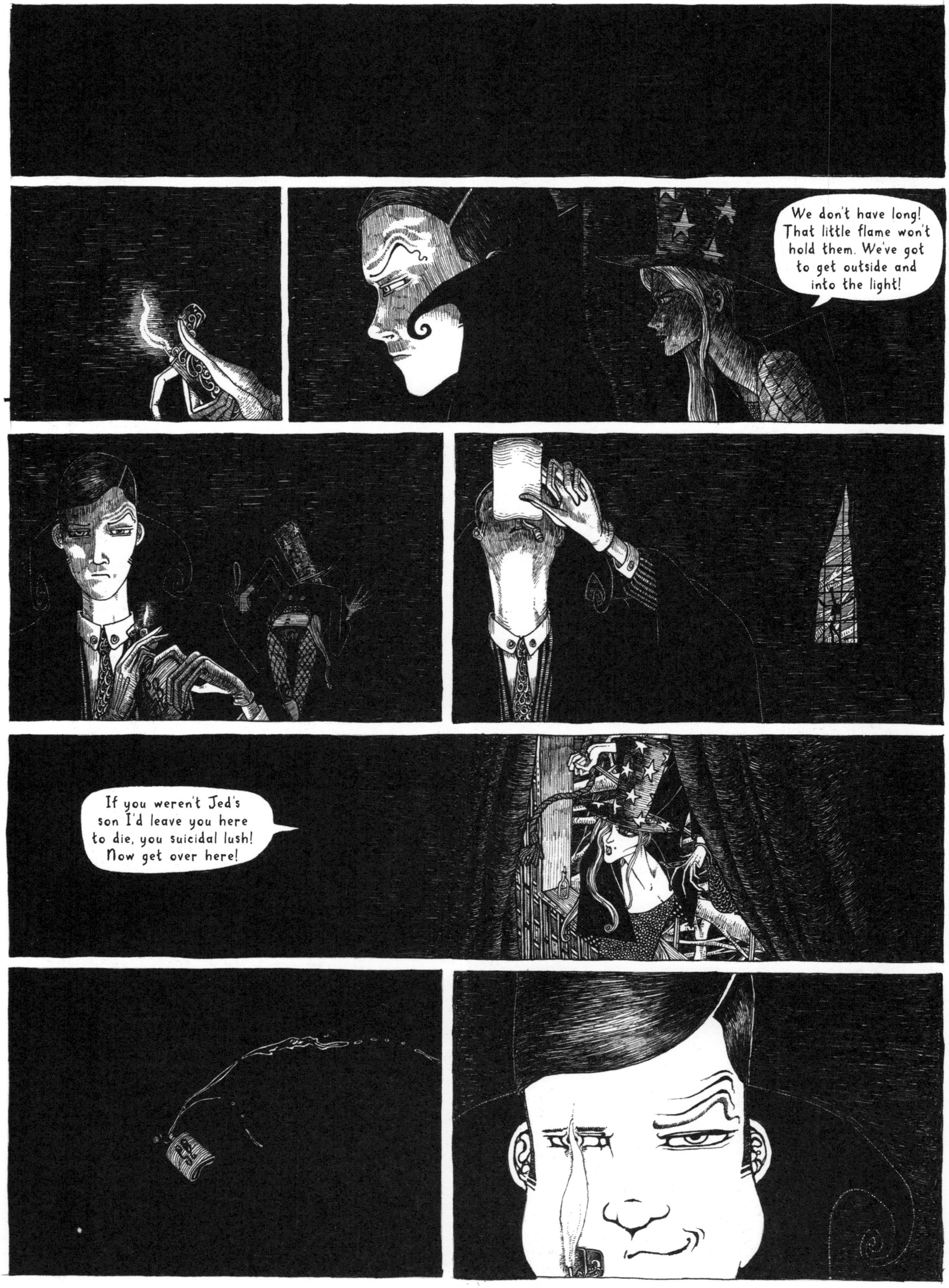
We don't have long! That little flame won't hold them. We've got to get outside and into the light!
If you weren't Jed's son I'd leave you here to die, you suicidal lush! Now get over here!

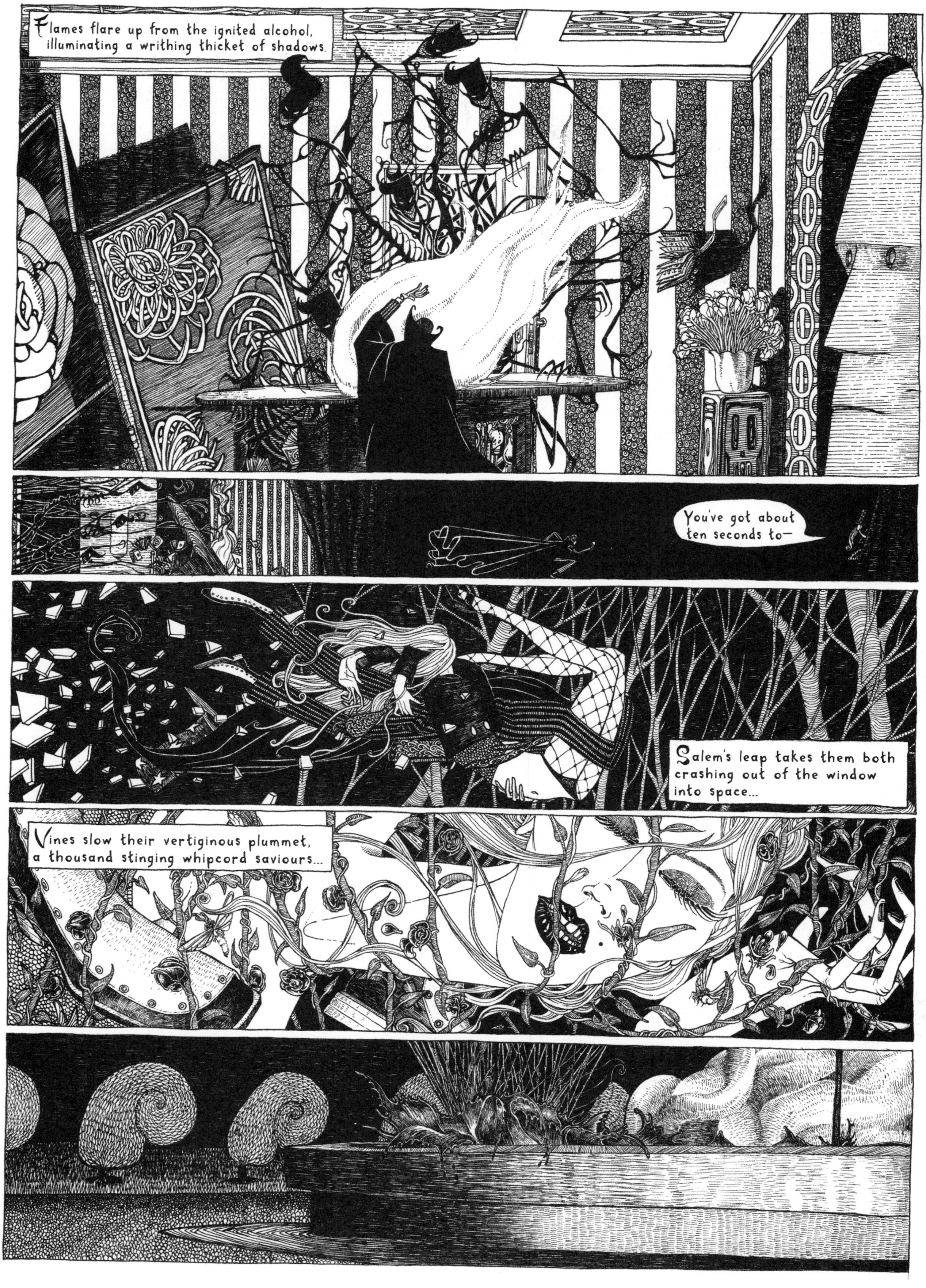
Flames flare up from the ignited alcohol, illuminating a writhing thicket of shadows.
You've got about ten seconds to—
Salem's leap takes them both crashing out of the window into space...
Vines slow their vertiginous plummet, a thousand stinging whipcord saviours...

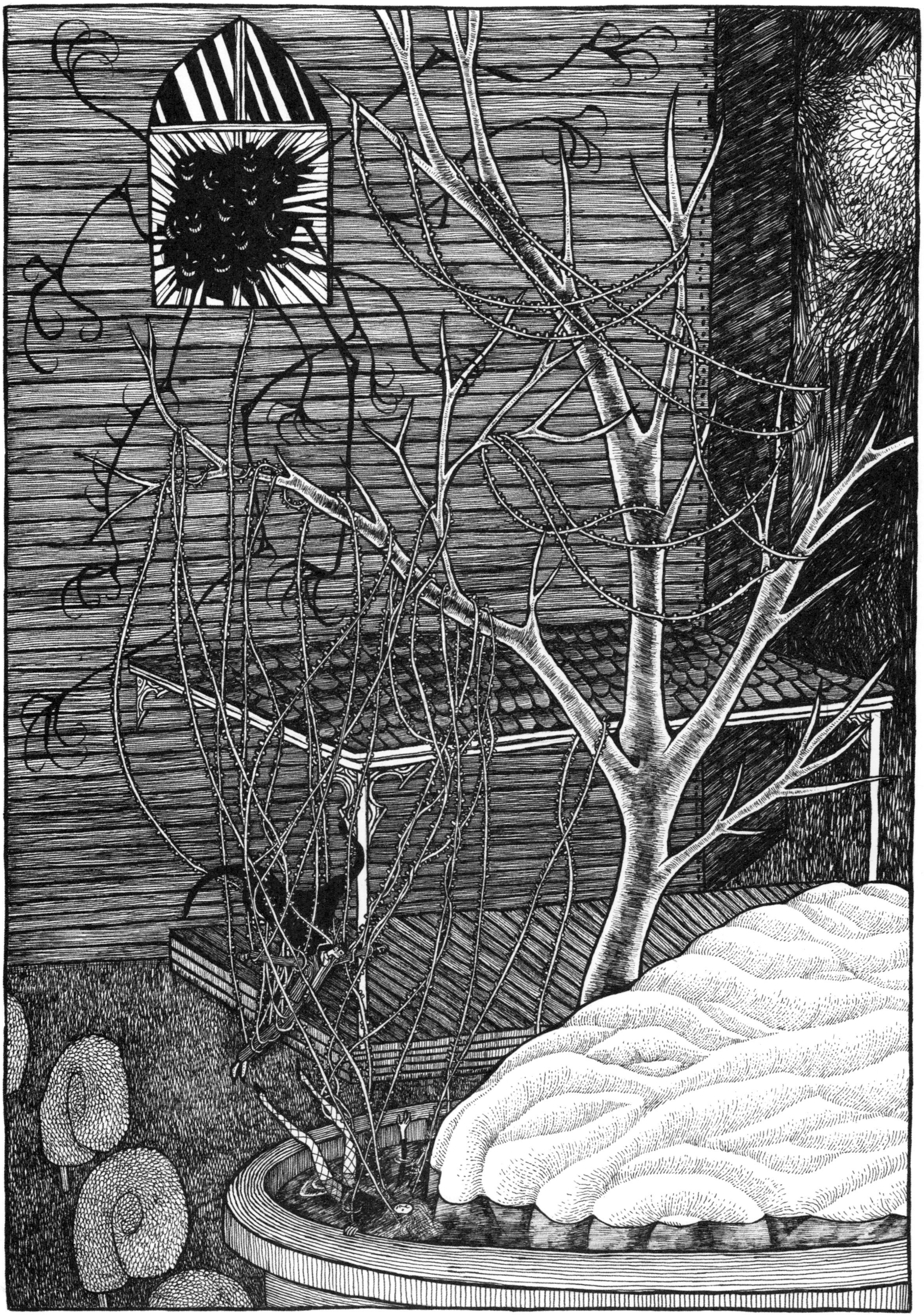

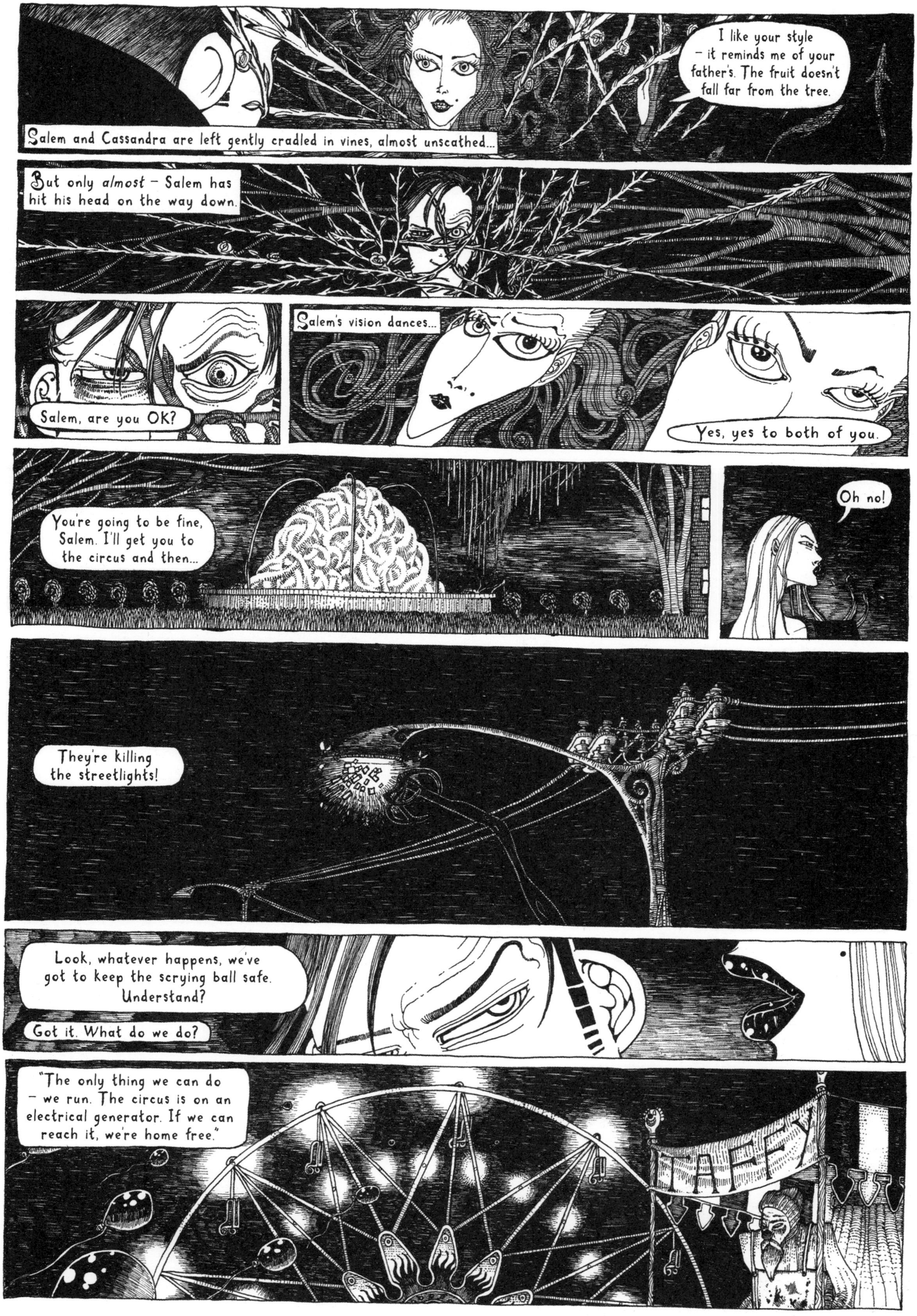
I like your style – it reminds me of your father's. The fruit doesn't fall far from the tree.
Salem and Cassandra are left gently cradled in vines, almost unscathed...
But only *almost* – Salem has hit his head on the way down.
Salem, are you OK?
Salem's vision dances...
Yes, yes to both of you.
You're going to be fine, Salem. I'll get you to the circus and then...
Oh no!
They're killing the streetlights!
Look, whatever happens, we've got to keep the scrying ball safe. Understand?
Got it. What do we do?
"The only thing we can do – we run. The circus is on an electrical generator. If we can reach it, we're home free."

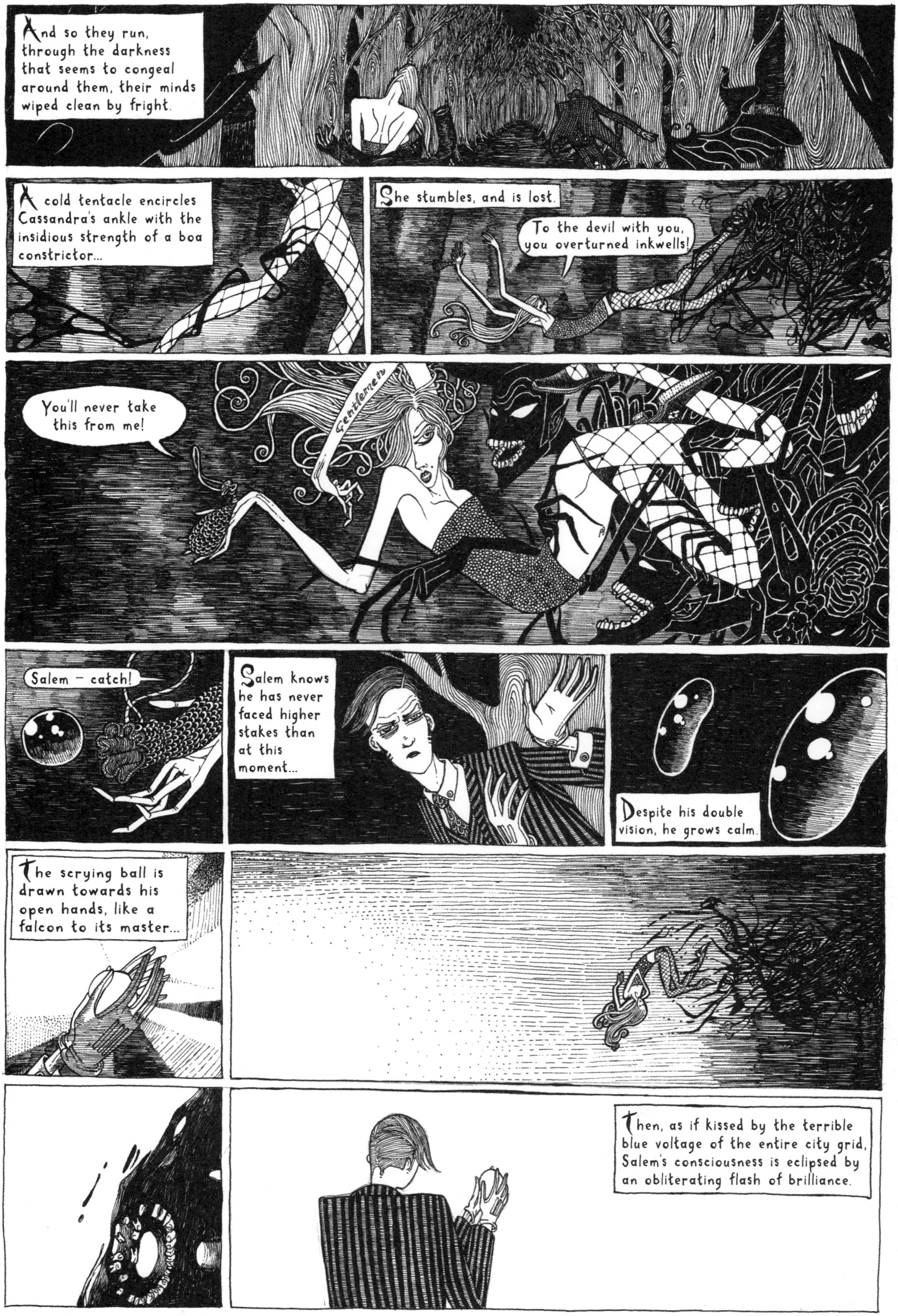
And so they run, through the darkness that seems to congeal around them, their minds wiped clean by fright.
A cold tentacle encircles Cassandra's ankle with the insidious strength of a boa constrictor...
She stumbles, and is lost.
To the devil with you, you overturned inkwells!
You'll never take this from me!
Gentlemen
Salem – catch!
Salem knows he has never faced higher stakes than at this moment...
Despite his double vision, he grows calm.
The scrying ball is drawn towards his open hands, like a falcon to its master...
Then, as if kissed by the terrible blue voltage of the entire city grid, Salem's consciousness is eclipsed by an obliterating flash of brilliance.

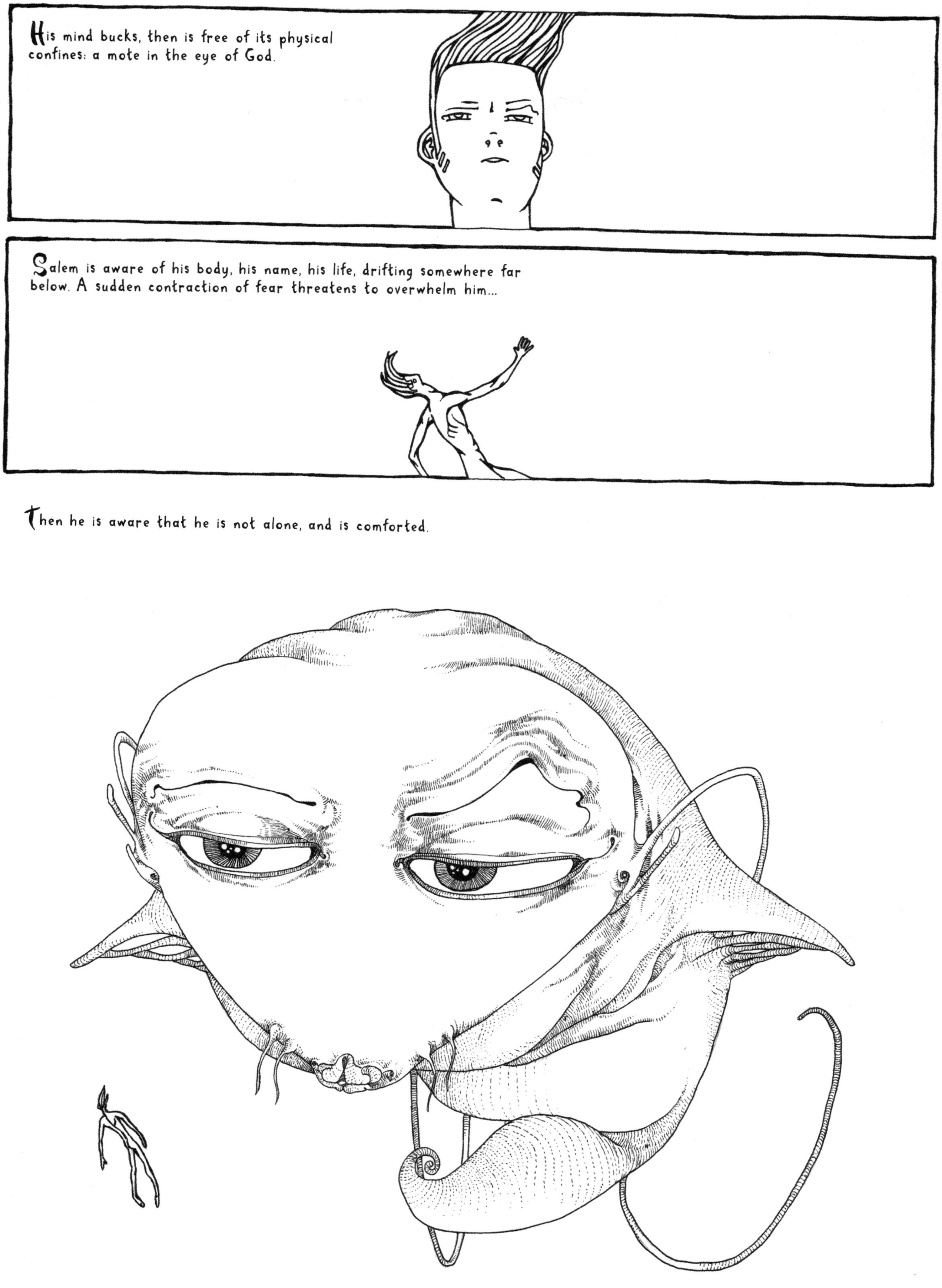
His mind bucks, then is free of its physical confines: a mote in the eye of God.
Salem is aware of his body, his name, his life, drifting somewhere far below. A sudden contraction of fear threatens to overwhelm him...
Then he is aware that he is not alone, and is comforted.

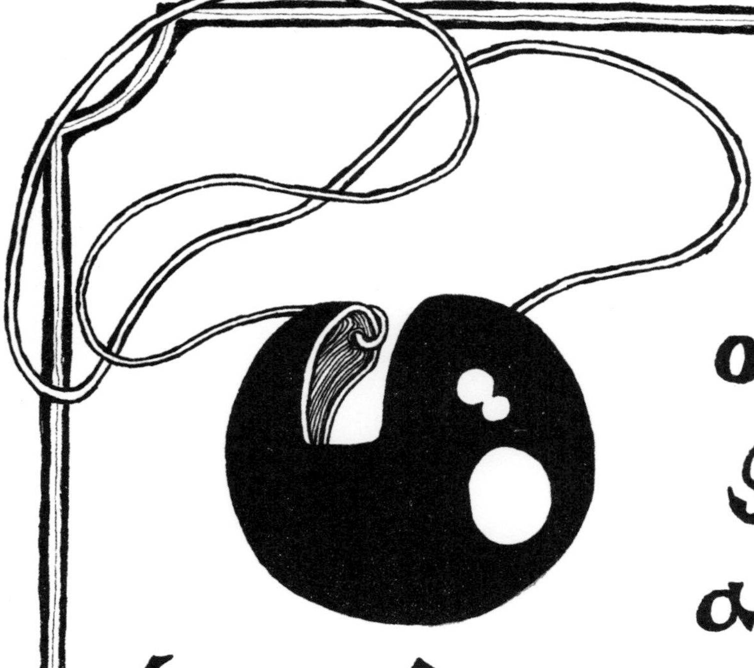

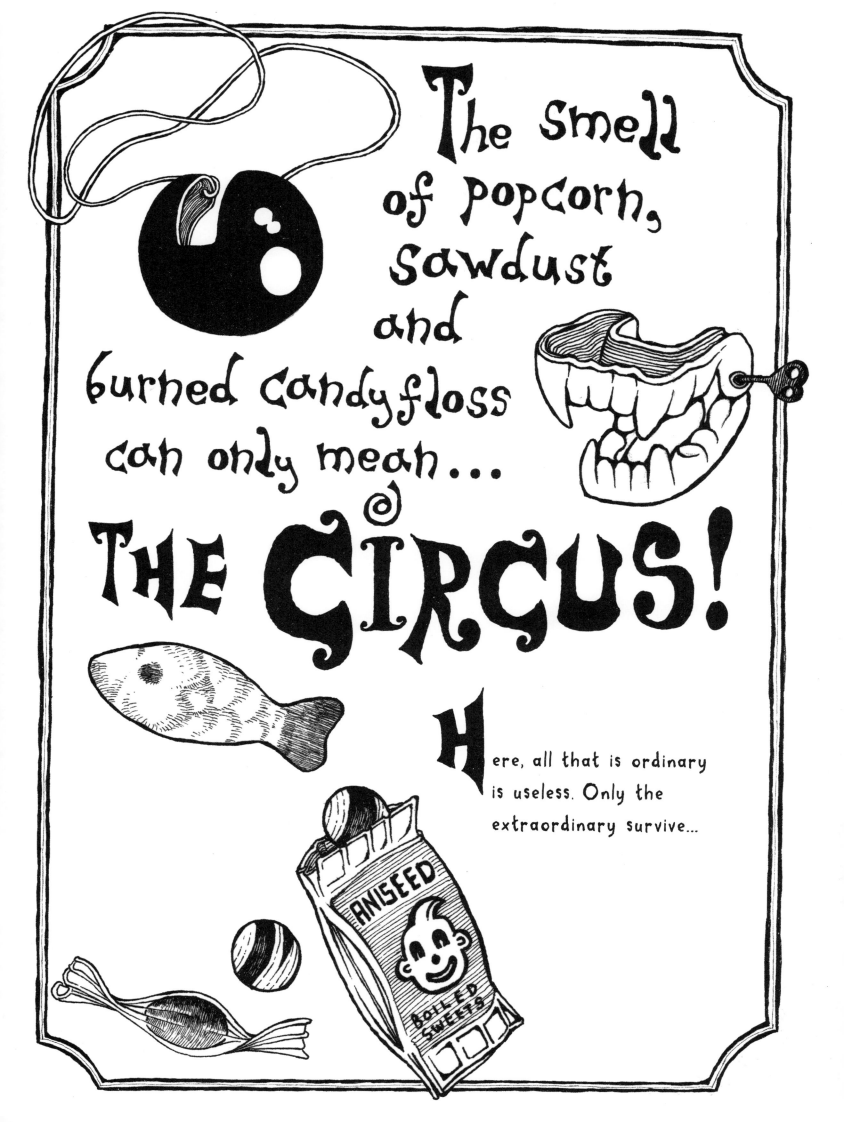

The smell of popcorn, sawdust and burned candyfloss can only mean...

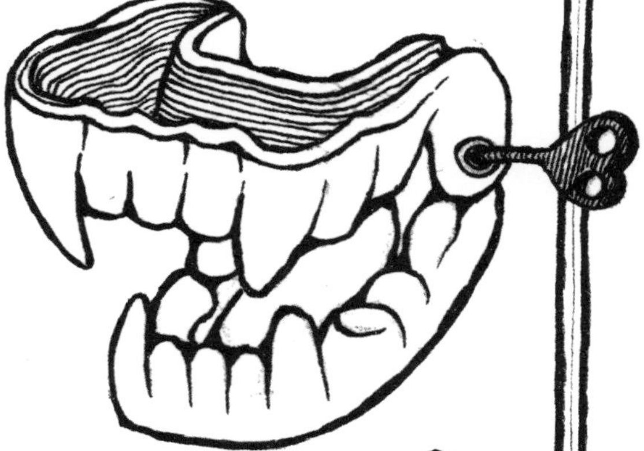

THE CIRCUS!

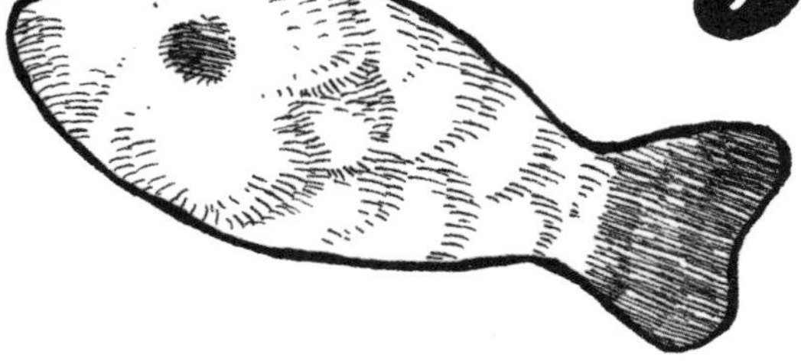

Here, all that is ordinary is useless. Only the extraordinary survive...

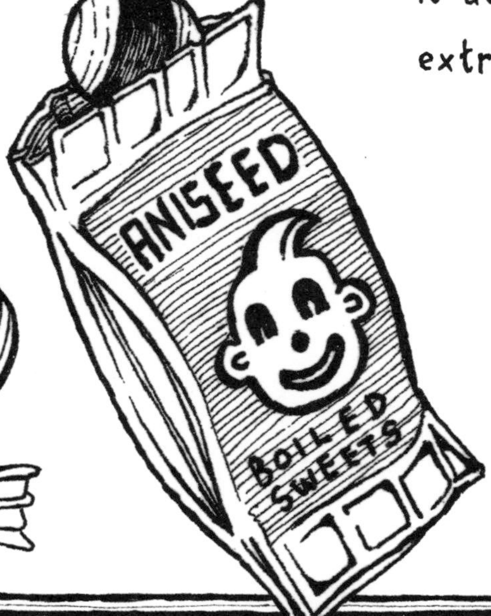
ANISEED
BOILED SWEETS

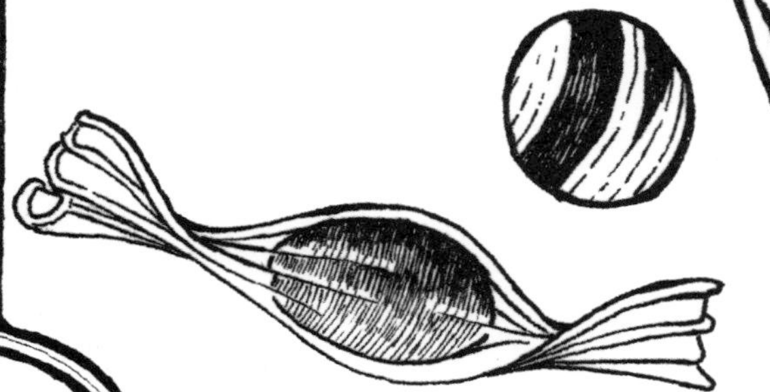

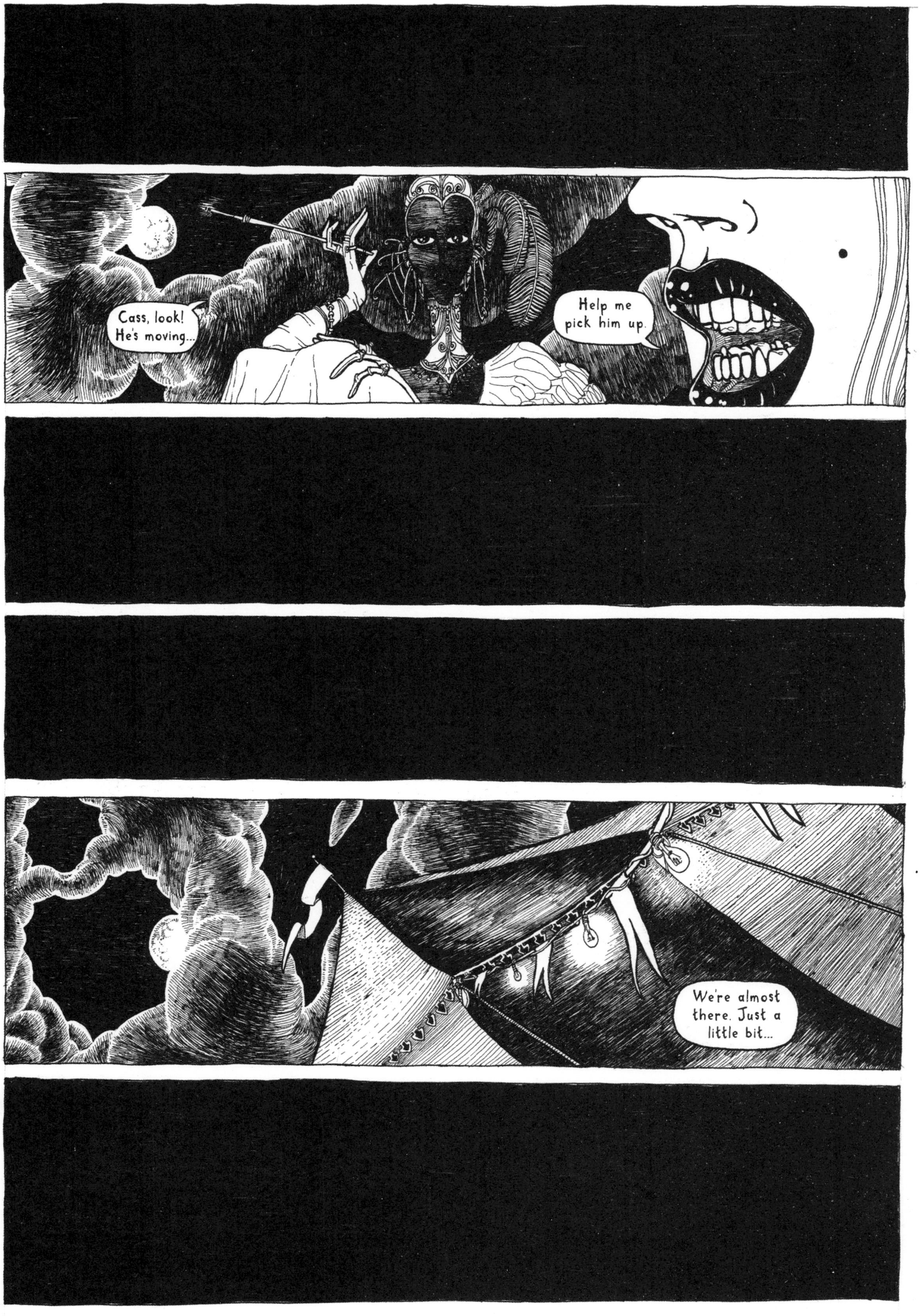
Cass, look! He's moving...
Help me pick him up.
We're almost there. Just a little bit...

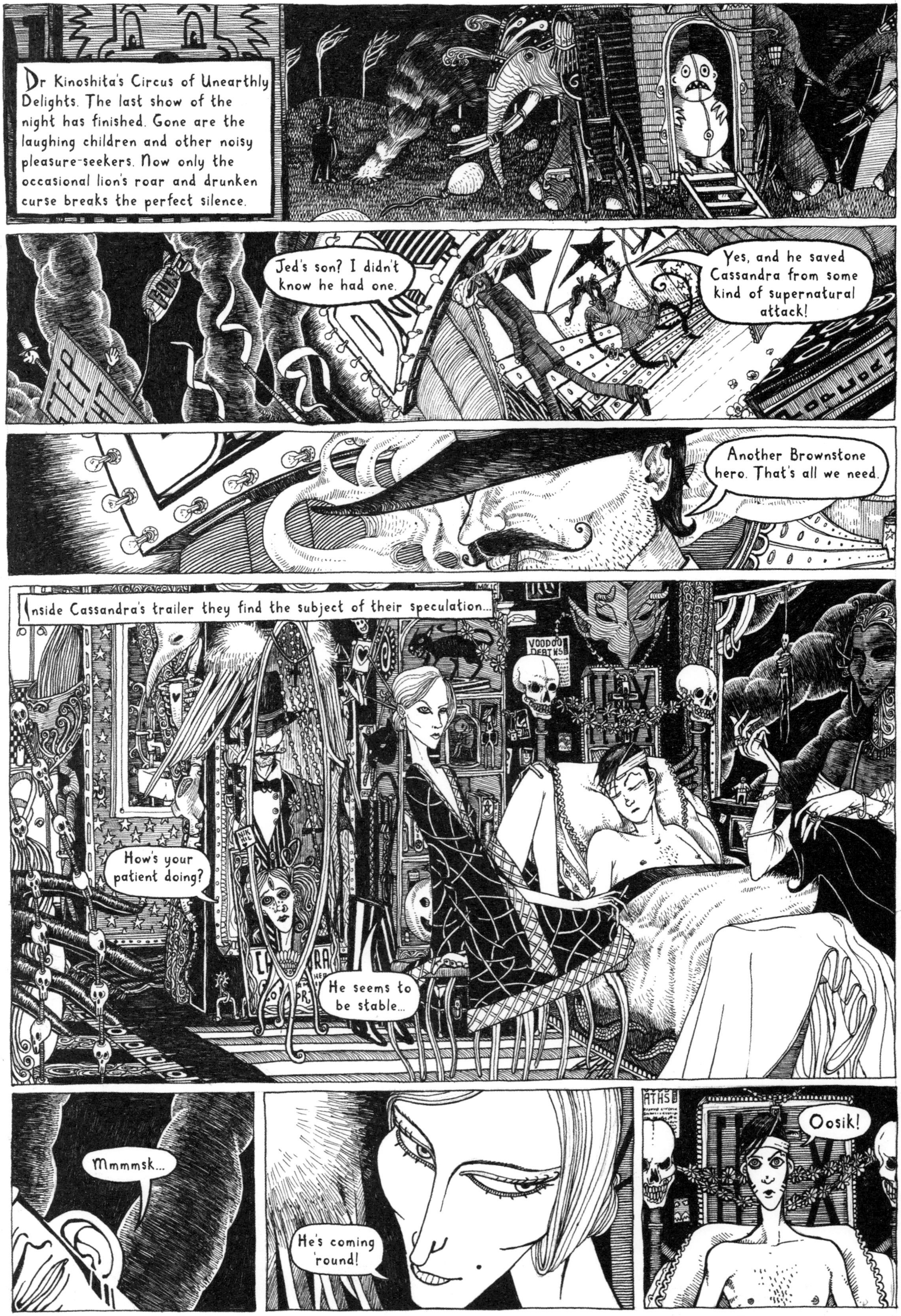
Dr Kinoshita's Circus of Unearthly Delights. The last show of the night has finished. Gone are the laughing children and other noisy pleasure-seekers. Now only the occasional lion's roar and drunken curse breaks the perfect silence.
Jed's son? I didn't know he had one.
Yes, and he saved Cassandra from some kind of supernatural attack!
Another Brownstone hero. That's all we need.
Inside Cassandra's trailer they find the subject of their speculation...
How's your patient doing?
He seems to be stable...
Mmmmsk...
He's coming 'round!
Oosik!

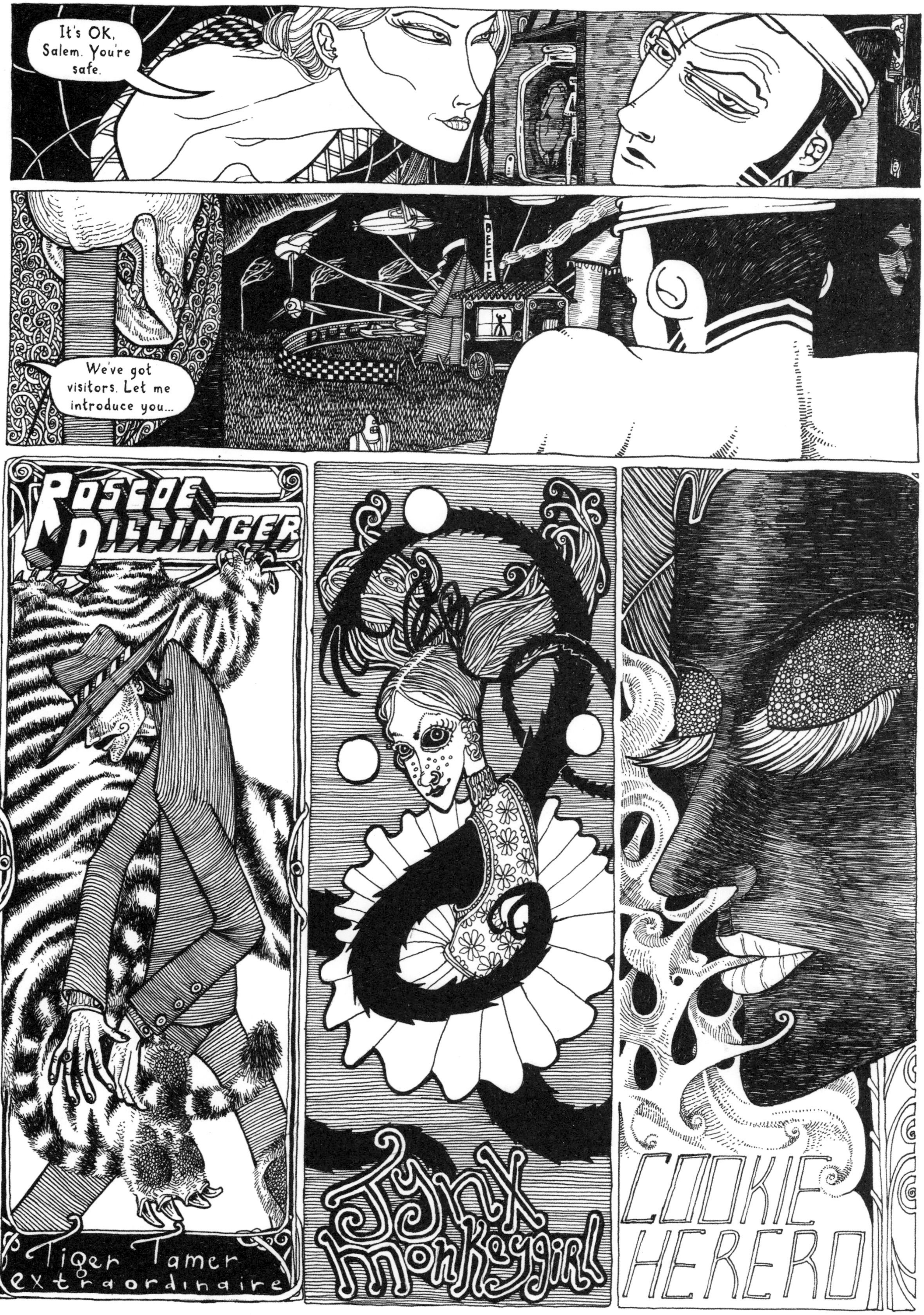
It's OK, Salem. You're safe.
We've got visitors. Let me introduce you...
ROSCOE DILLINGER
Tiger Tamer extraordinaire
Jynx Monkeygirl
COOKIE HERERO

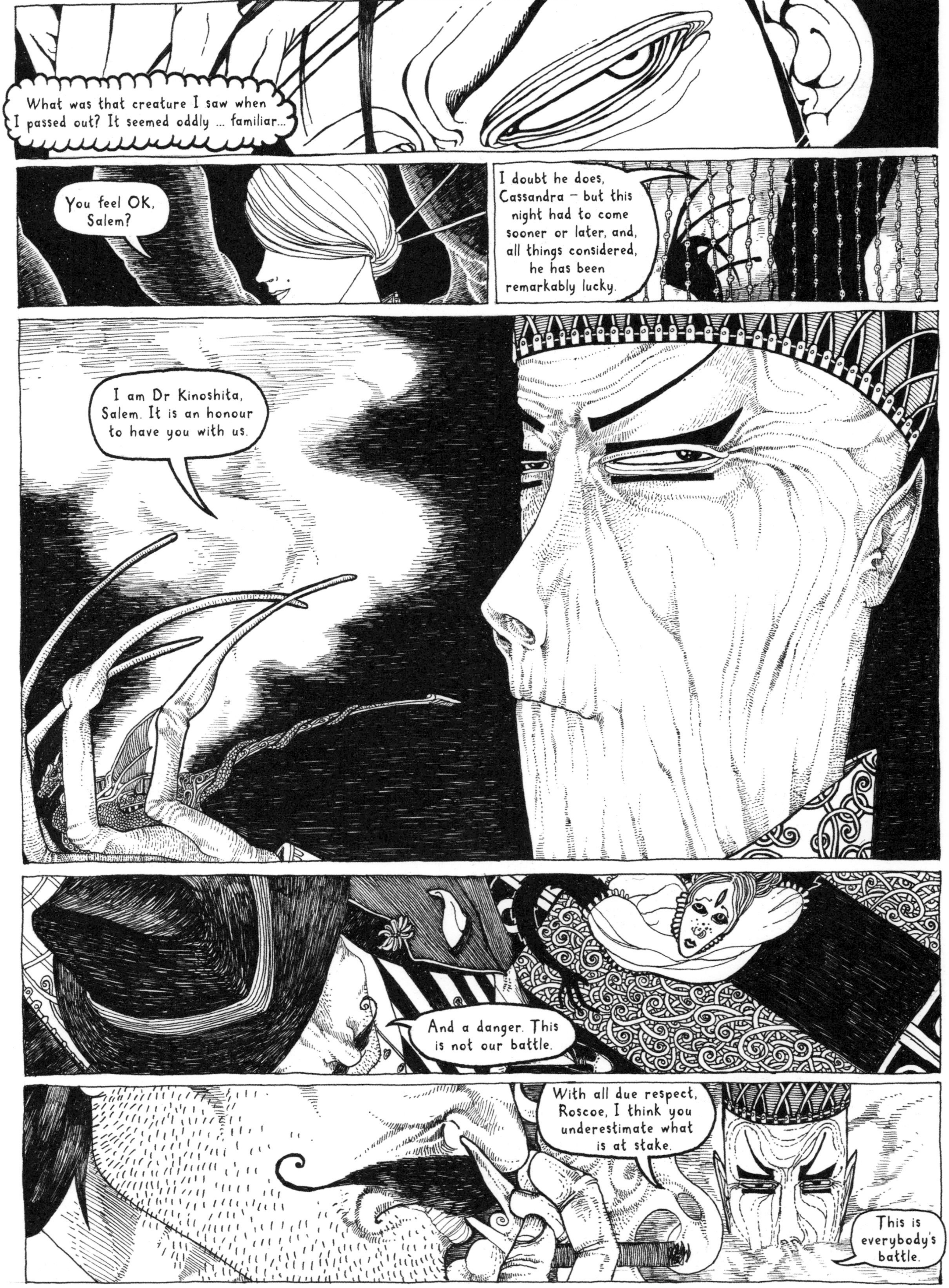
What was that creature I saw when I passed out? It seemed oddly ... familiar...
You feel OK, Salem?
I doubt he does, Cassandra – but this night had to come sooner or later, and, all things considered, he has been remarkably lucky.
I am Dr Kinoshita, Salem. It is an honour to have you with us.
And a danger. This is not our battle.
With all due respect, Roscoe, I think you underestimate what is at stake.
This is everybody's battle.

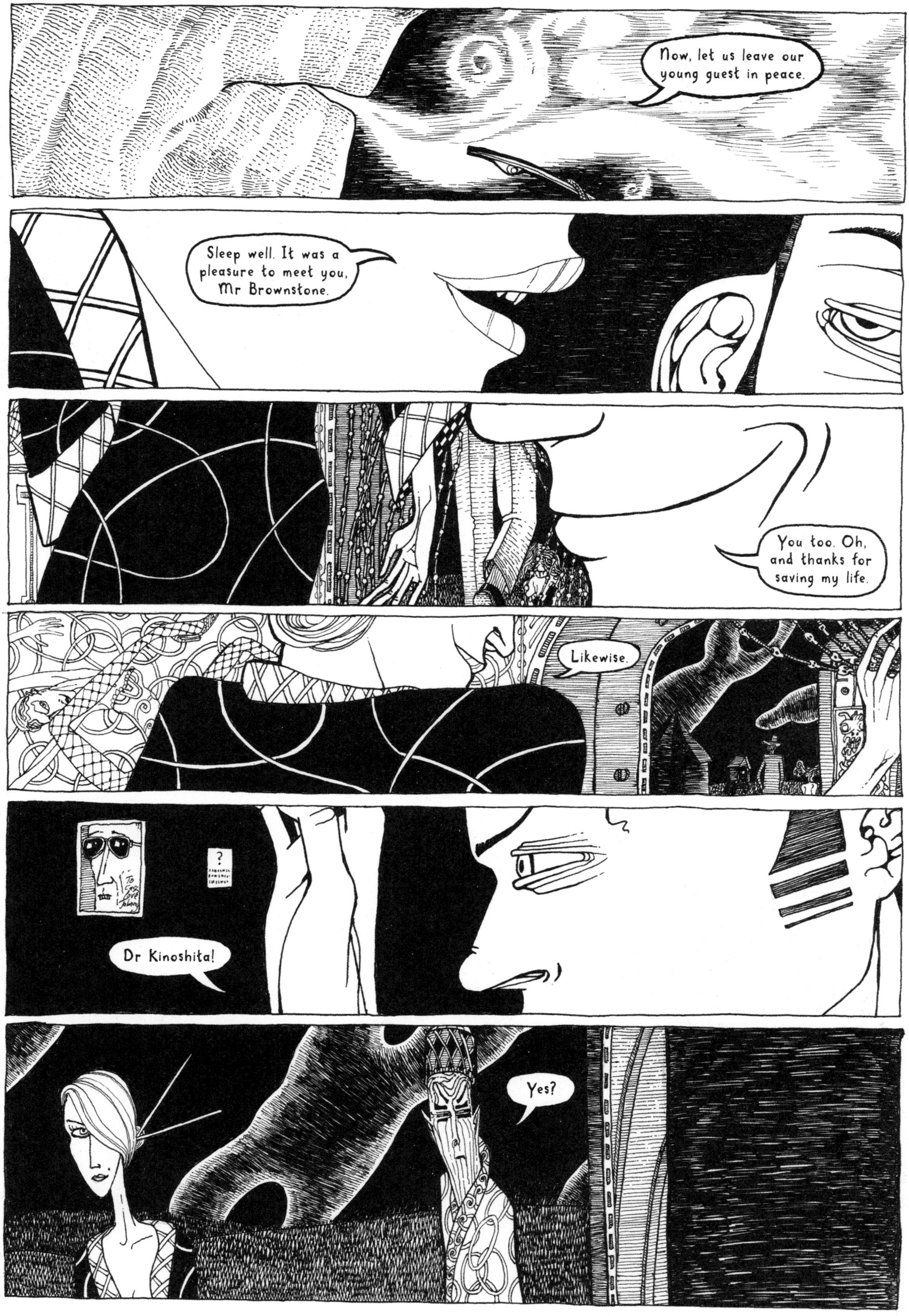

Now, let us leave our young guest in peace.
Sleep well. It was a pleasure to meet you, Mr Brownstone.
You too. Oh, and thanks for saving my life.
Likewise.
Dr Kinoshita!
Yes?

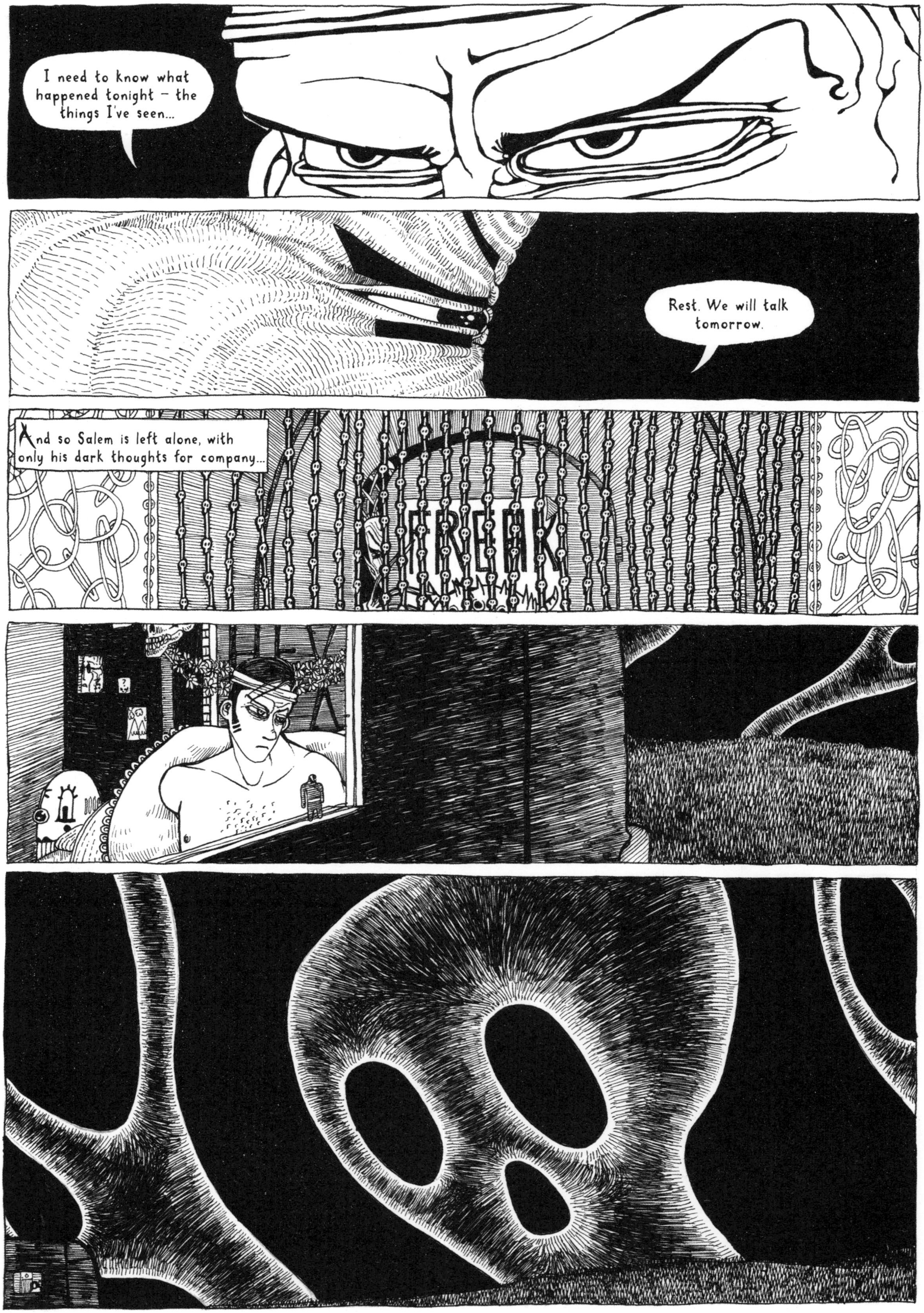
I need to know what happened tonight – the things I've seen...
Rest. We will talk tomorrow.
And so Salem is left alone, with only his dark thoughts for company...
FREAK

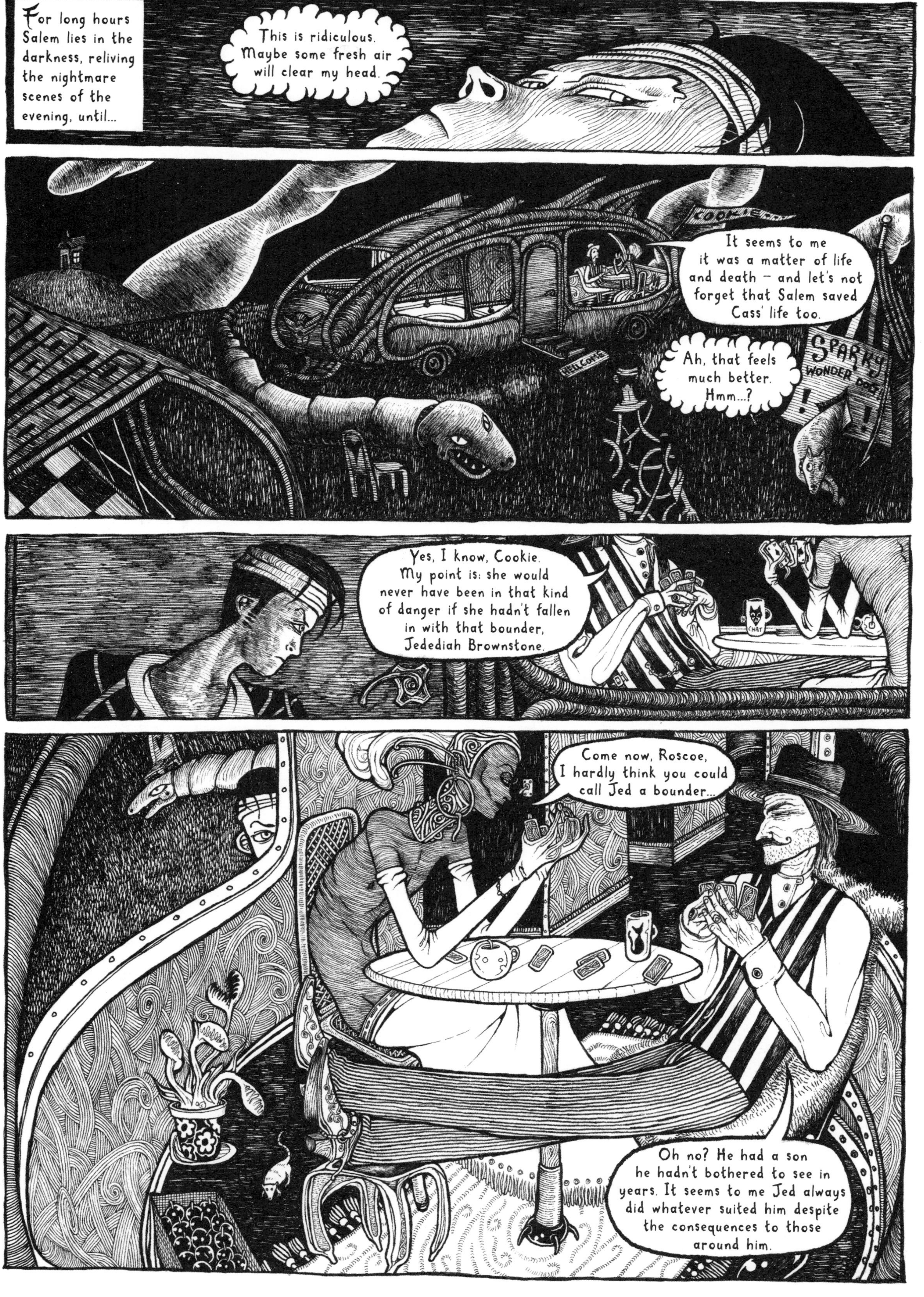

For long hours Salem lies in the darkness, reliving the nightmare scenes of the evening, until...
This is ridiculous. Maybe some fresh air will clear my head.
It seems to me it was a matter of life and death – and let's not forget that Salem saved Cass' life too.
Ah, that feels much better. Hmm...?
SPARKY
WONDER
Yes, I know, Cookie. My point is: she would never have been in that kind of danger if she hadn't fallen in with that bounder, Jedediah Brownstone.
Come now, Roscoe, I hardly think you could call Jed a bounder...
Oh no? He had a son he hadn't bothered to see in years. It seems to me Jed always did whatever suited him despite the consequences to those around him.

"I mean, remember the time he conjured up a double of Cassandra who then ran amok?"

I know — but he only conjured her up as a birthday present for Cass in the first place.

Some birthday present — she almost ended up being cooked in her own birthday cake! And what about those giant ectoplasmic serpents that attacked him here at the circus?

That was terrible — but there was no harm done...

"No harm done?! They ate two of my tigers!!"

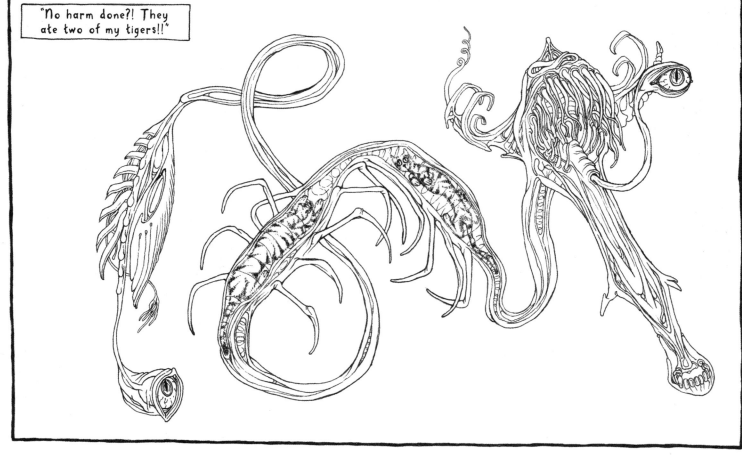

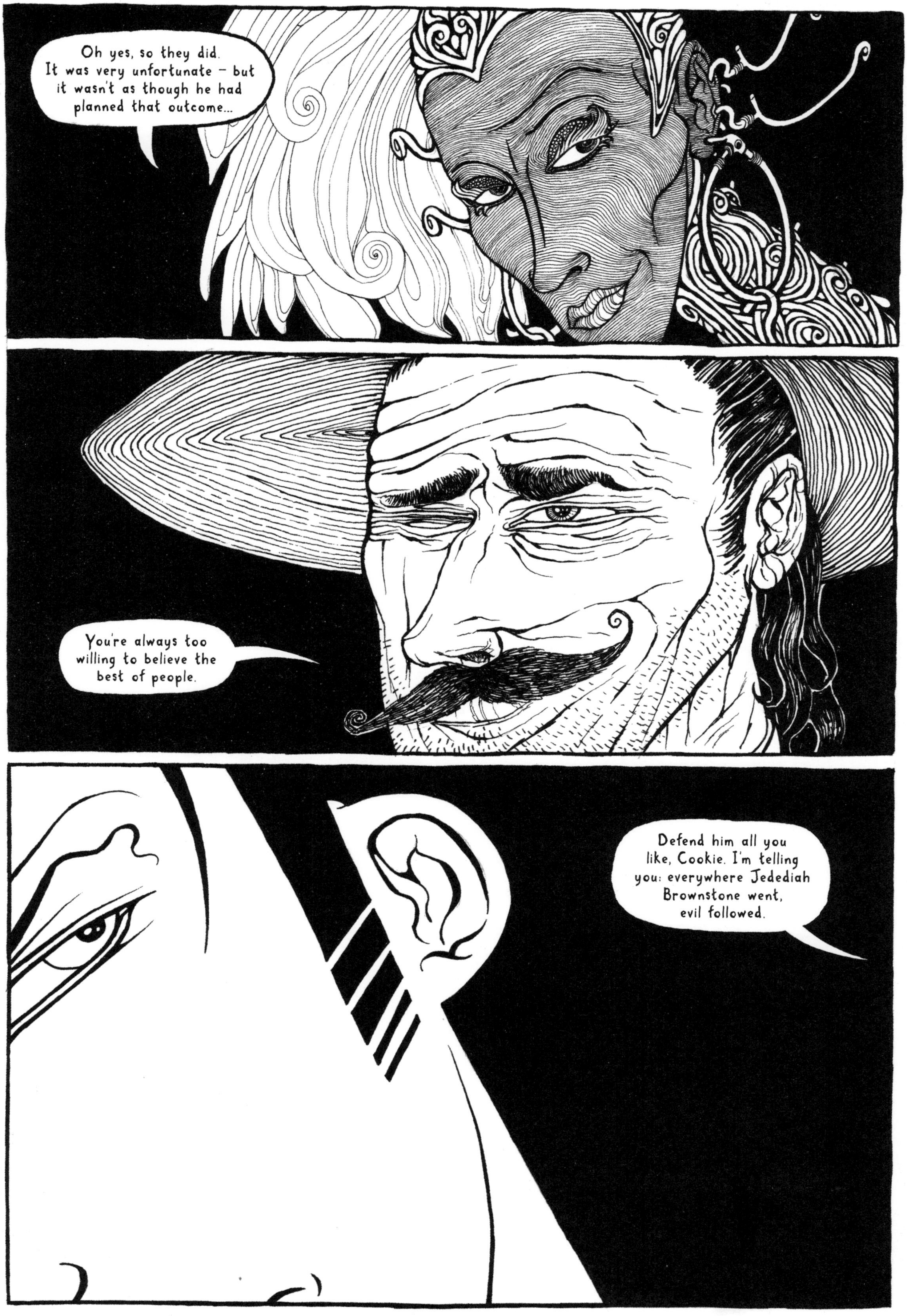
Oh yes, so they did. It was very unfortunate – but it wasn't as though he had planned that outcome...
You're always too willing to believe the best of people.
Defend him all you like, Cookie. I'm telling you: everywhere Jedediah Brownstone went, evil followed.

Meanwhile, smoke hangs over the Brownstone manse...

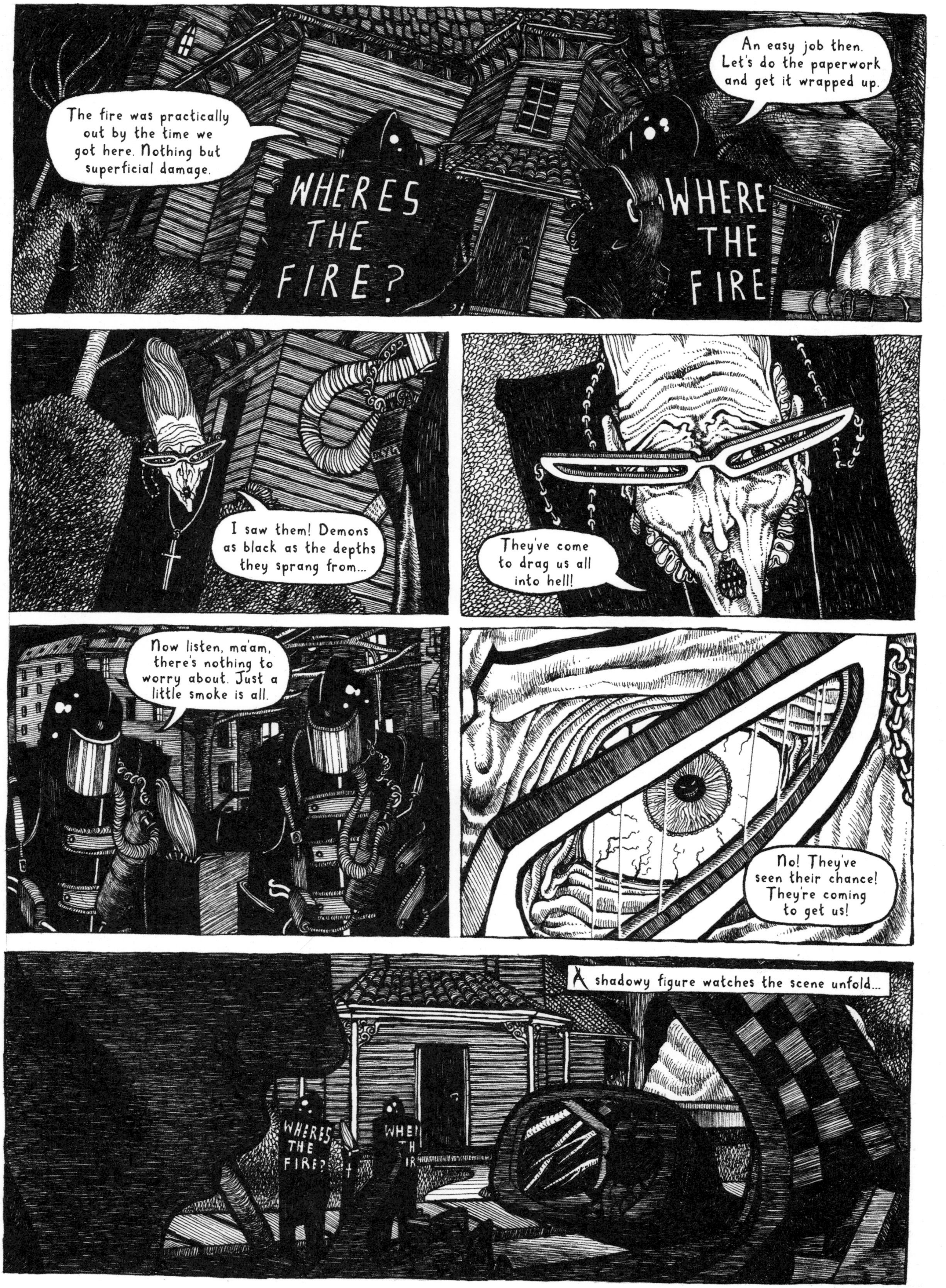
The fire was practically out by the time we got here. Nothing but superficial damage.
An easy job then. Let's do the paperwork and get it wrapped up.
WHERES THE FIRE?
WHERE THE FIRE
I saw them! Demons as black as the depths they sprang from...
They've come to drag us all into hell!
Now listen, ma'am, there's nothing to worry about. Just a little smoke is all.
No! They've seen their chance! They're coming to get us!
A shadowy figure watches the scene unfold...
WHERES THE FIRE?

Lola Q's snake-like gaze is unwavering...

Her hand returns again and again to the dossier at her side.

DOSSIER-7-42

SALEM DROWNSTONE

Hey there, pretty lady, we're going downtown.

Suddenly...

THE WILD EYES

I'm off duty.

She says she's off duty — can you believe that?!

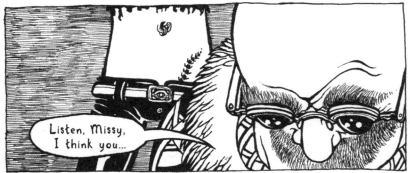

Listen, Missy, I think you...

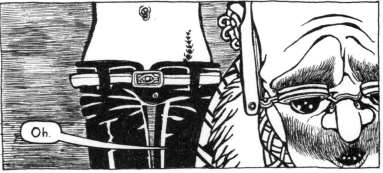

Oh.

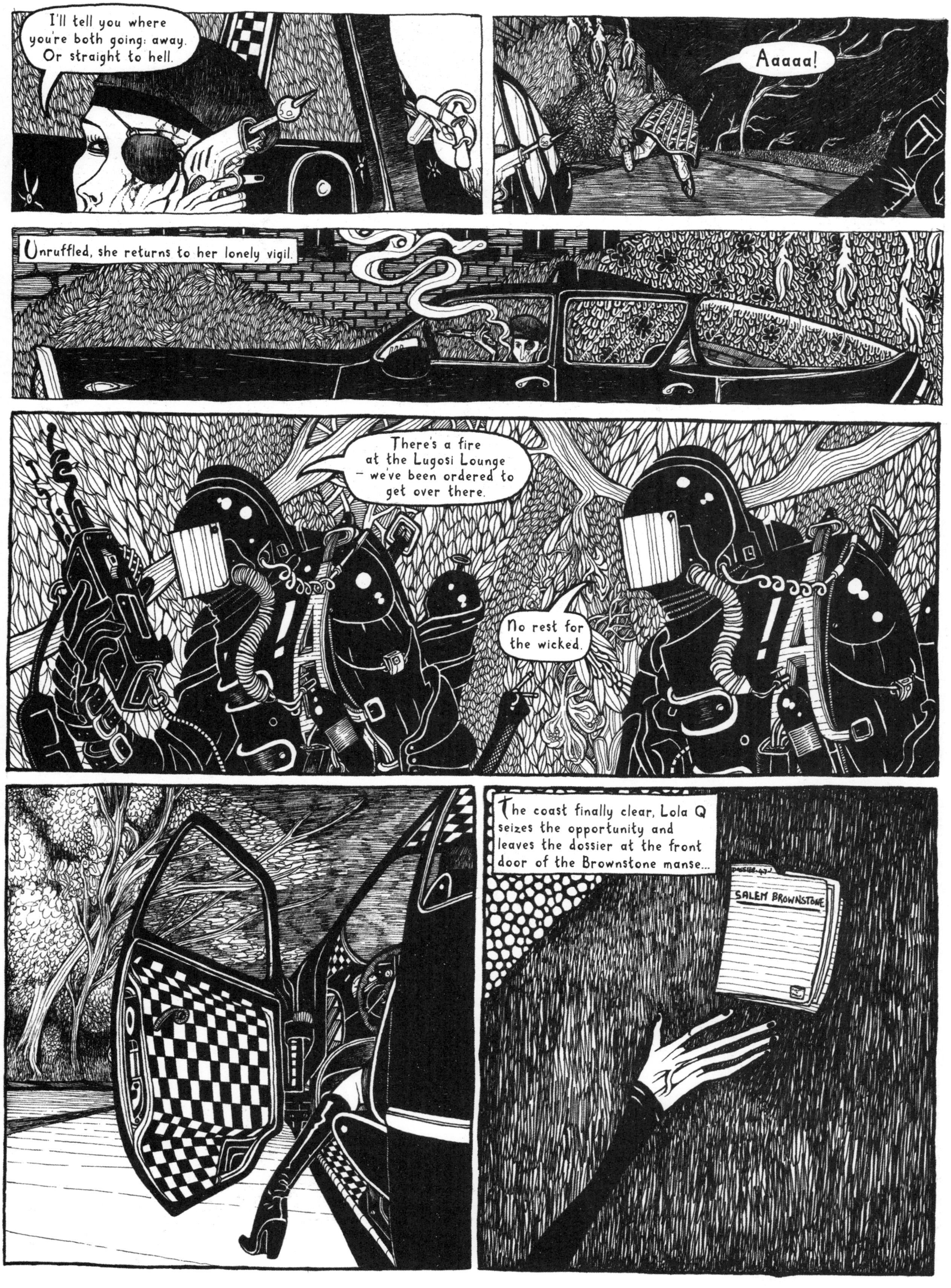
I'll tell you where you're both going: away. Or straight to hell.
Aaaaa!
Unruffled, she returns to her lonely vigil.
There's a fire at the Lugosi Lounge — we've been ordered to get over there.
No rest for the wicked.
The coast finally clear, Lola Q seizes the opportunity and leaves the dossier at the front door of the Brownstone manse...
SALEM BROWNSTONE

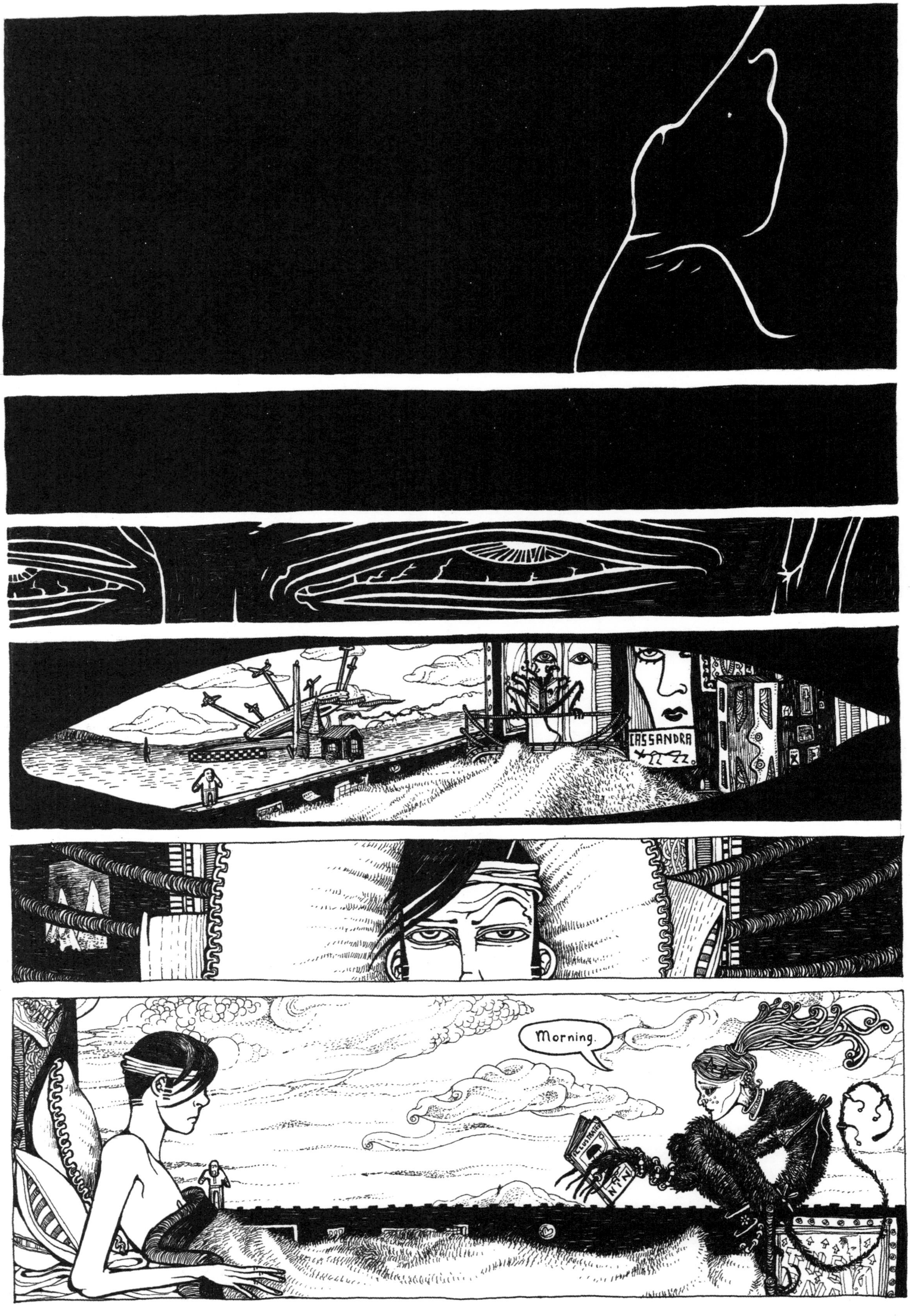
CASSANDRA
Morning.

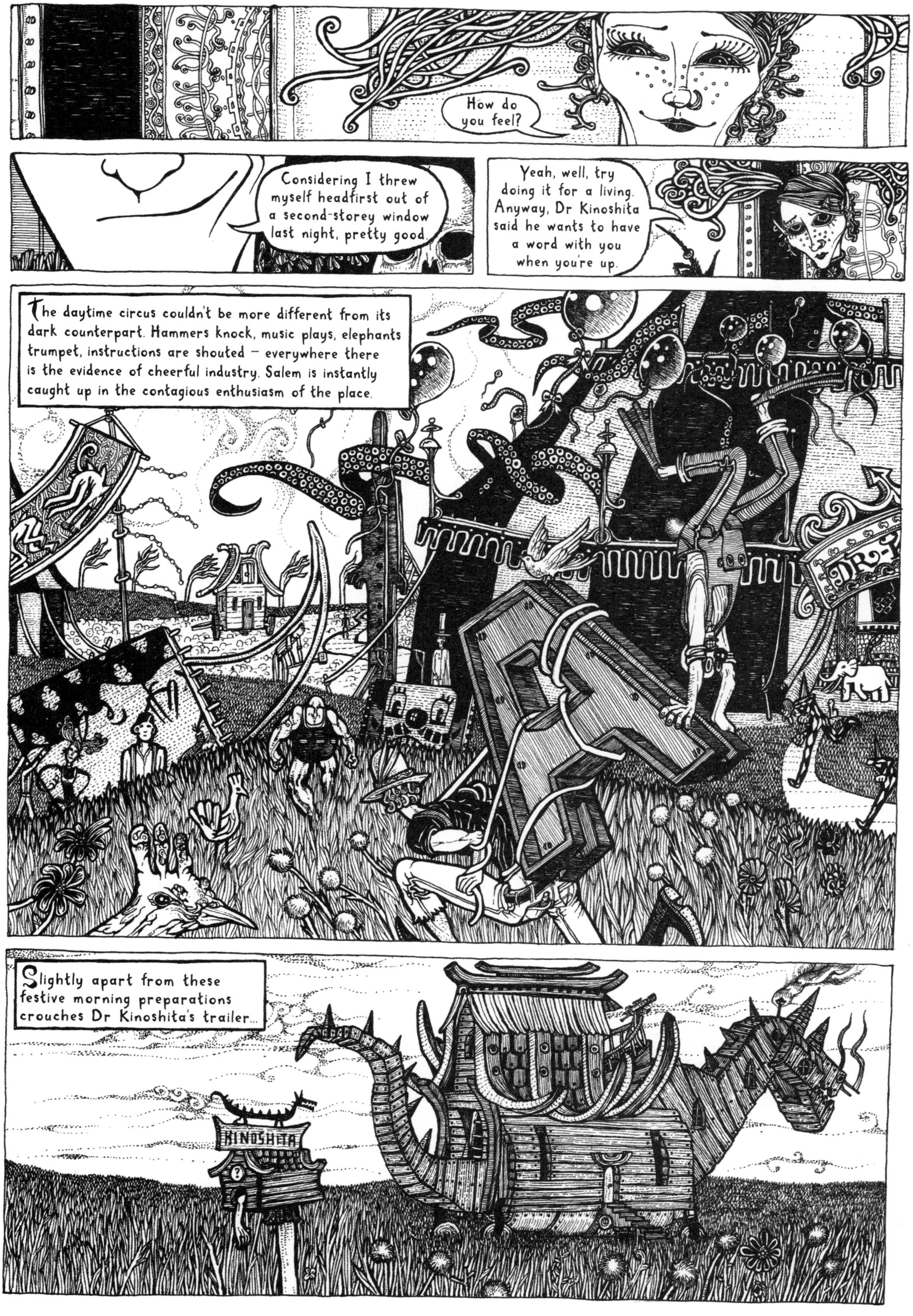
How do you feel?
Considering I threw myself headfirst out of a second-storey window last night, pretty good.
Yeah, well, try doing it for a living. Anyway, Dr Kinoshita said he wants to have a word with you when you're up.
The daytime circus couldn't be more different from its dark counterpart. Hammers knock, music plays, elephants trumpet, instructions are shouted – everywhere there is the evidence of cheerful industry. Salem is instantly caught up in the contagious enthusiasm of the place.
Slightly apart from these festive morning preparations crouches Dr Kinoshita's trailer...
KINOSHITA

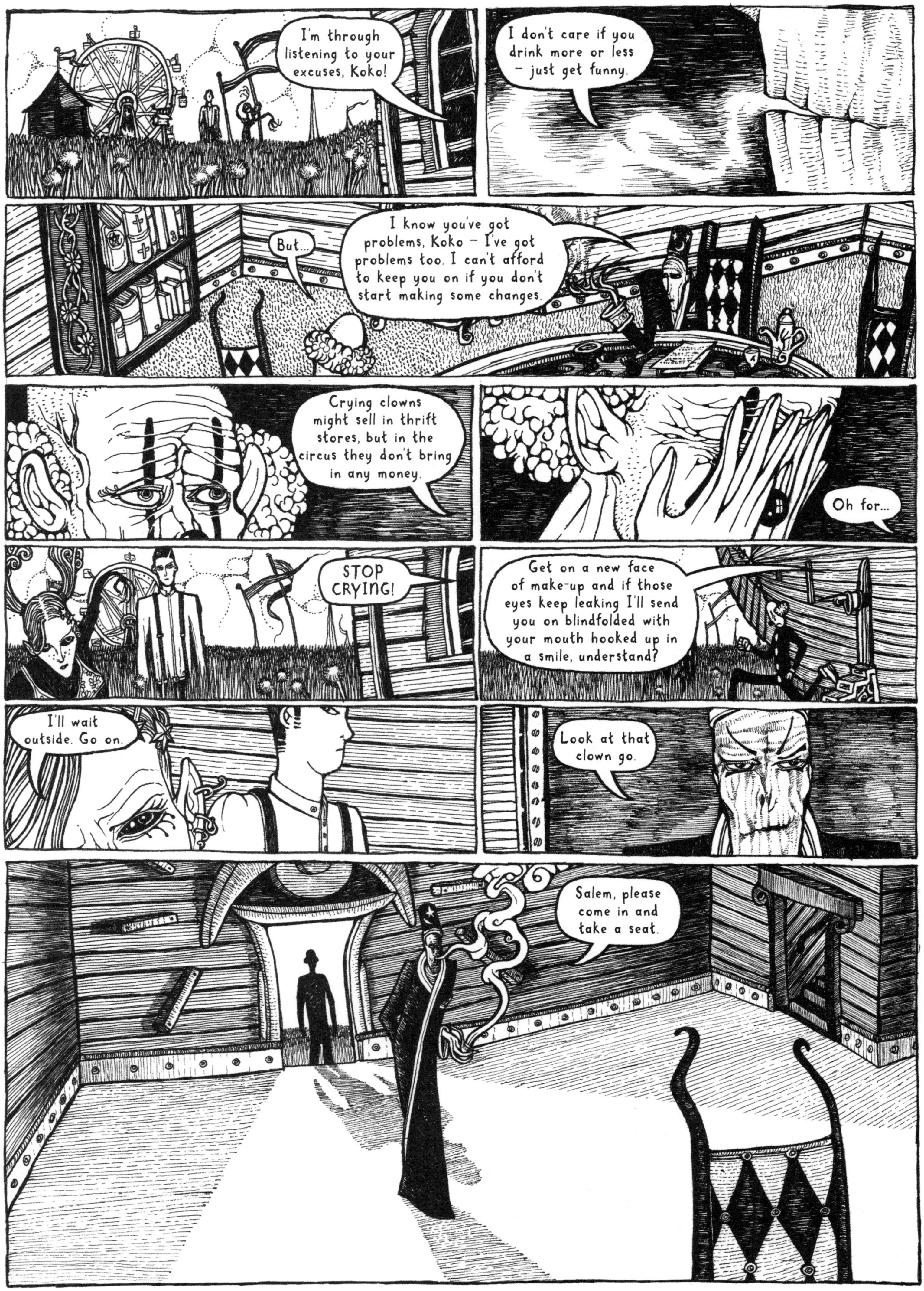
I'm through listening to your excuses, Koko!
I don't care if you drink more or less – just get funny.
But...
I know you've got problems, Koko – I've got problems too. I can't afford to keep you on if you don't start making some changes.
Crying clowns might sell in thrift stores, but in the circus they don't bring in any money.
Oh for...
STOP CRYING!
Get on a new face of make-up and if those eyes keep leaking I'll send you on blindfolded with your mouth hooked up in a smile, understand?
I'll wait outside. Go on.
Look at that clown go.
Salem, please come in and take a seat.

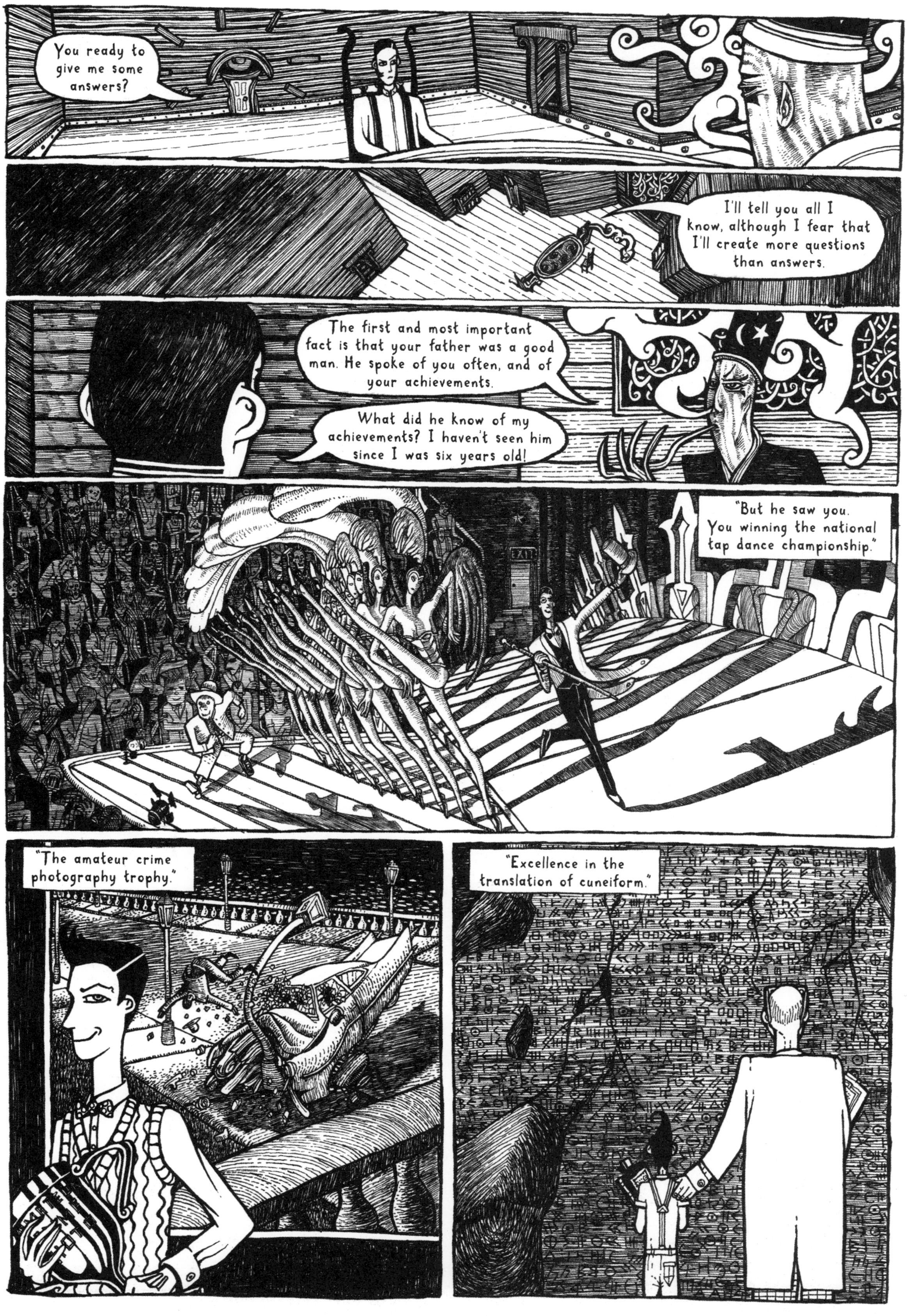
You ready to give me some answers?
I'll tell you all I know, although I fear that I'll create more questions than answers.
The first and most important fact is that your father was a good man. He spoke of you often, and of your achievements.
What did he know of my achievements? I haven't seen him since I was six years old!
"But he saw you. You winning the national tap dance championship."
EXIT
"The amateur crime photography trophy."
"Excellence in the translation of cuneiform."

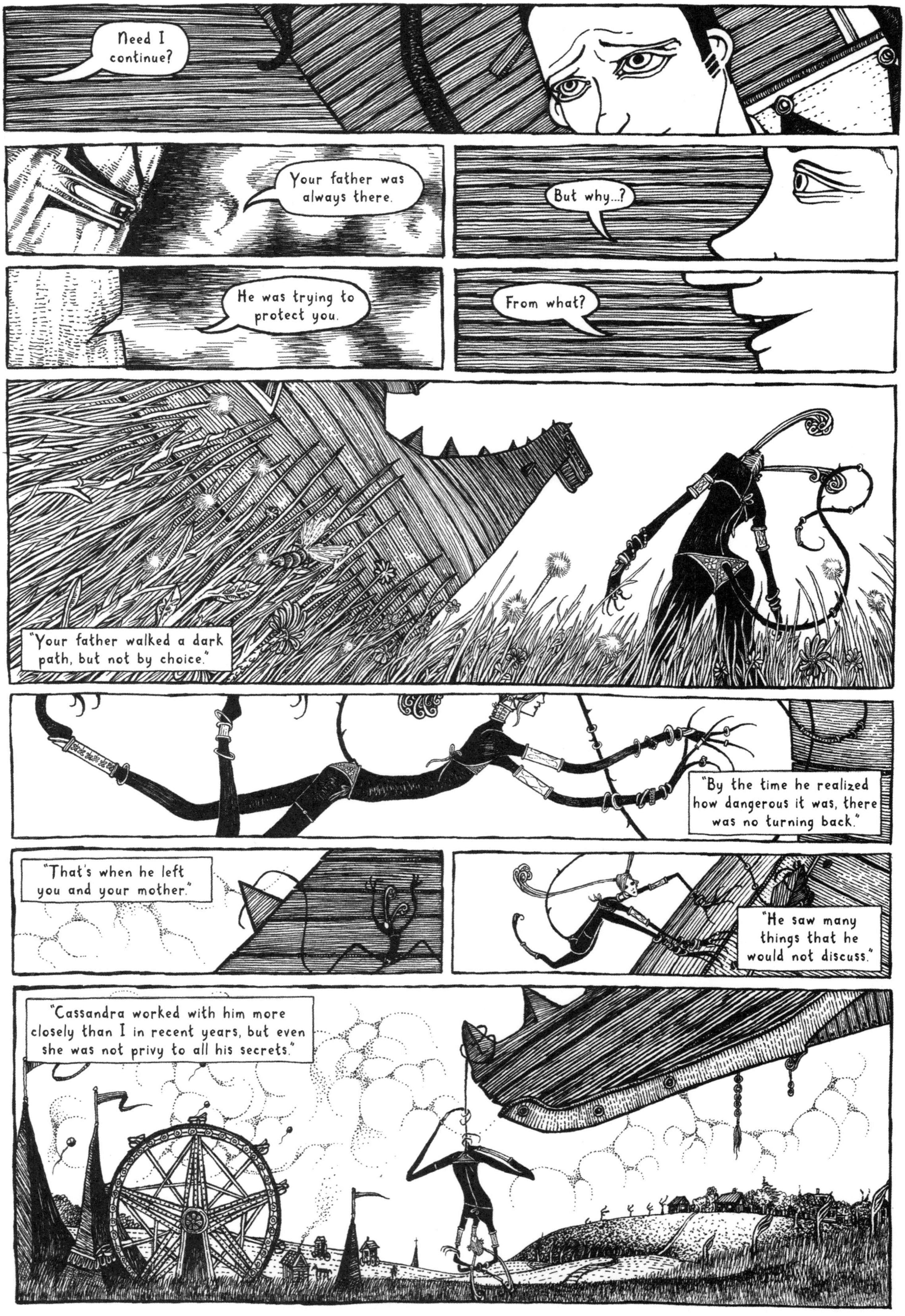
Need I continue?
Your father was always there.
But why...?
He was trying to protect you.
From what?
"Your father walked a dark path, but not by choice."
"By the time he realized how dangerous it was, there was no turning back."
"That's when he left you and your mother."
"He saw many things that he would not discuss."
"Cassandra worked with him more closely than I in recent years, but even she was not privy to all his secrets."

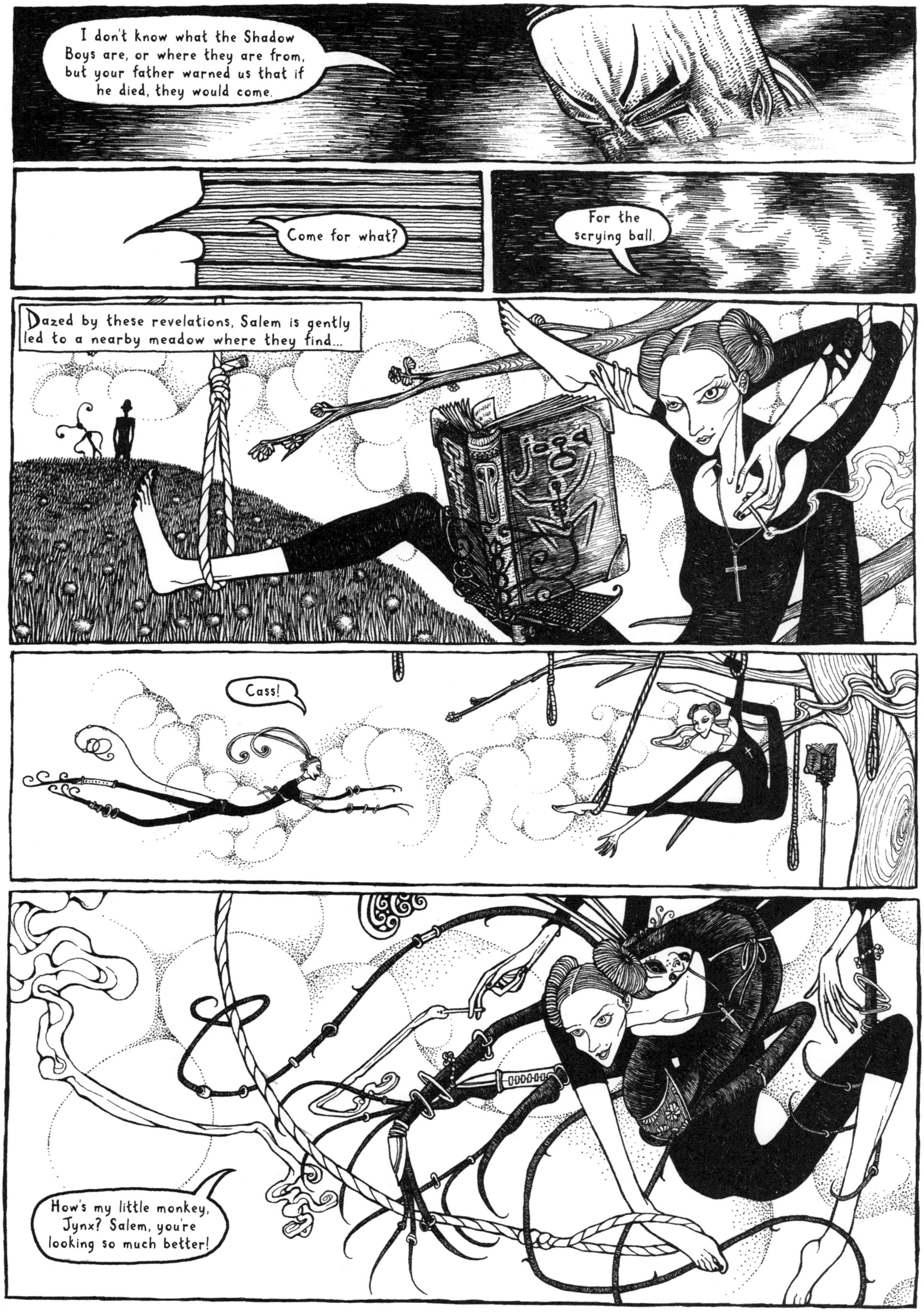
I don't know what the Shadow Boys are, or where they are from, but your father warned us that if he died, they would come.
Come for what?
For the scrying ball.
Dazed by these revelations, Salem is gently led to a nearby meadow where they find...
Cass!
How's my little monkey, Jynx? Salem, you're looking so much better!

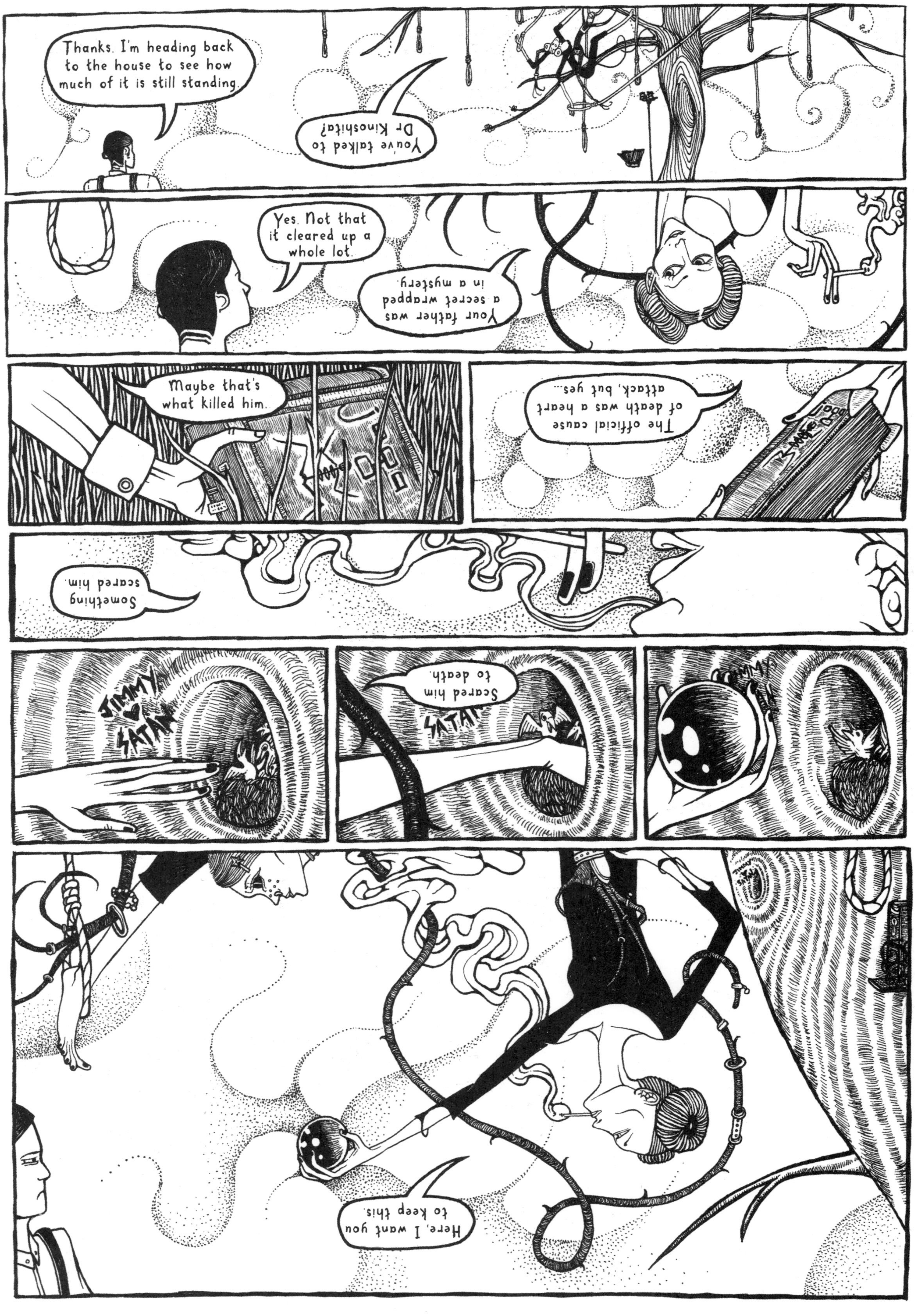

Thanks. I'm heading back to the house to see how much of it is still standing.
You've talked to Dr Kinoshita?
Yes. Not that it cleared up a whole lot.
Your father was a secret wrapped in a mystery.
Maybe that's what killed him.
The official cause of death was a heart attack, but yes...
Something scared him.
JIMMY ♥ SATAN
Scared him to death.
SATAN
Here, I want you to keep this.

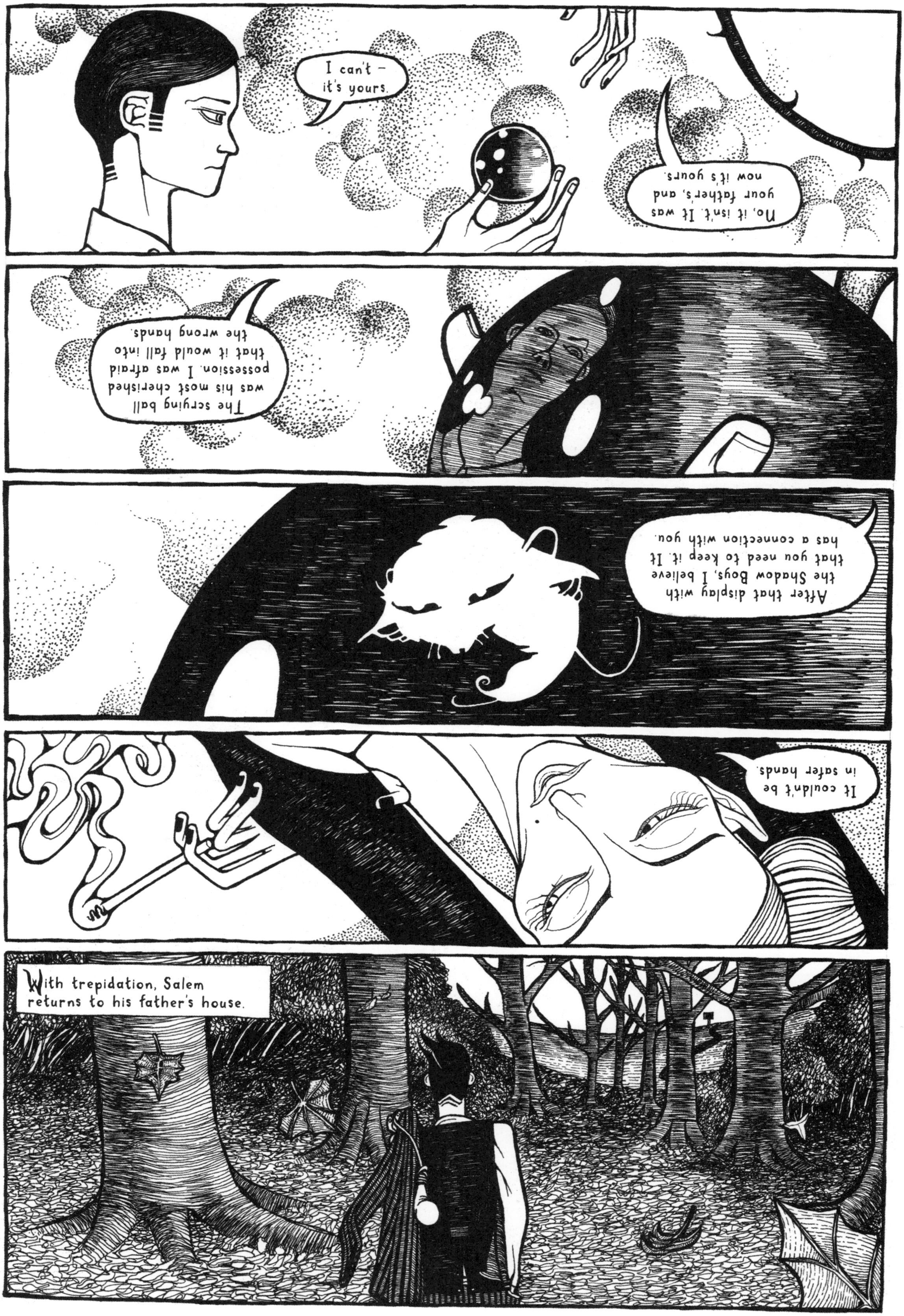
I can't – it's yours.
No, it isn't. It was your father's, and now it's yours.
The scrying ball was his most cherished possession. I was afraid that it would fall into the wrong hands.
After that display with the Shadow Boys, I believe that you need to keep it. It has a connection with you.
It couldn't be in safer hands.
With trepidation, Salem returns to his father's house.

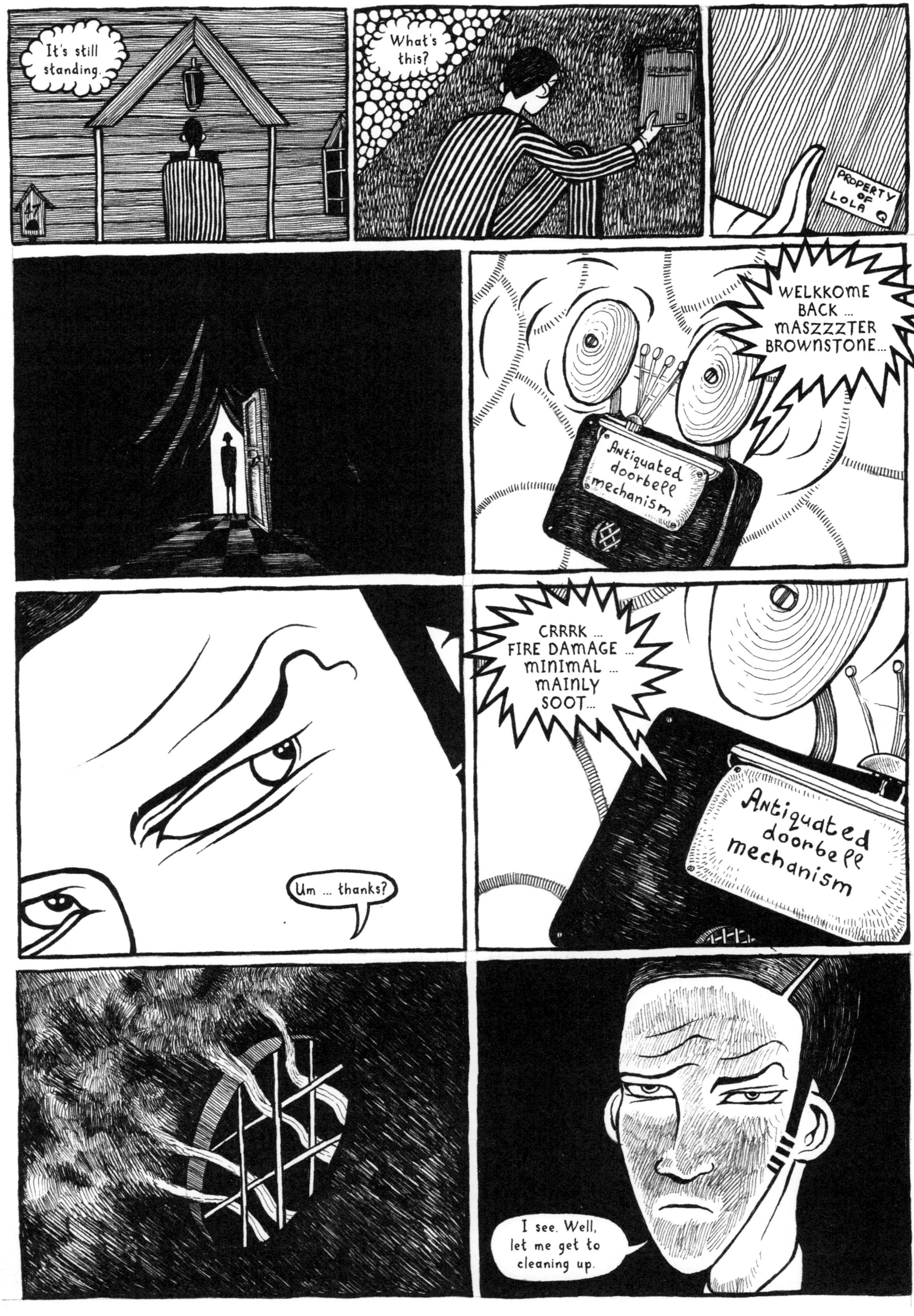
It's still standing.
17
What's this?
PROPERTY OF LOLA Q
WELKKOME BACK ... MASZZZTER BROWNSTONE...
Antiquated doorbell mechanism
CRRRK ... FIRE DAMAGE ... MINIMAL ... MAINLY SOOT...
Antiquated doorbell mechanism
Um ... thanks?
I see. Well, let me get to cleaning up.

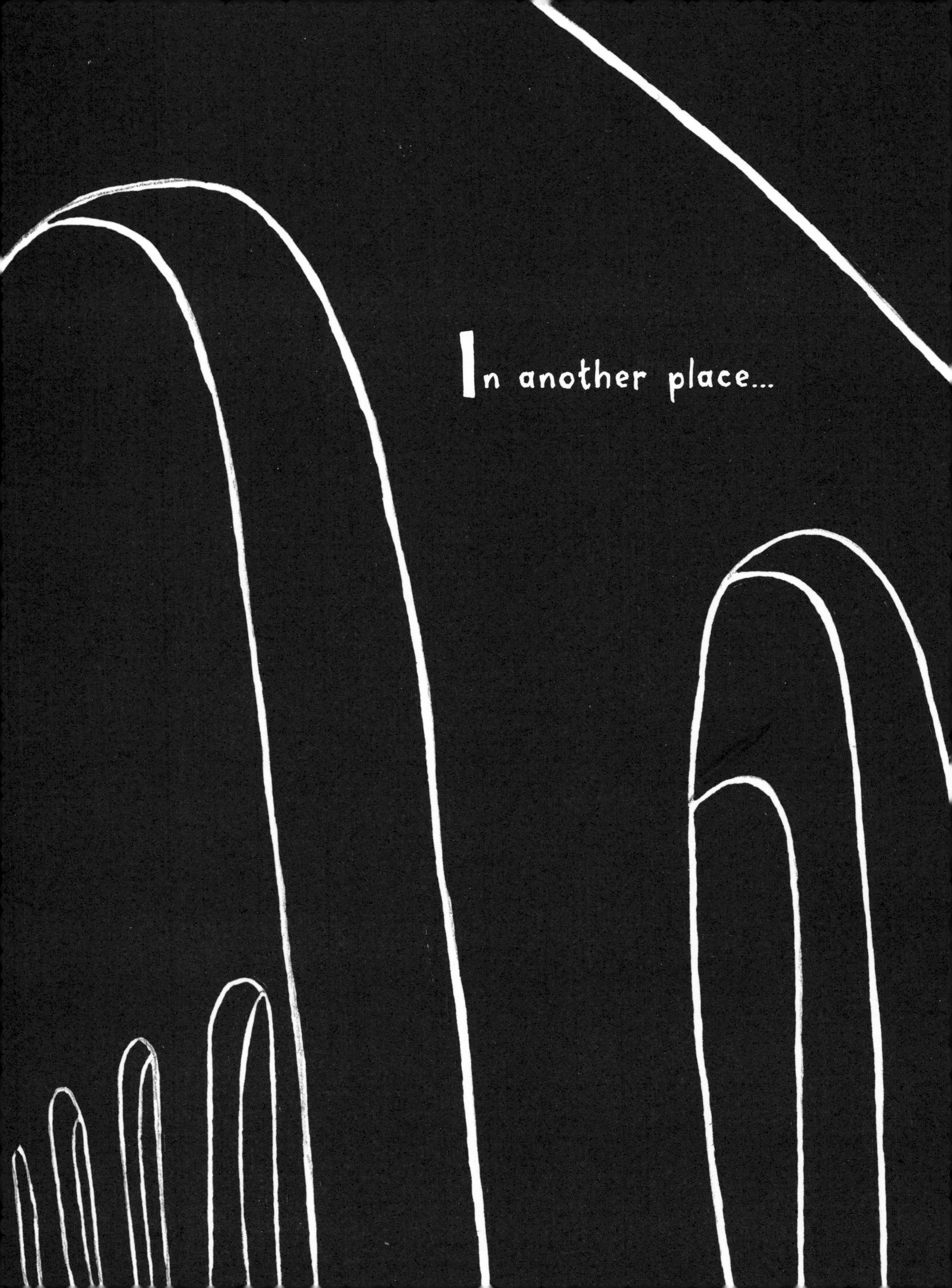
In another place...

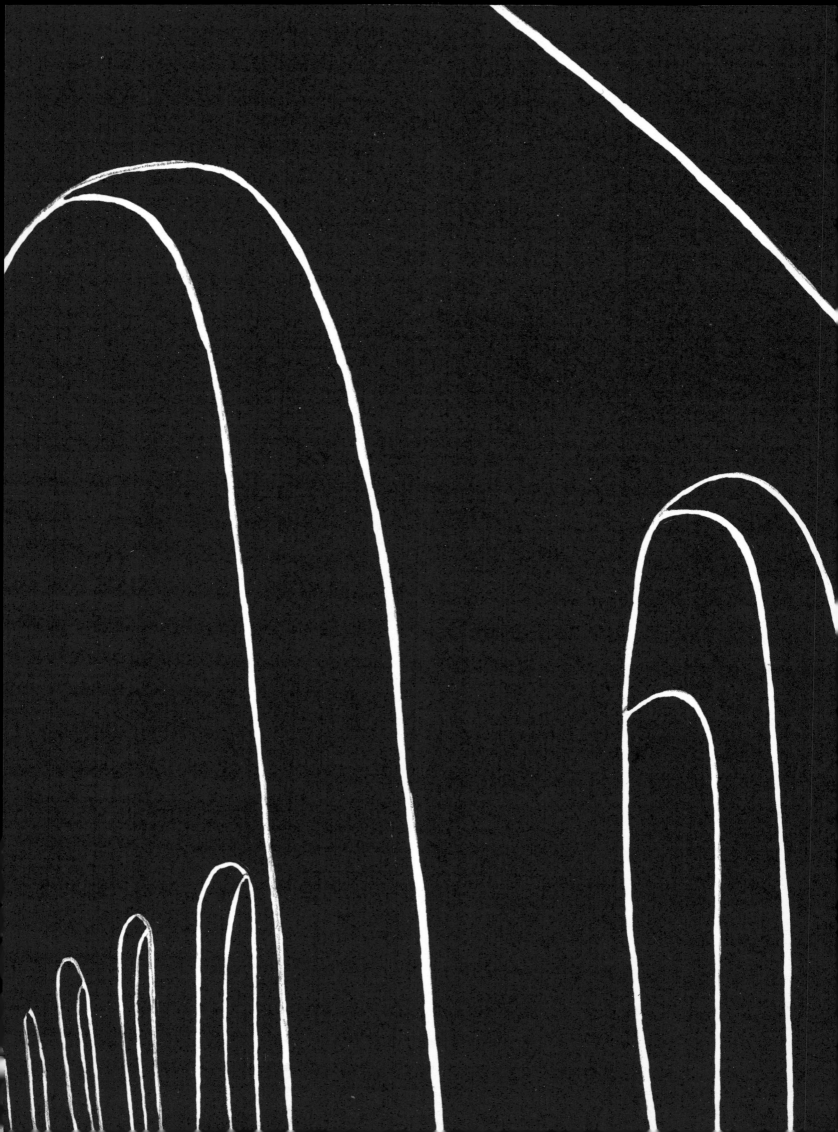

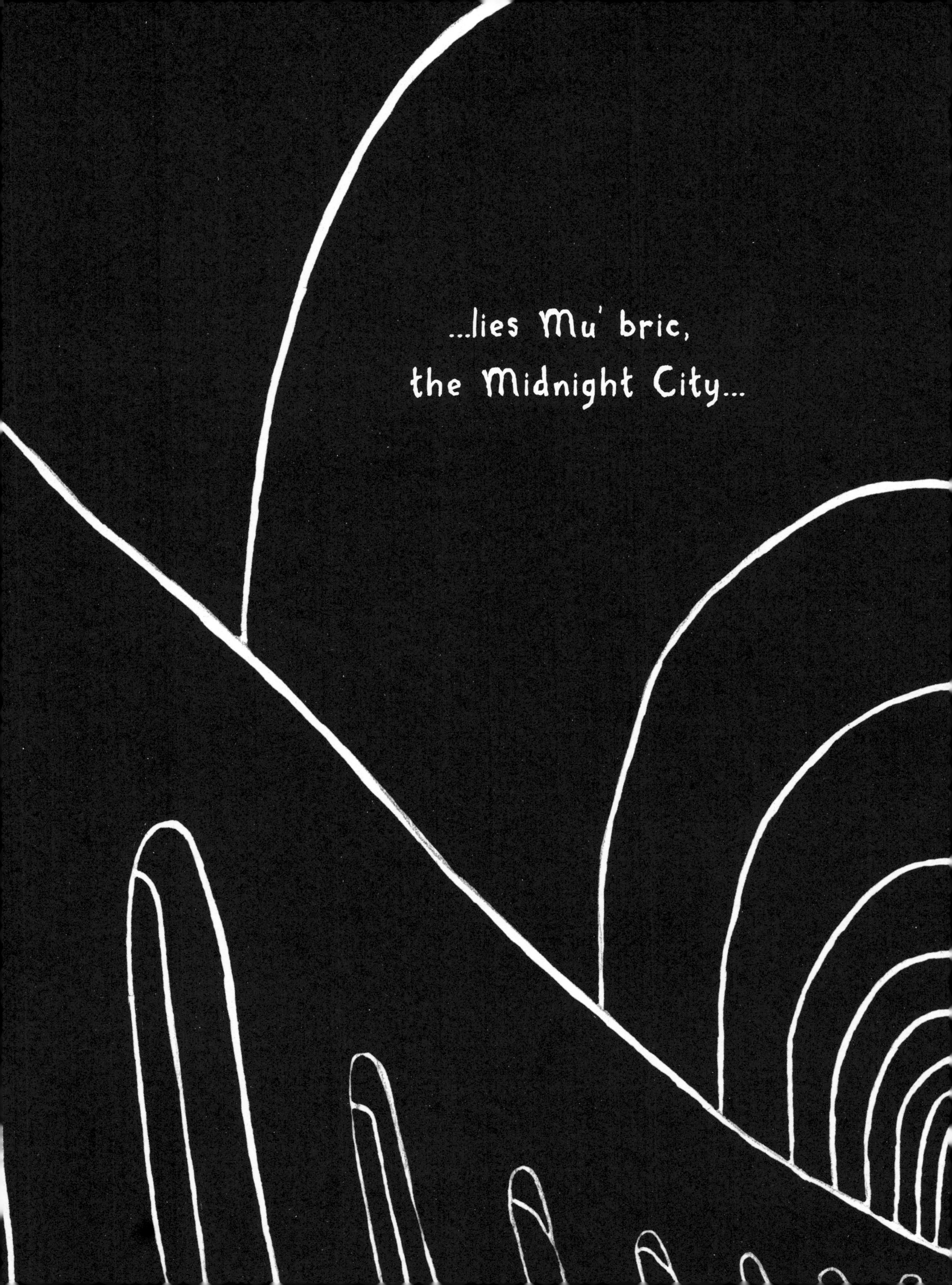
...lies Mu' bric,
the Midnight City...

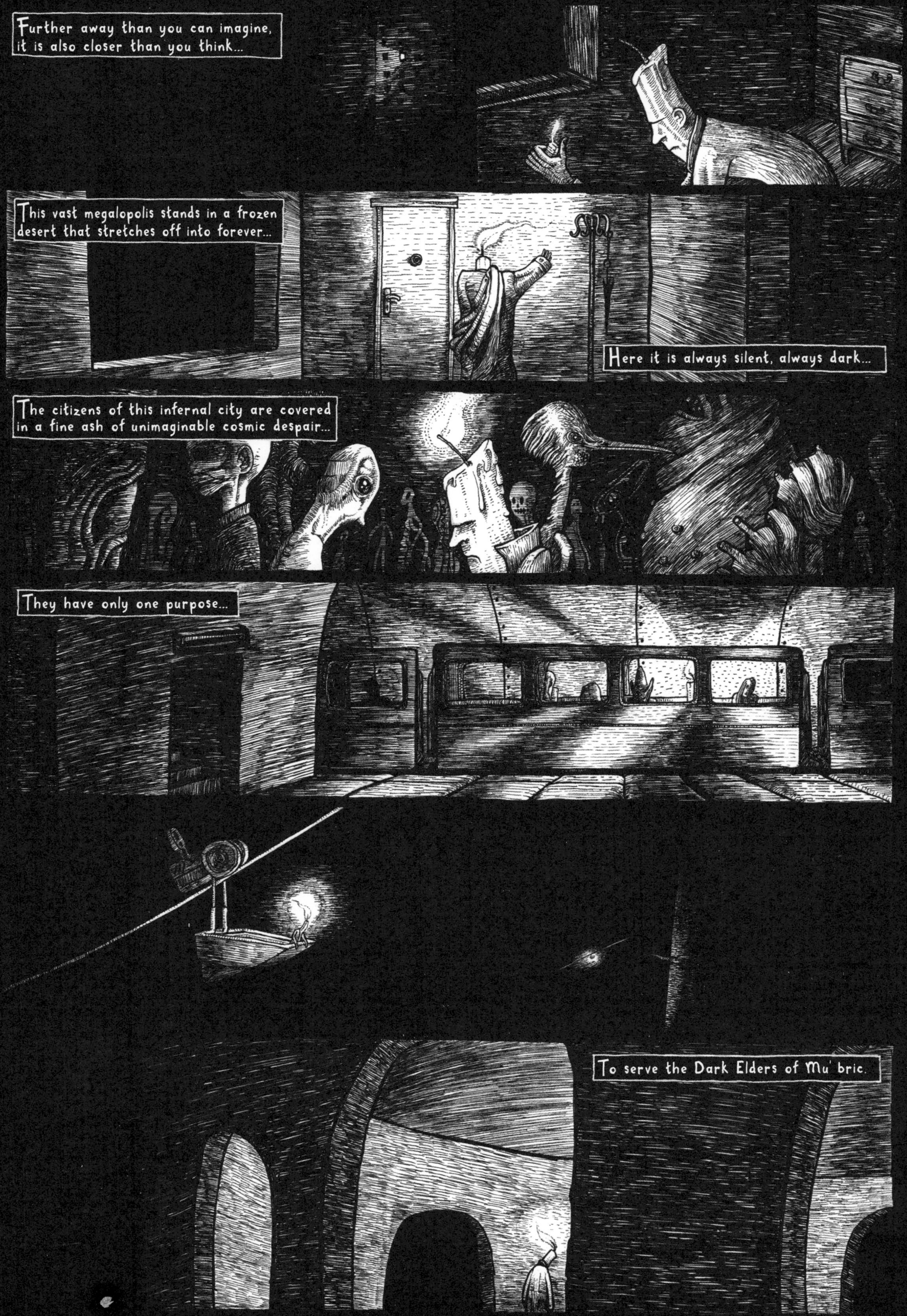
Further away than you can imagine, it is also closer than you think...
This vast megalopolis stands in a frozen desert that stretches off into forever...
Here it is always silent, always dark...
The citizens of this infernal city are covered in a fine ash of unimaginable cosmic despair...
They have only one purpose...
To serve the Dark Elders of Mu'bric.

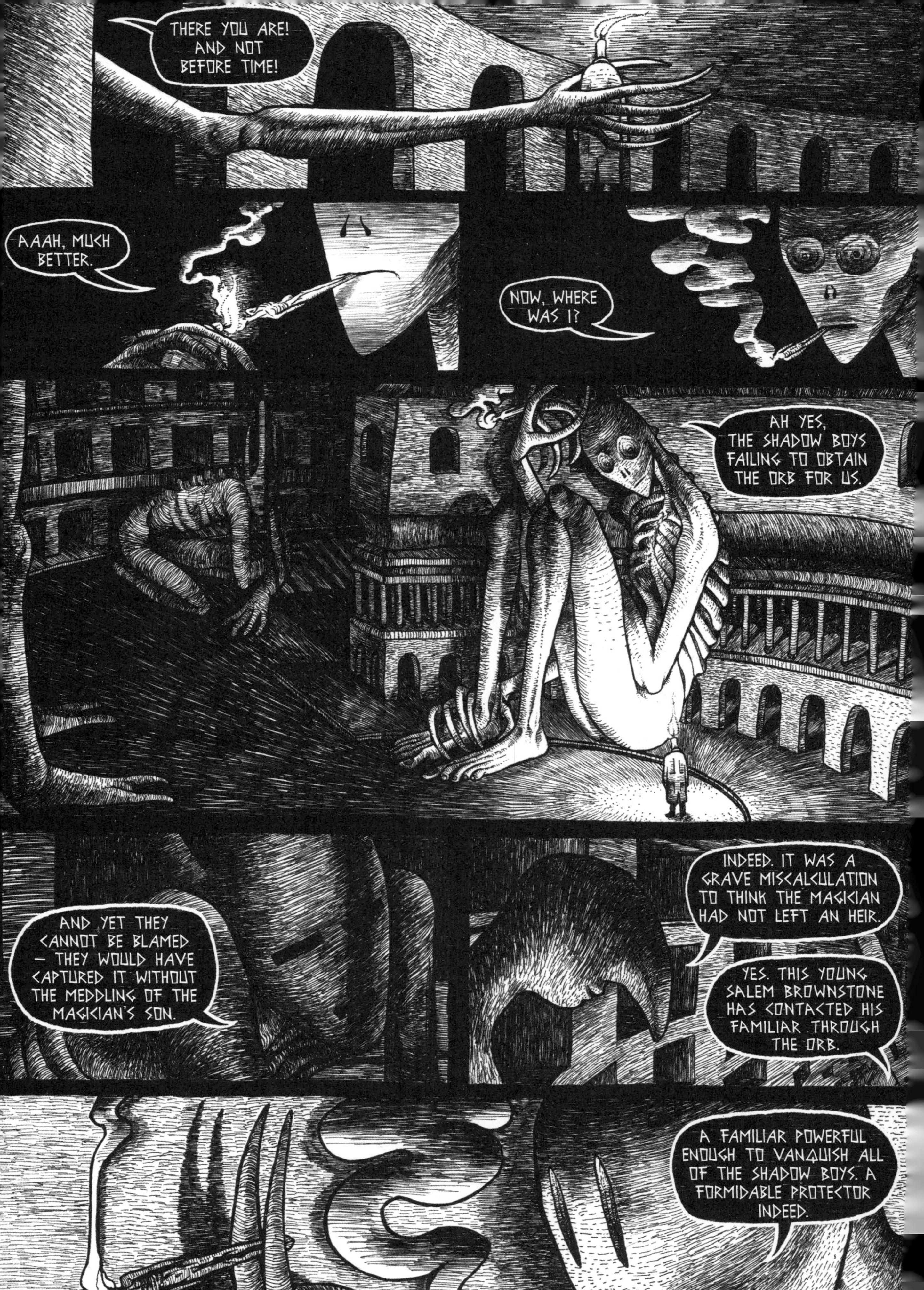
THERE YOU ARE! AND NOT BEFORE TIME!
AAAH, MUCH BETTER.
NOW, WHERE WAS I?
AH YES, THE SHADOW BOYS FAILING TO OBTAIN THE ORB FOR US.
AND YET THEY CANNOT BE BLAMED – THEY WOULD HAVE CAPTURED IT WITHOUT THE MEDDLING OF THE MAGICIAN'S SON.
INDEED. IT WAS A GRAVE MISCALCULATION TO THINK THE MAGICIAN HAD NOT LEFT AN HEIR.
YES. THIS YOUNG SALEM BROWNSTONE HAS CONTACTED HIS FAMILIAR THROUGH THE ORB.
A FAMILIAR POWERFUL ENOUGH TO VANQUISH ALL OF THE SHADOW BOYS. A FORMIDABLE PROTECTOR INDEED.

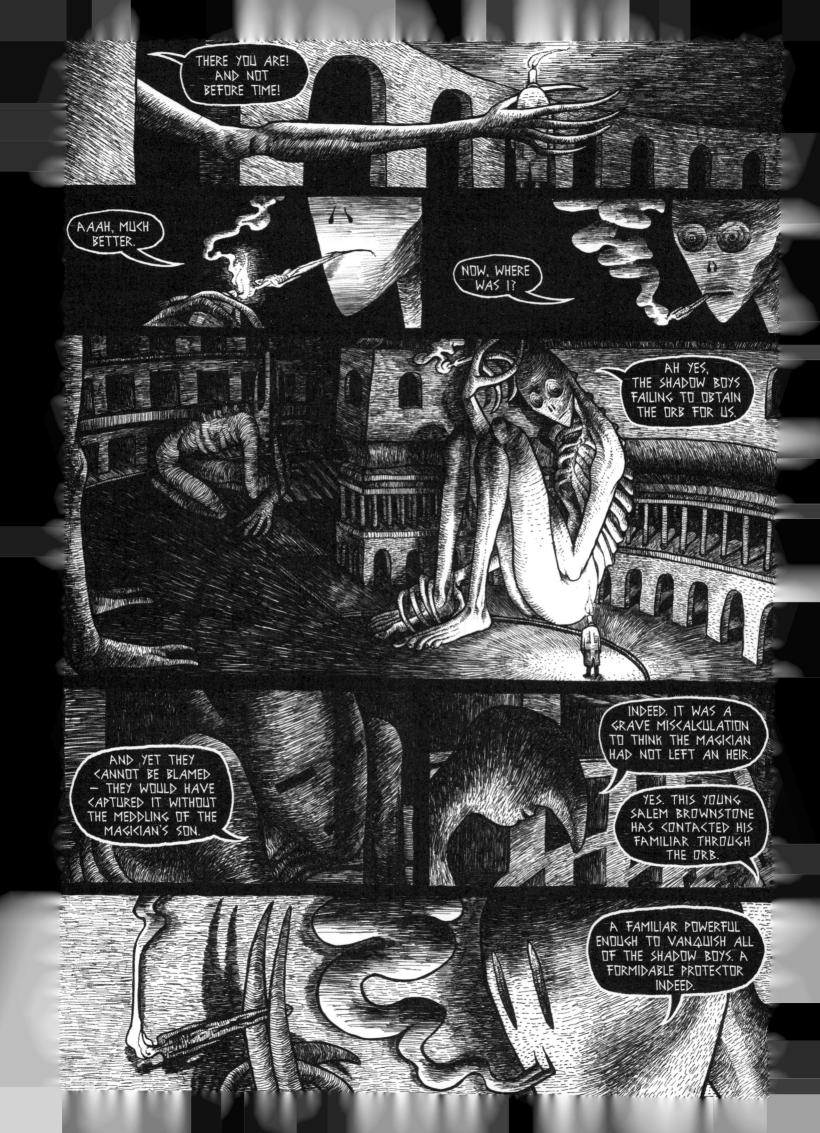

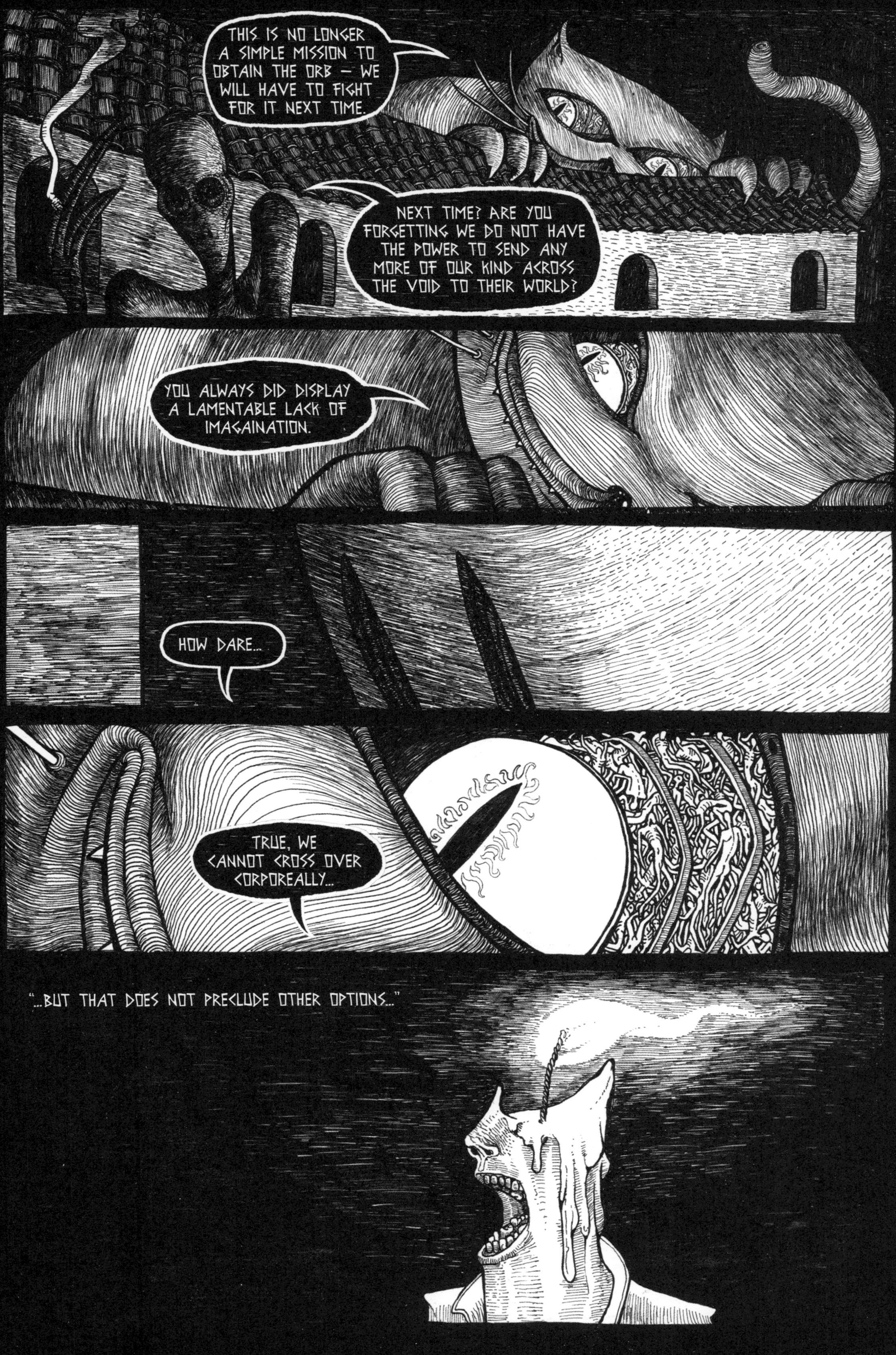
THIS IS NO LONGER A SIMPLE MISSION TO OBTAIN THE ORB — WE WILL HAVE TO FIGHT FOR IT NEXT TIME.
NEXT TIME? ARE YOU FORGETTING WE DO NOT HAVE THE POWER TO SEND ANY MORE OF OUR KIND ACROSS THE VOID TO THEIR WORLD?
YOU ALWAYS DID DISPLAY A LAMENTABLE LACK OF IMAGAINATION.
HOW DARE...
TRUE, WE CANNOT CROSS OVER CORPOREALLY...
"...BUT THAT DOES NOT PRECLUDE OTHER OPTIONS..."

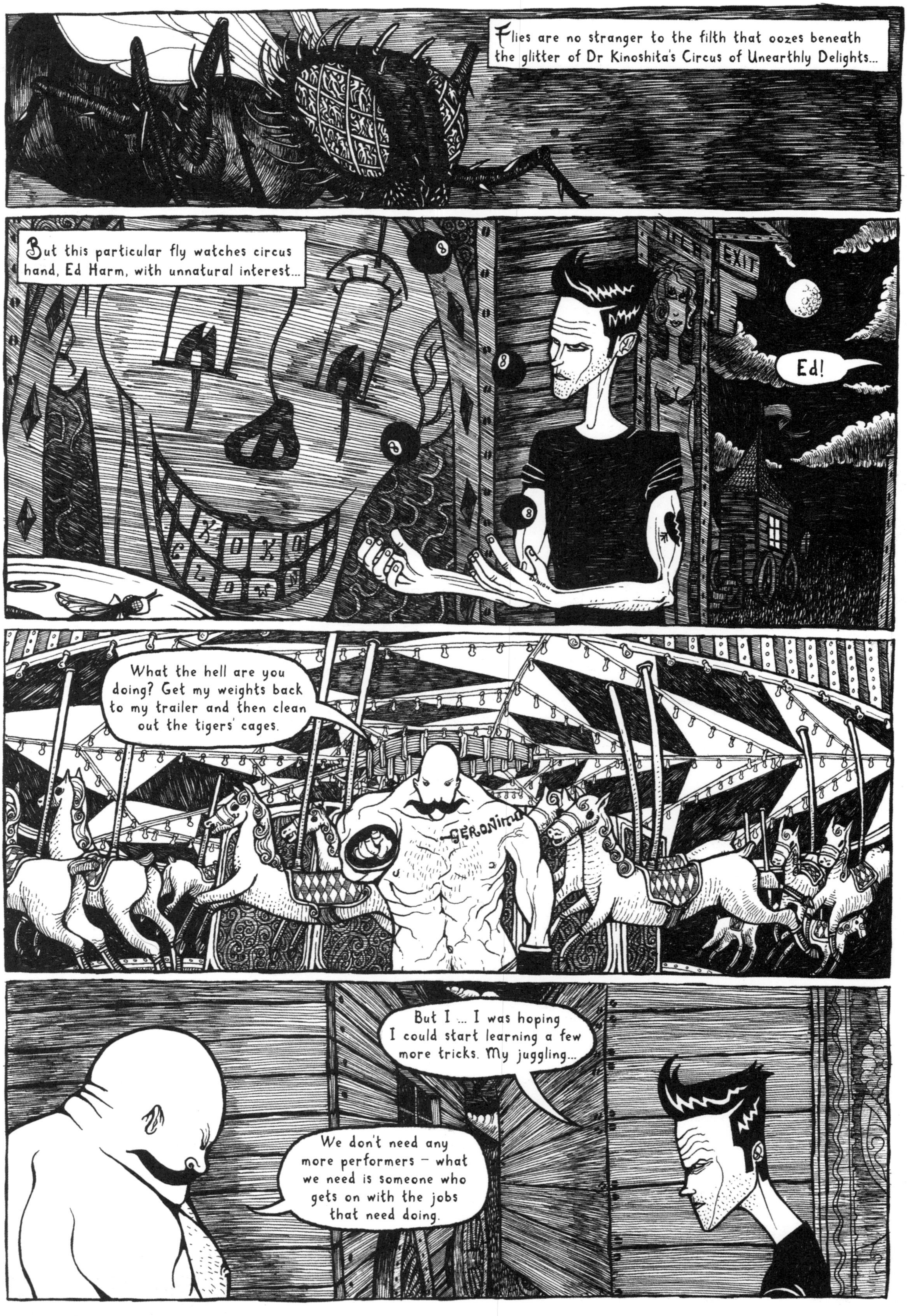
Flies are no stranger to the filth that oozes beneath the glitter of Dr Kinoshita's Circus of Unearthly Delights...
But this particular fly watches circus hand, Ed Harm, with unnatural interest...
Ed!
What the hell are you doing? Get my weights back to my trailer and then clean out the tigers' cages.
GERONIMO
But I ... I was hoping I could start learning a few more tricks. My juggling...
We don't need any more performers – what we need is someone who gets on with the jobs that need doing.

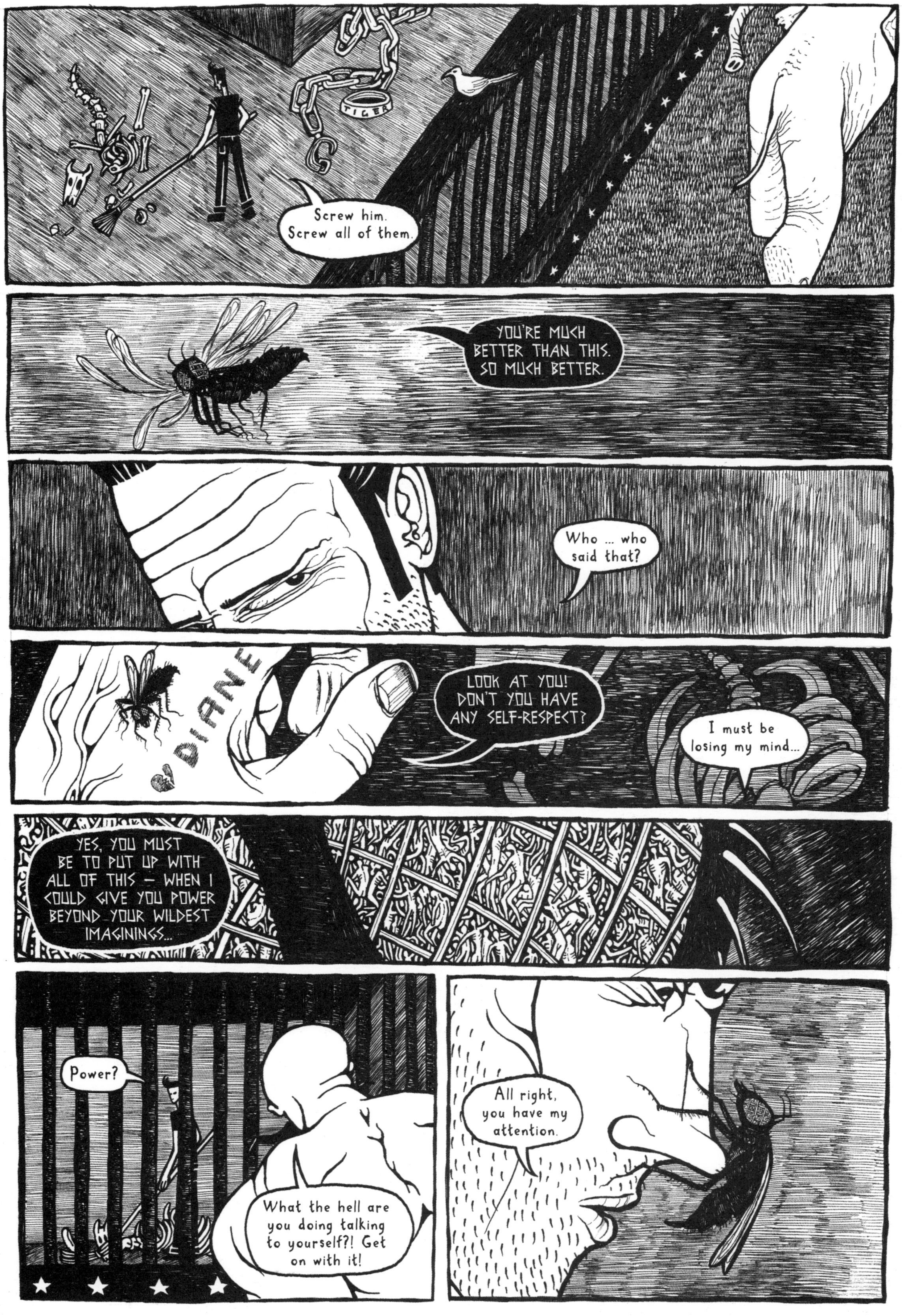
Screw him. Screw all of them.
YOU'RE MUCH BETTER THAN THIS. SO MUCH BETTER.
Who ... who said that?
DIANE
LOOK AT YOU! DON'T YOU HAVE ANY SELF-RESPECT?
I must be losing my mind...
YES, YOU MUST BE TO PUT UP WITH ALL OF THIS — WHEN I COULD GIVE YOU POWER BEYOND YOUR WILDEST IMAGININGS...
Power?
What the hell are you doing talking to yourself?! Get on with it!
All right, you have my attention.

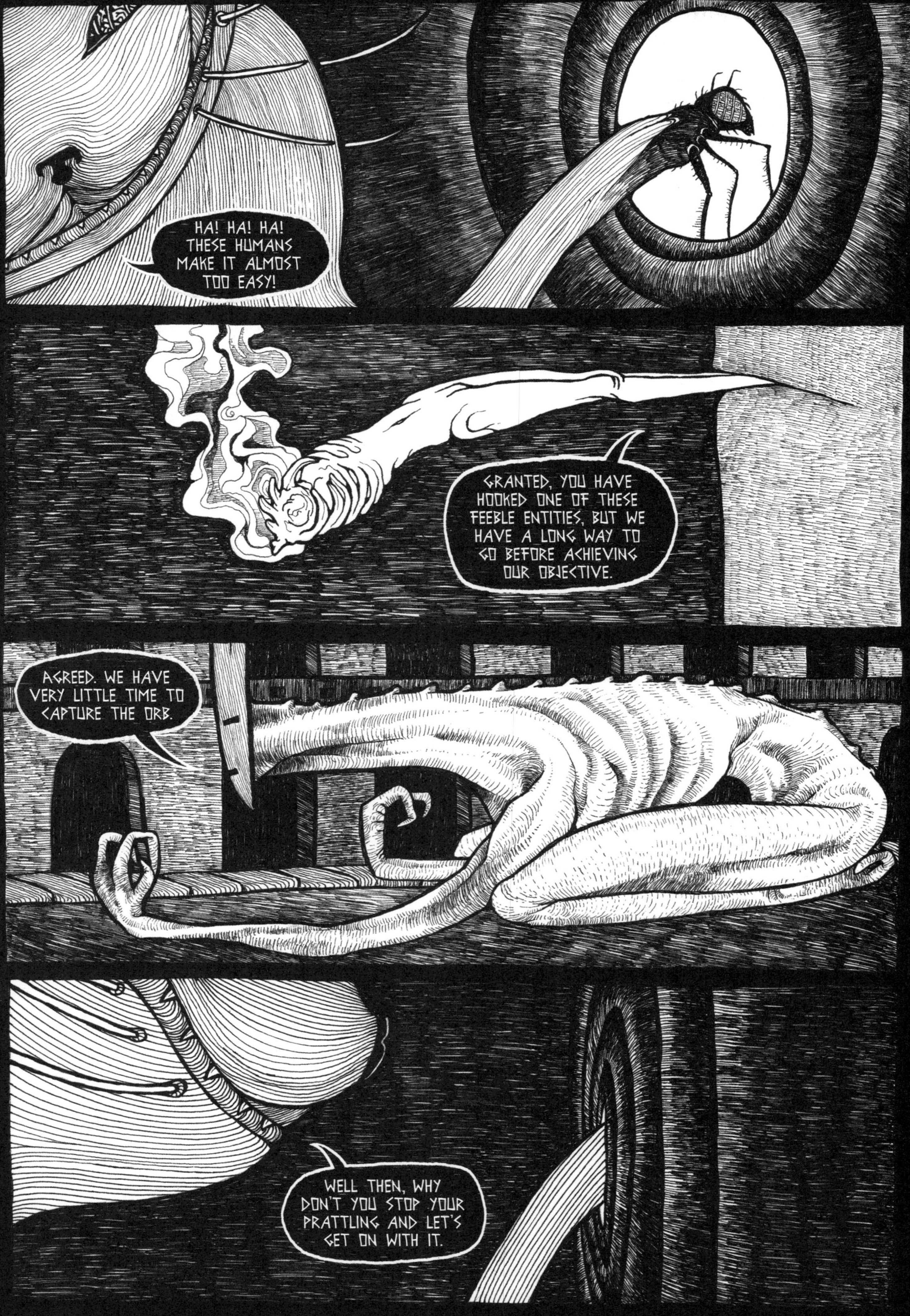
HA! HA! HA! THESE HUMANS MAKE IT ALMOST TOO EASY!
GRANTED, YOU HAVE HOOKED ONE OF THESE FEEBLE ENTITIES, BUT WE HAVE A LONG WAY TO GO BEFORE ACHIEVING OUR OBJECTIVE.
AGREED. WE HAVE VERY LITTLE TIME TO CAPTURE THE ORB.
WELL THEN, WHY DON'T YOU STOP YOUR PRATTLING AND LET'S GET ON WITH IT.

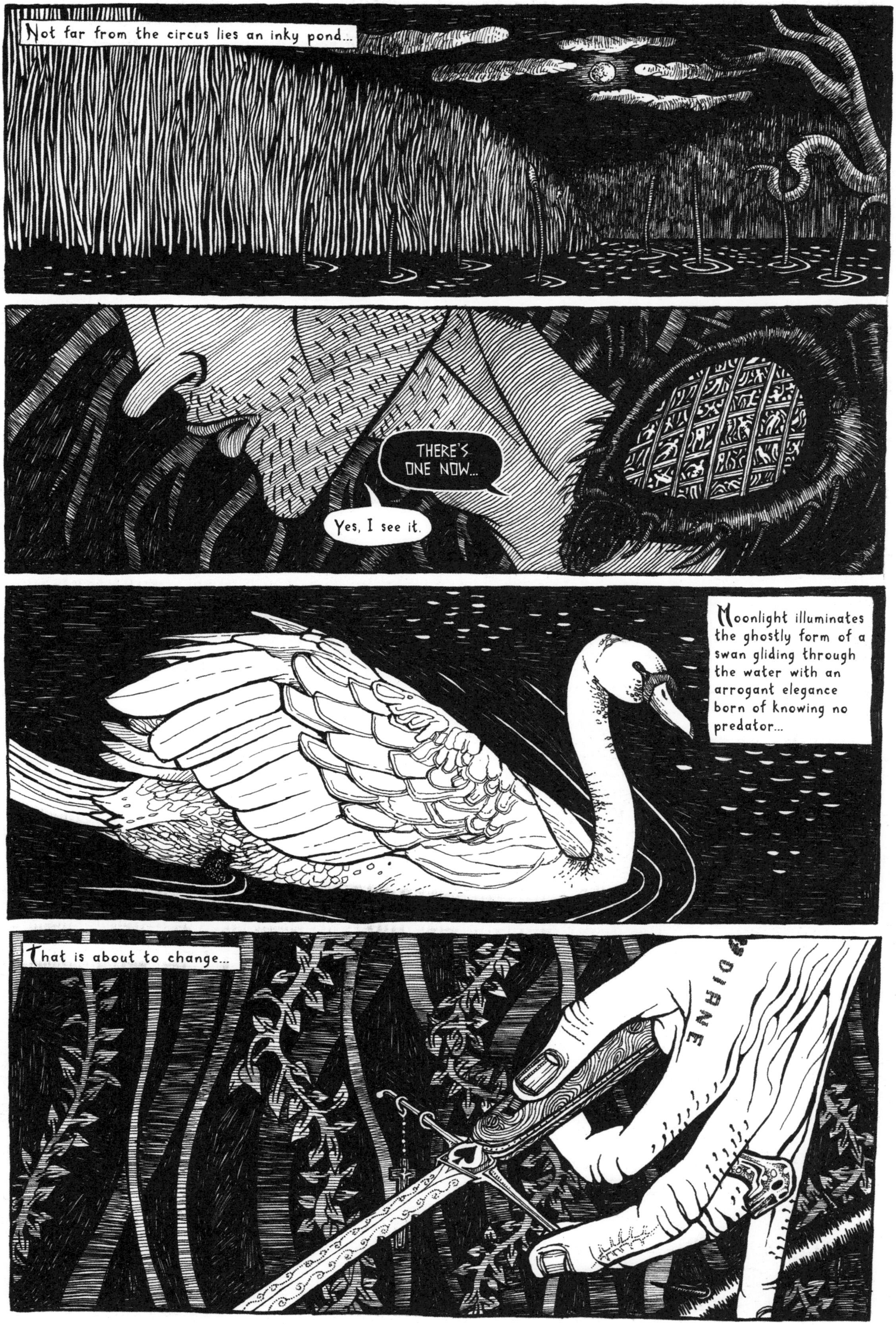
Not far from the circus lies an inky pond...
THERE'S ONE NOW...
Yes, I see it.
Moonlight illuminates the ghostly form of a swan gliding through the water with an arrogant elegance born of knowing no predator...
That is about to change...

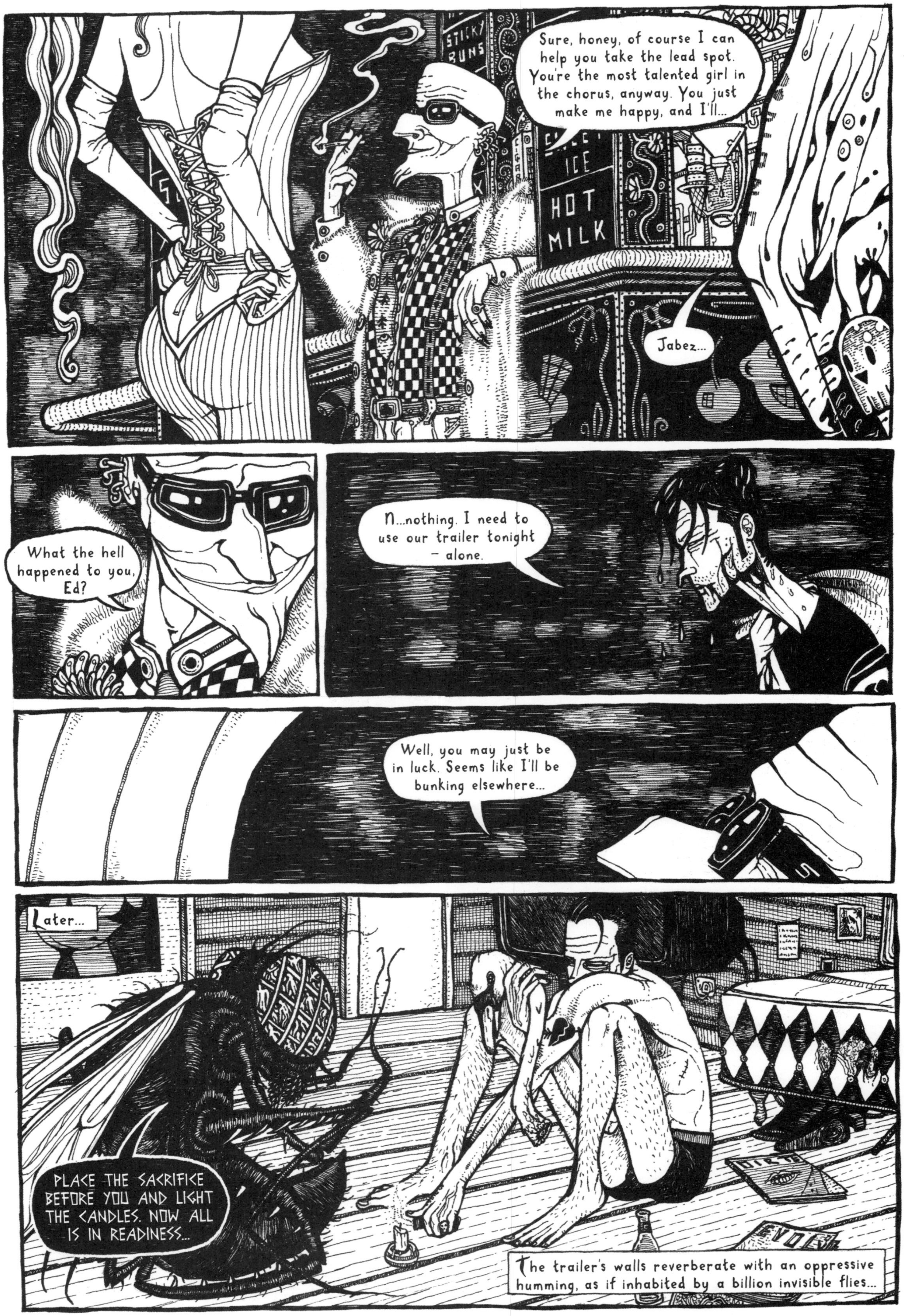

Sure, honey, of course I can help you take the lead spot. You're the most talented girl in the chorus, anyway. You just make me happy, and I'll...
STICKY BUNS
ICE
HOT MILK
Jabez...
What the hell happened to you, Ed?
N...nothing. I need to use our trailer tonight — alone.
Well, you may just be in luck. Seems like I'll be bunking elsewhere...
Later...
PLACE THE SACRIFICE BEFORE YOU AND LIGHT THE CANDLES. NOW ALL IS IN READINESS...
The trailer's walls reverberate with an oppressive humming, as if inhabited by a billion invisible flies...

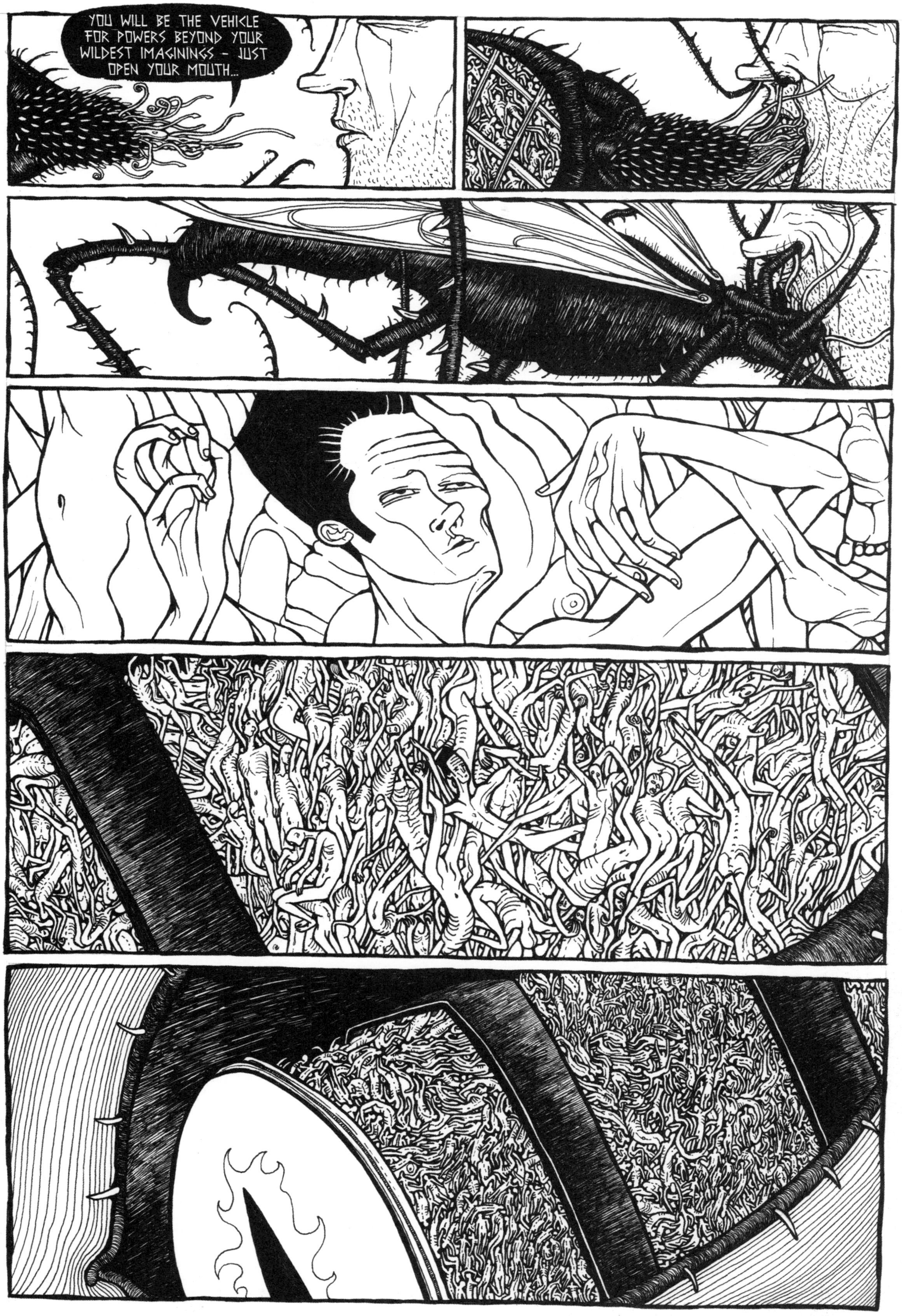
YOU WILL BE THE VEHICLE FOR POWERS BEYOND YOUR WILDEST IMAGININGS – JUST OPEN YOUR MOUTH...

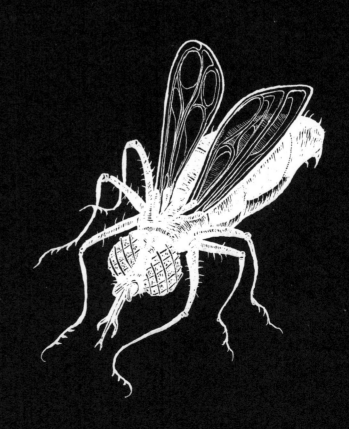

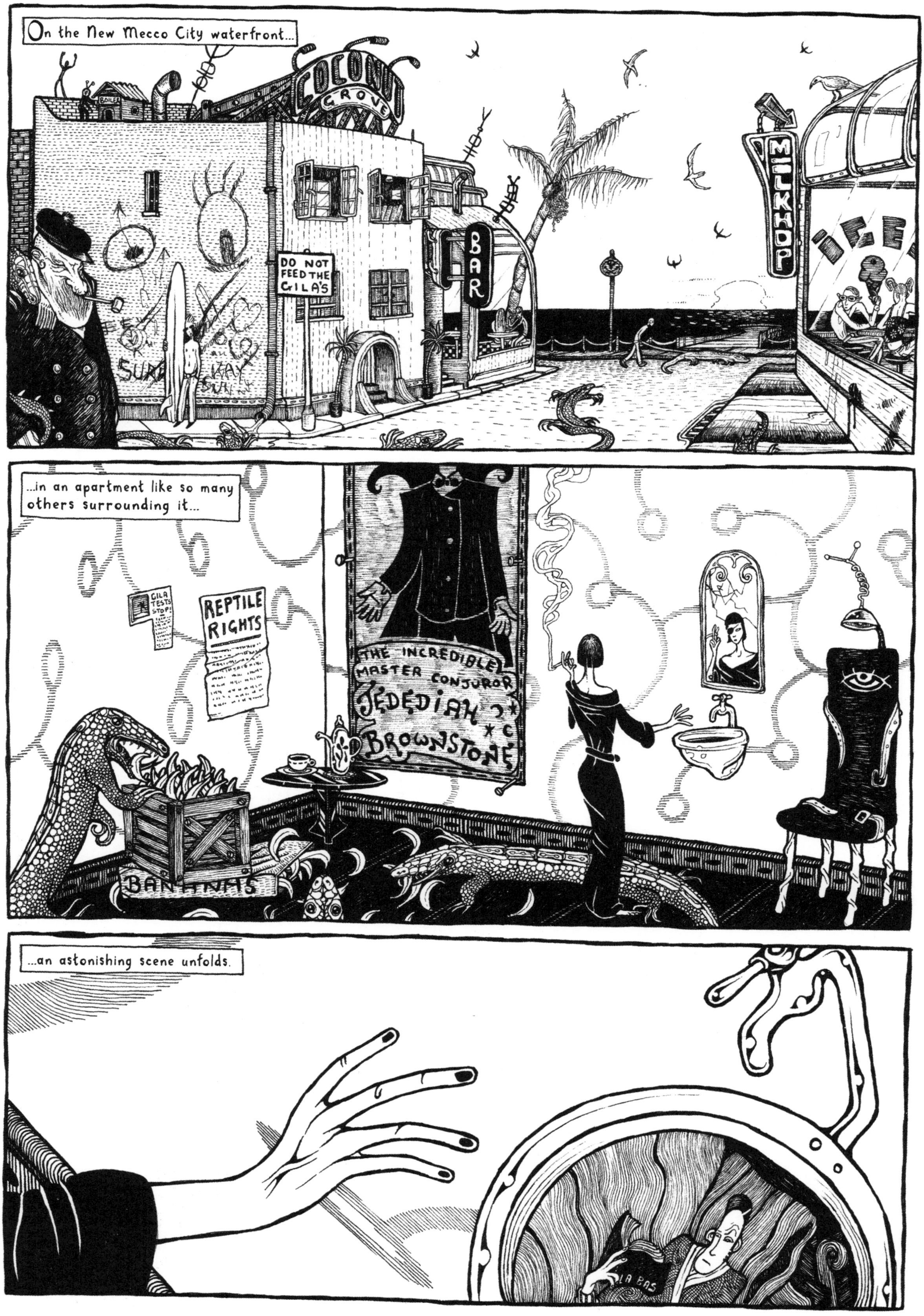
On the New Mecco City waterfront...
BOILER
COCONUT GROVE
DO NOT FEED THE GILA'S
BAR
MILKHOP
ICE
...in an apartment like so many others surrounding it...
GILA TESTS STOP!
REPTILE RIGHTS
THE INCREDIBLE MASTER CONJUROR JEDEDIAH BROWNSTONE
BANANAS
...an astonishing scene unfolds.
LA BAS

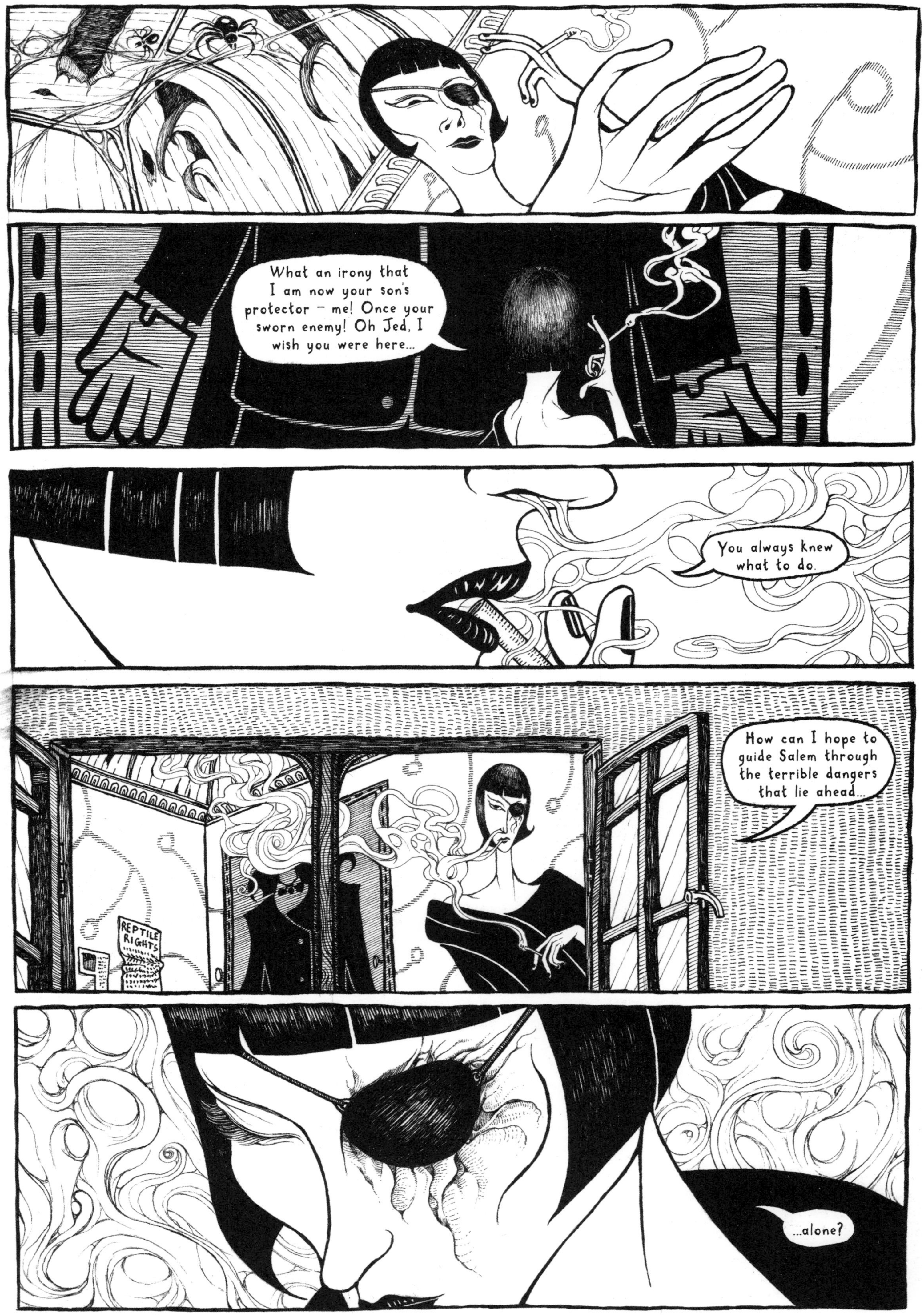
What an irony that I am now your son's protector – me! Once your sworn enemy! Oh Jed, I wish you were here...
You always knew what to do.
REPTILE RIGHTS
How can I hope to guide Salem through the terrible dangers that lie ahead...
...alone?

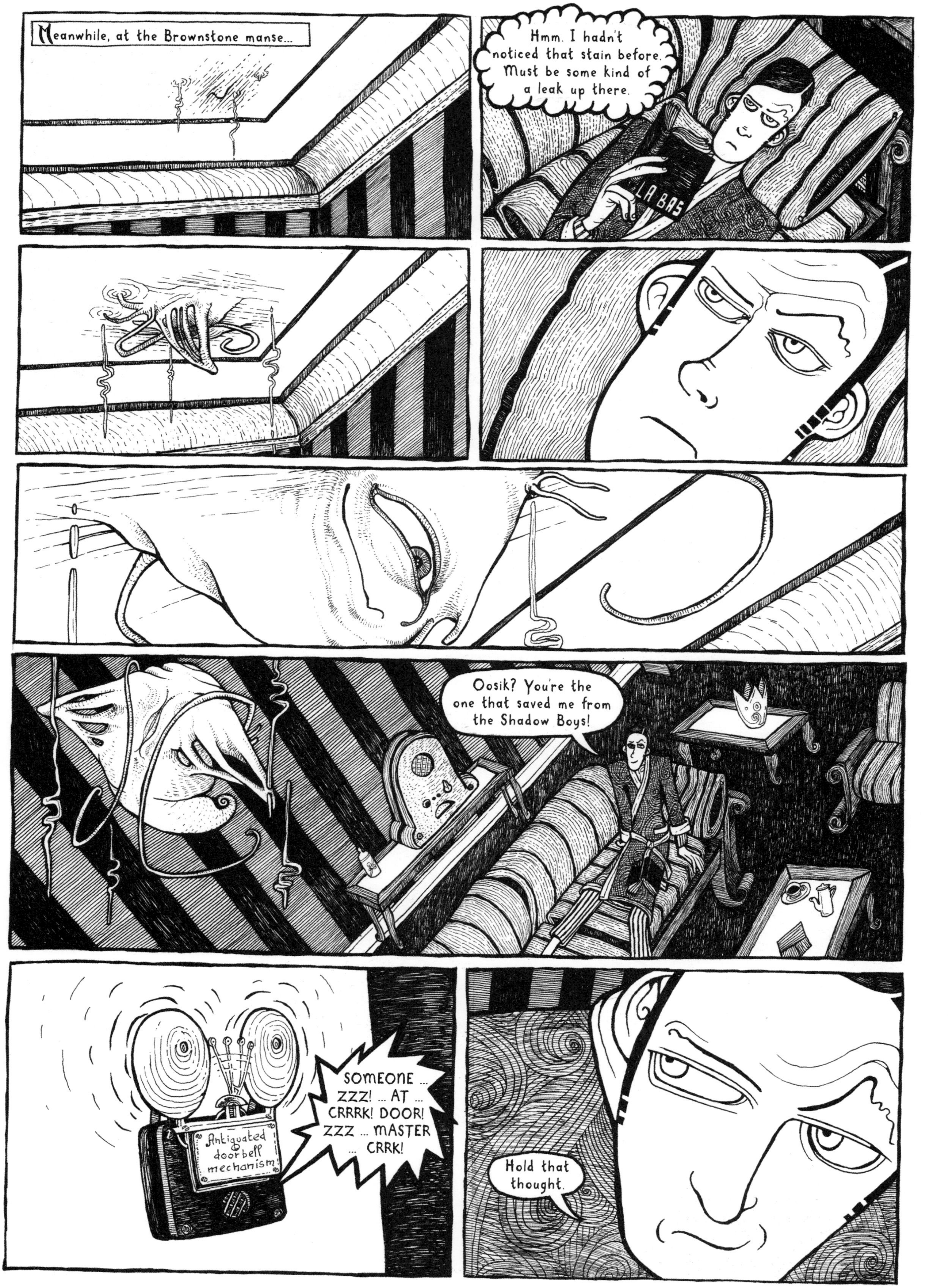
Meanwhile, at the Brownstone manse...
Hmm. I hadn't noticed that stain before. Must be some kind of a leak up there.
LA BAS
Oosik? You're the one that saved me from the Shadow Boys!
Antiquated doorbell mechanism
SOMEONE ... ZZZ! ... AT ... CRRRK! DOOR! ZZZ ... MASTER ... CRRK!
Hold that thought.

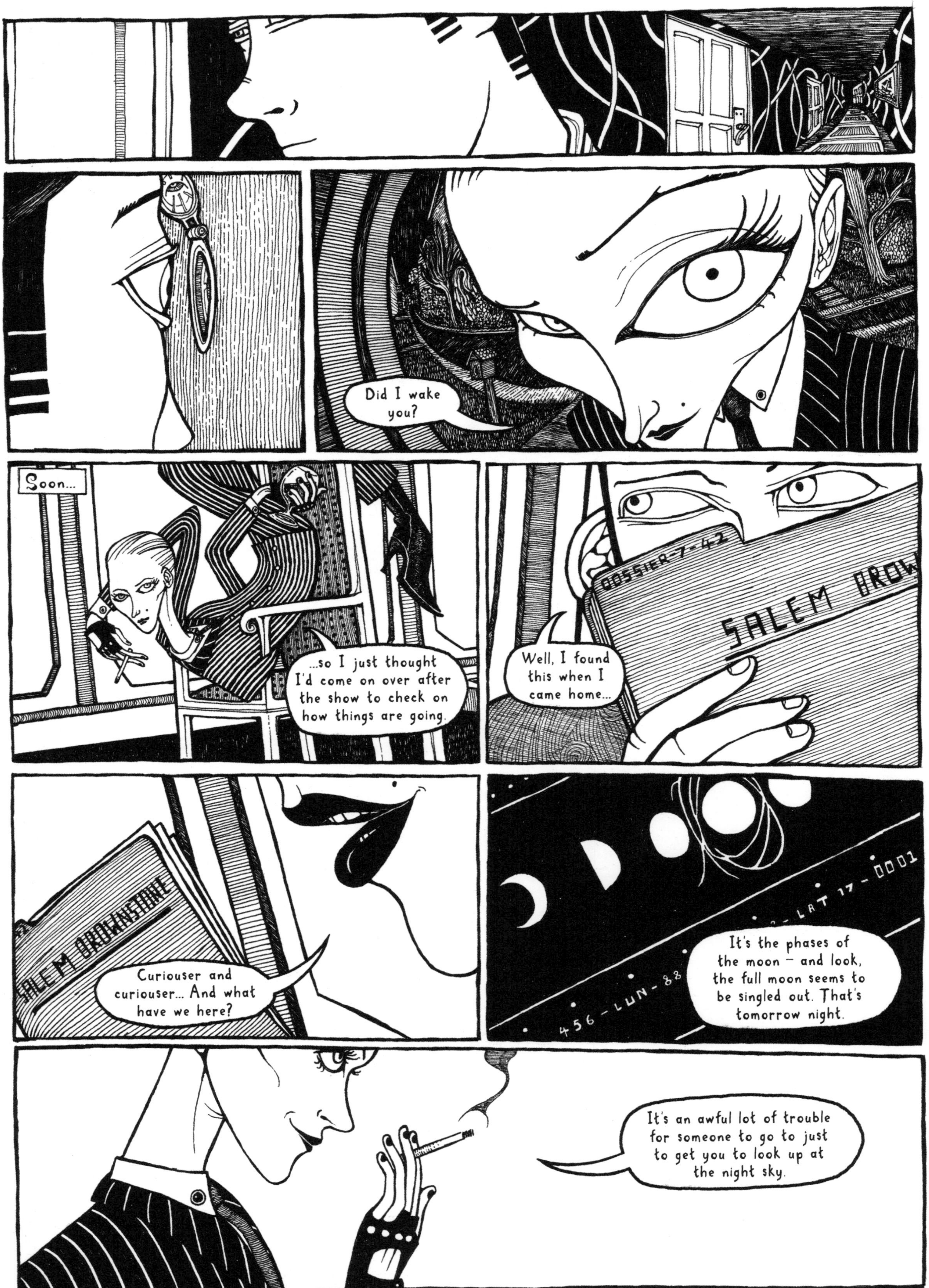
Did I wake you?
Soon...
...so I just thought I'd come on over after the show to check on how things are going.
Well, I found this when I came home...
DOSSIER-7-42
SALEM BROW
SALEM BROWNSTONE
Curiouser and curiouser... And what have we here?
LAT 17-0001
456-LUN-88
It's the phases of the moon – and look, the full moon seems to be singled out. That's tomorrow night.
It's an awful lot of trouble for someone to go to just to get you to look up at the night sky.

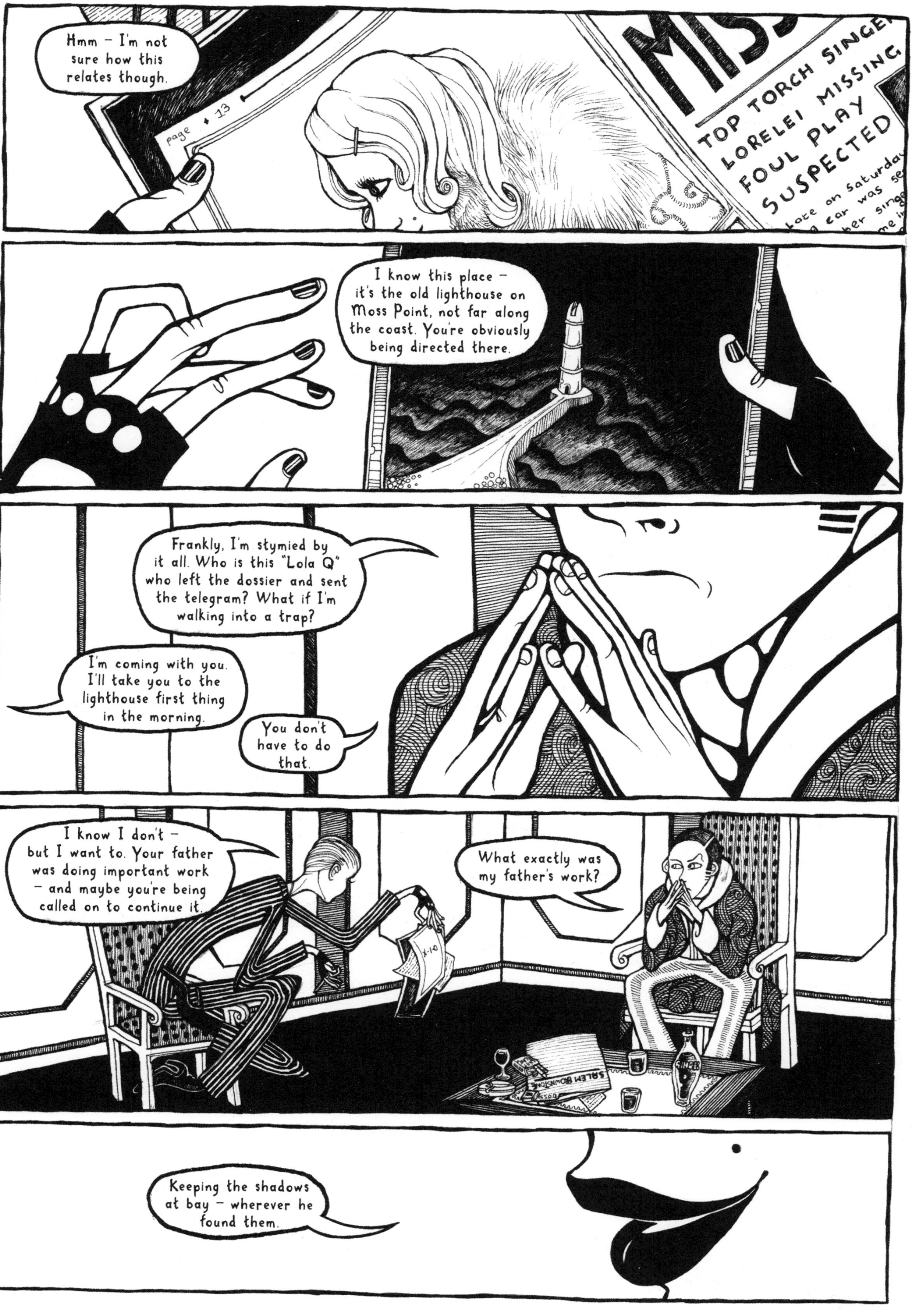
Hmm – I'm not sure how this relates though.
page 13
MISS
TOP TORCH SINGER LORELEI MISSING
FOUL PLAY SUSPECTED
I know this place – it's the old lighthouse on Moss Point, not far along the coast. You're obviously being directed there.
Frankly, I'm stymied by it all. Who is this "Lola Q" who left the dossier and sent the telegram? What if I'm walking into a trap?
I'm coming with you. I'll take you to the lighthouse first thing in the morning.
You don't have to do that.
I know I don't – but I want to. Your father was doing important work – and maybe you're being called on to continue it.
What exactly was my father's work?
Keeping the shadows at bay – wherever he found them.

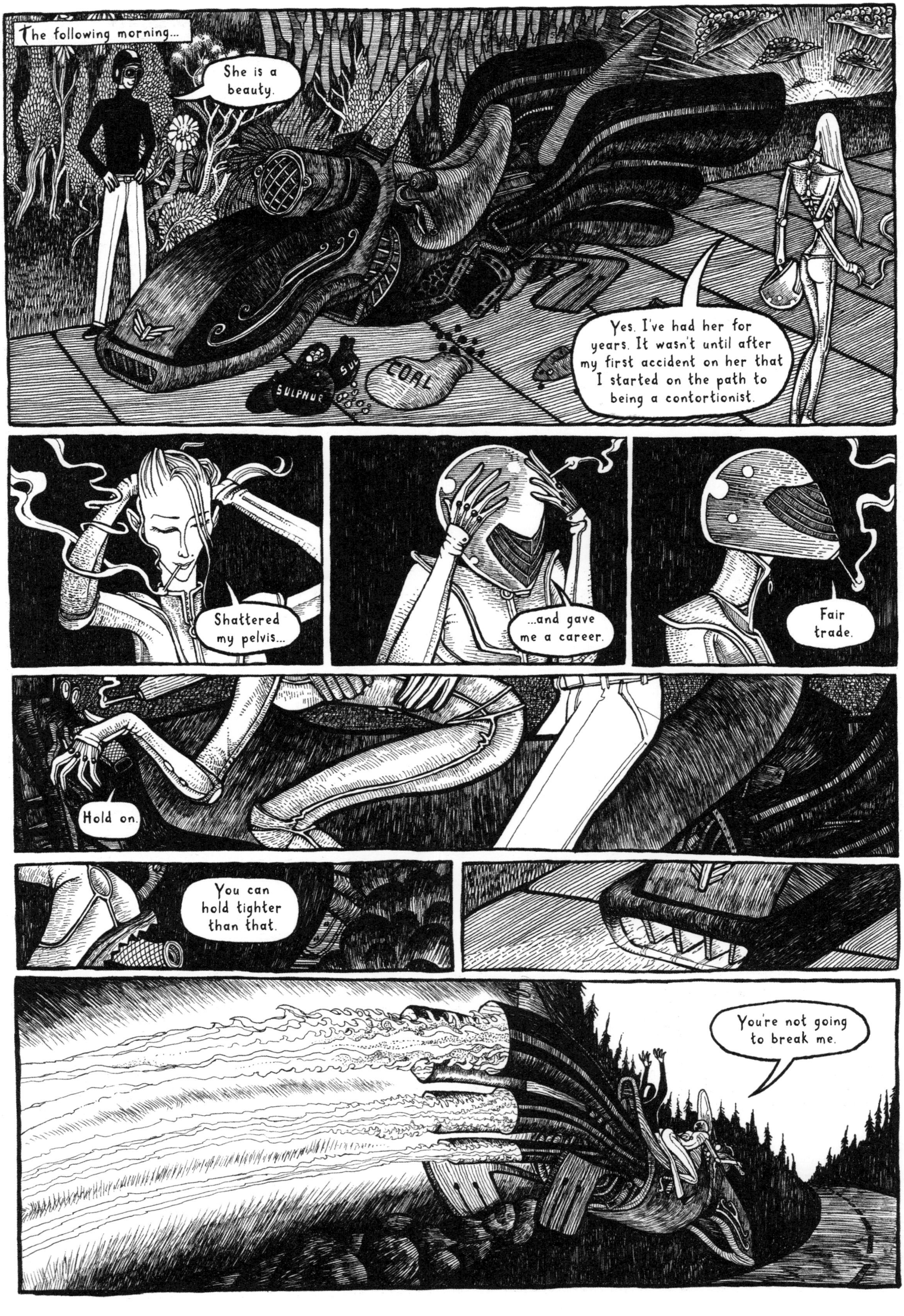
The following morning...
She is a beauty.
Yes. I've had her for years. It wasn't until after my first accident on her that I started on the path to being a contortionist.
SULPHUR
SUL
COAL
Shattered my pelvis...
...and gave me a career.
Fair trade.
Hold on.
You can hold tighter than that.
You're not going to break me.

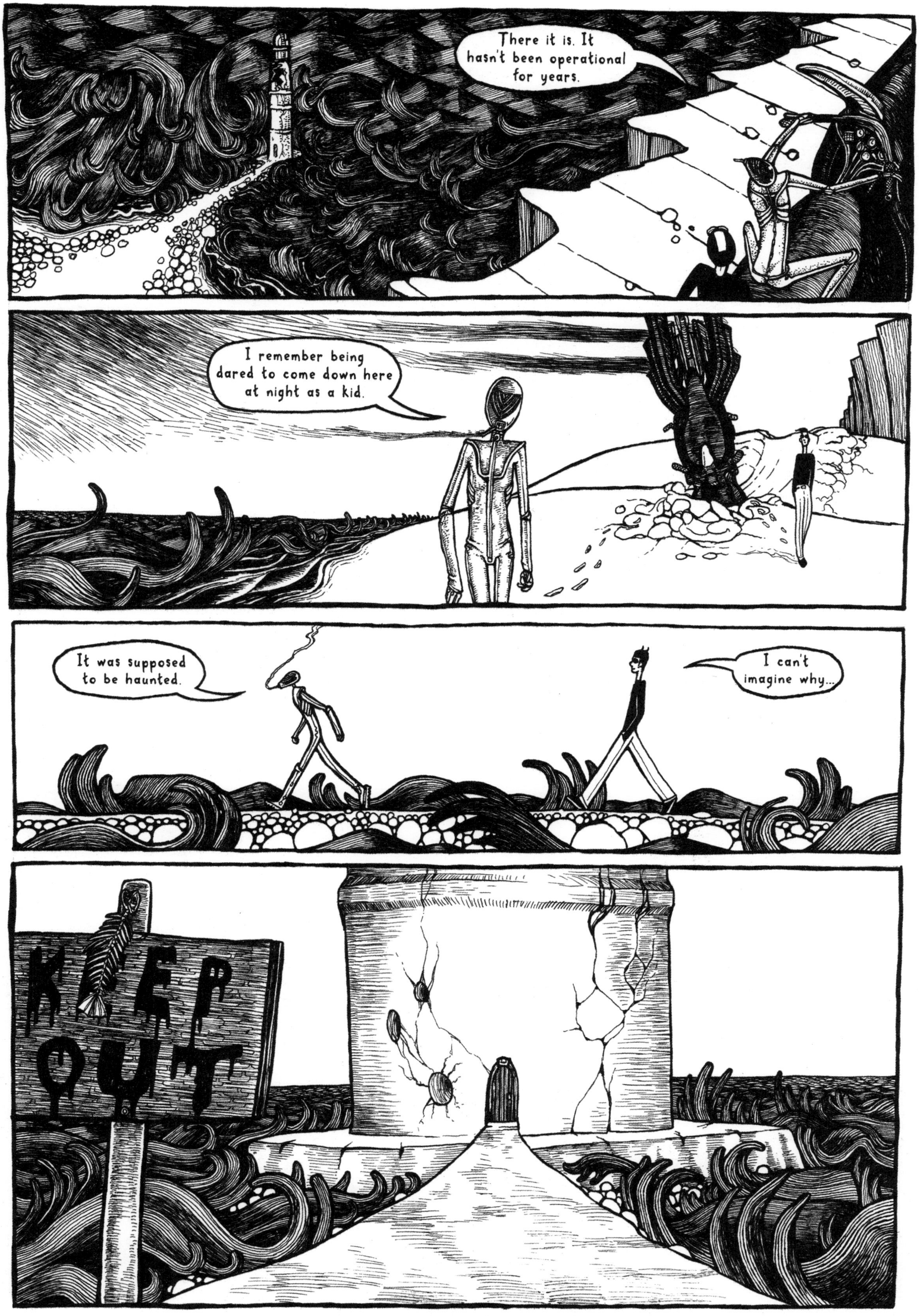
There it is. It hasn't been operational for years.
I remember being dared to come down here at night as a kid.
It was supposed to be haunted.
I can't imagine why...
KEEP OUT

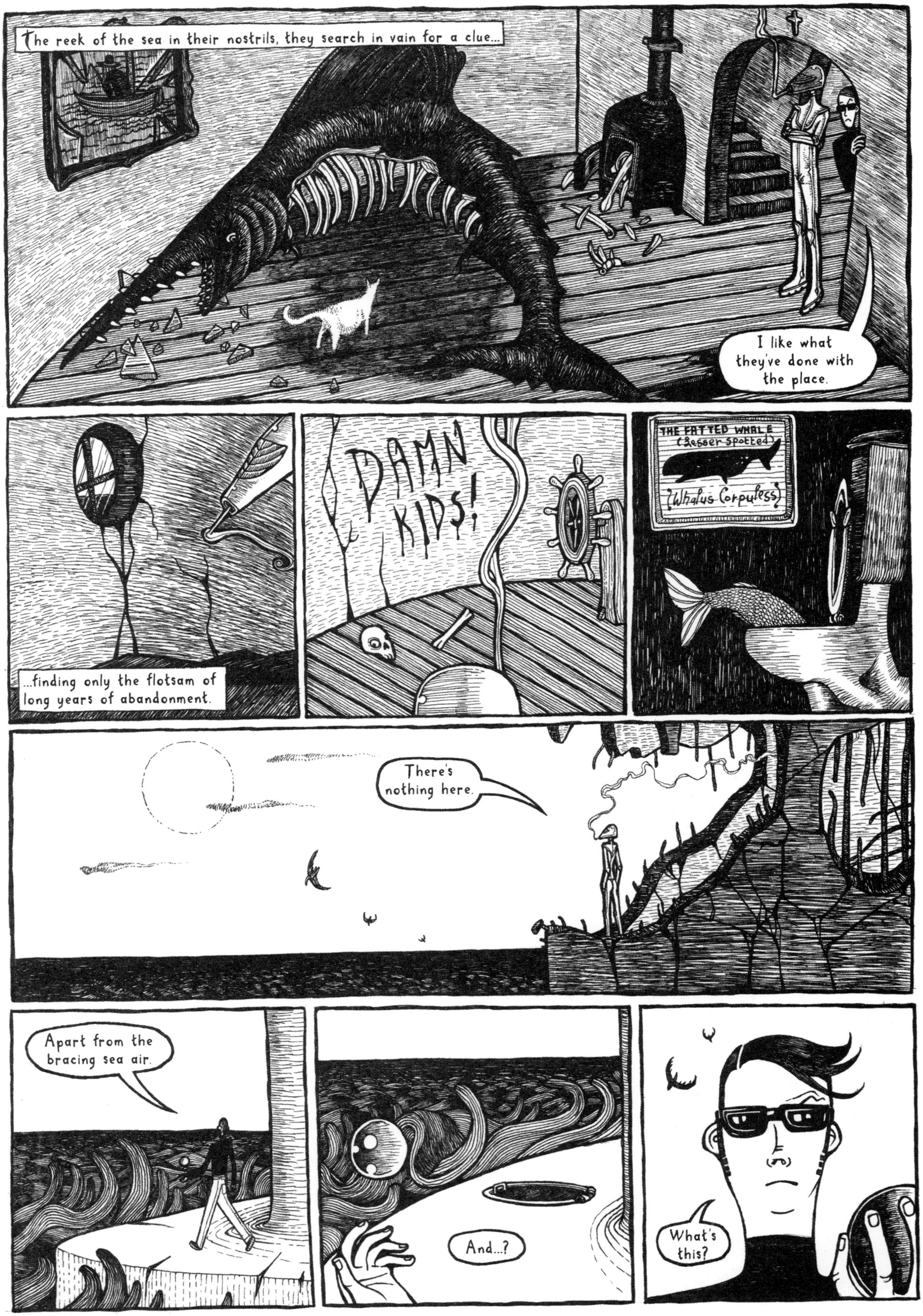
The reek of the sea in their nostrils, they search in vain for a clue...
I like what they've done with the place.
...finding only the flotsam of long years of abandonment.
DAMN KIDS!
THE FATTED WHALE
(Lesser Spotted)
Whalus Corpuless
There's nothing here.
Apart from the bracing sea air.
And...?
What's this?

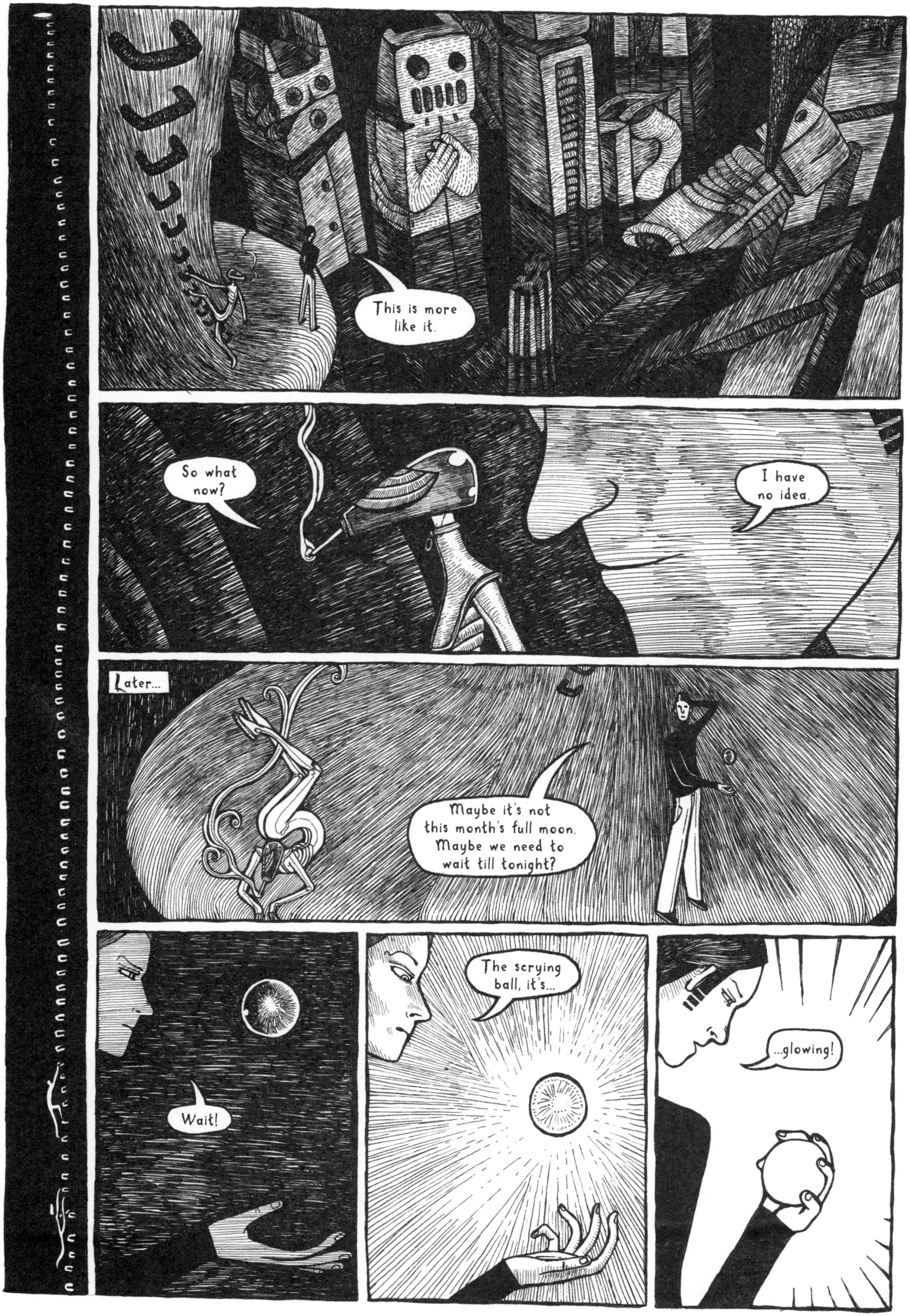
This is more like it.
So what now?
I have no idea.
Later...
Maybe it's not this month's full moon. Maybe we need to wait till tonight?
Wait!
The scrying ball, it's...
...glowing!

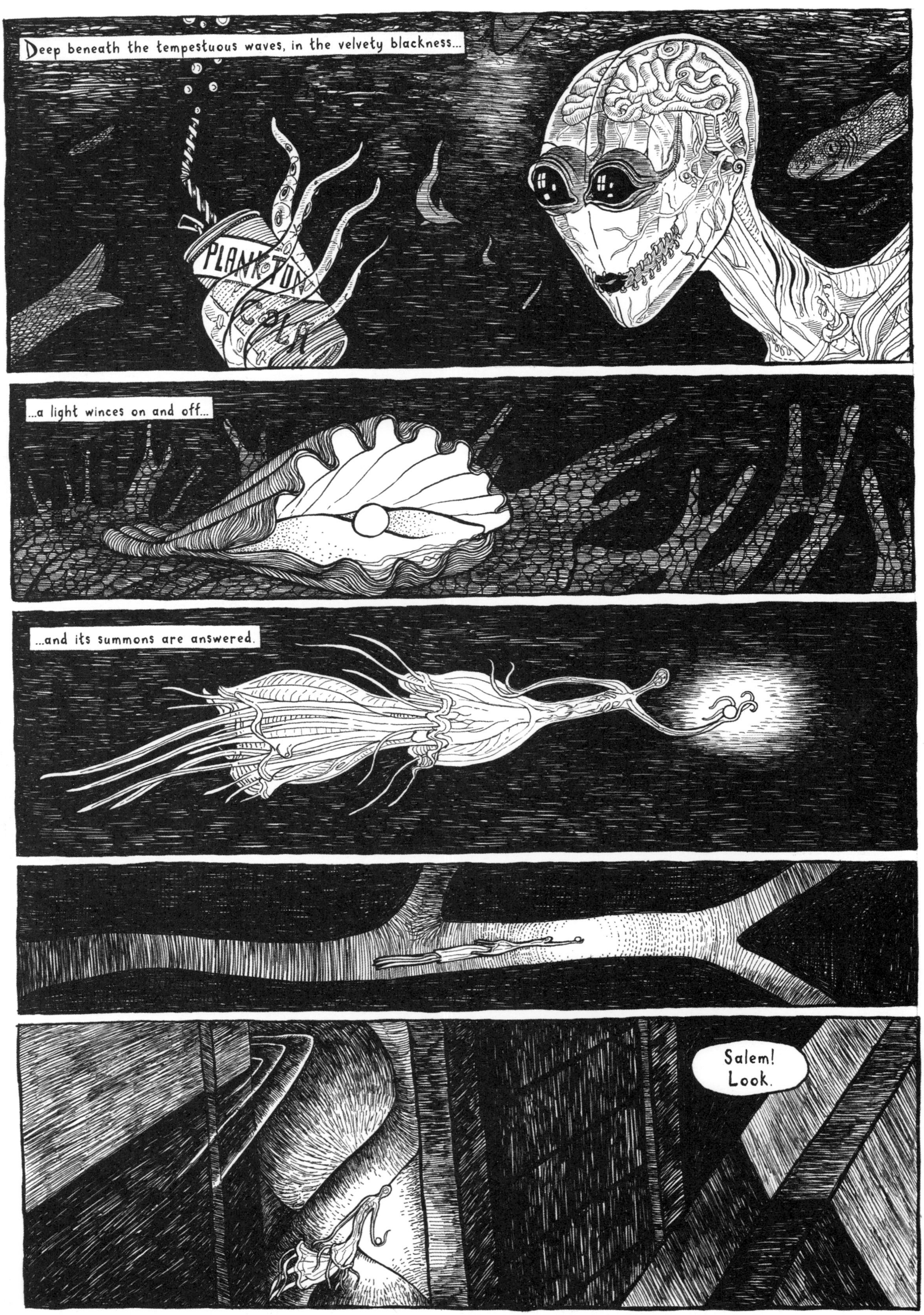
Deep beneath the tempestuous waves, in the velvety blackness...
PLANKTON COLA
...a light winces on and off...
...and its summons are answered.
Salem! Look.

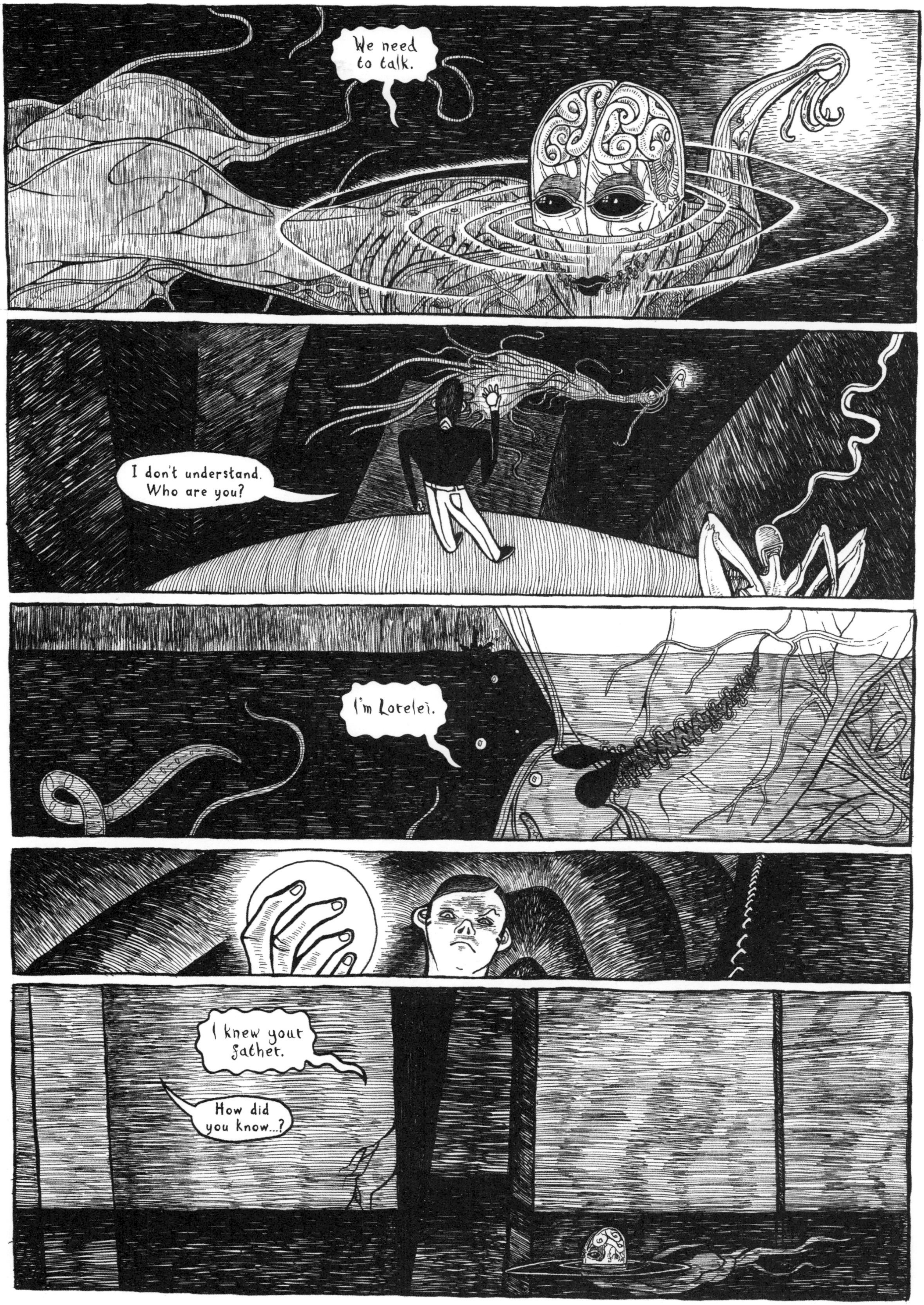
We need to talk.
I don't understand. Who are you?
I'm Lorelei.
I knew your father.
How did you know...?

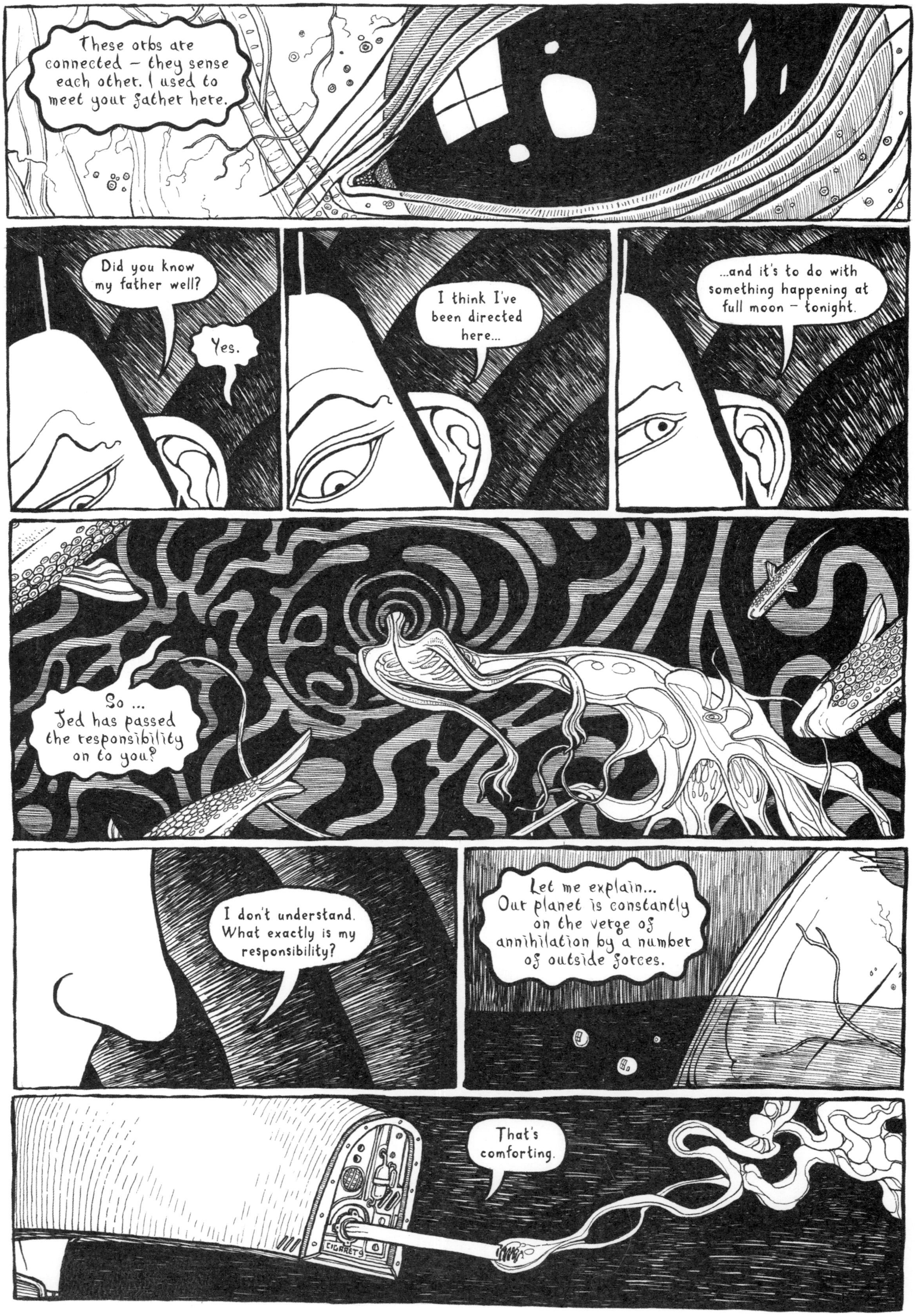
These orbs are connected – they sense each other. I used to meet your father here.
Did you know my father well?
Yes.
I think I've been directed here...
...and it's to do with something happening at full moon – tonight.
So ... Jed has passed the responsibility on to you?
I don't understand. What exactly is my responsibility?
Let me explain... Our planet is constantly on the verge of annihilation by a number of outside forces.
That's comforting.
CIGRRETS

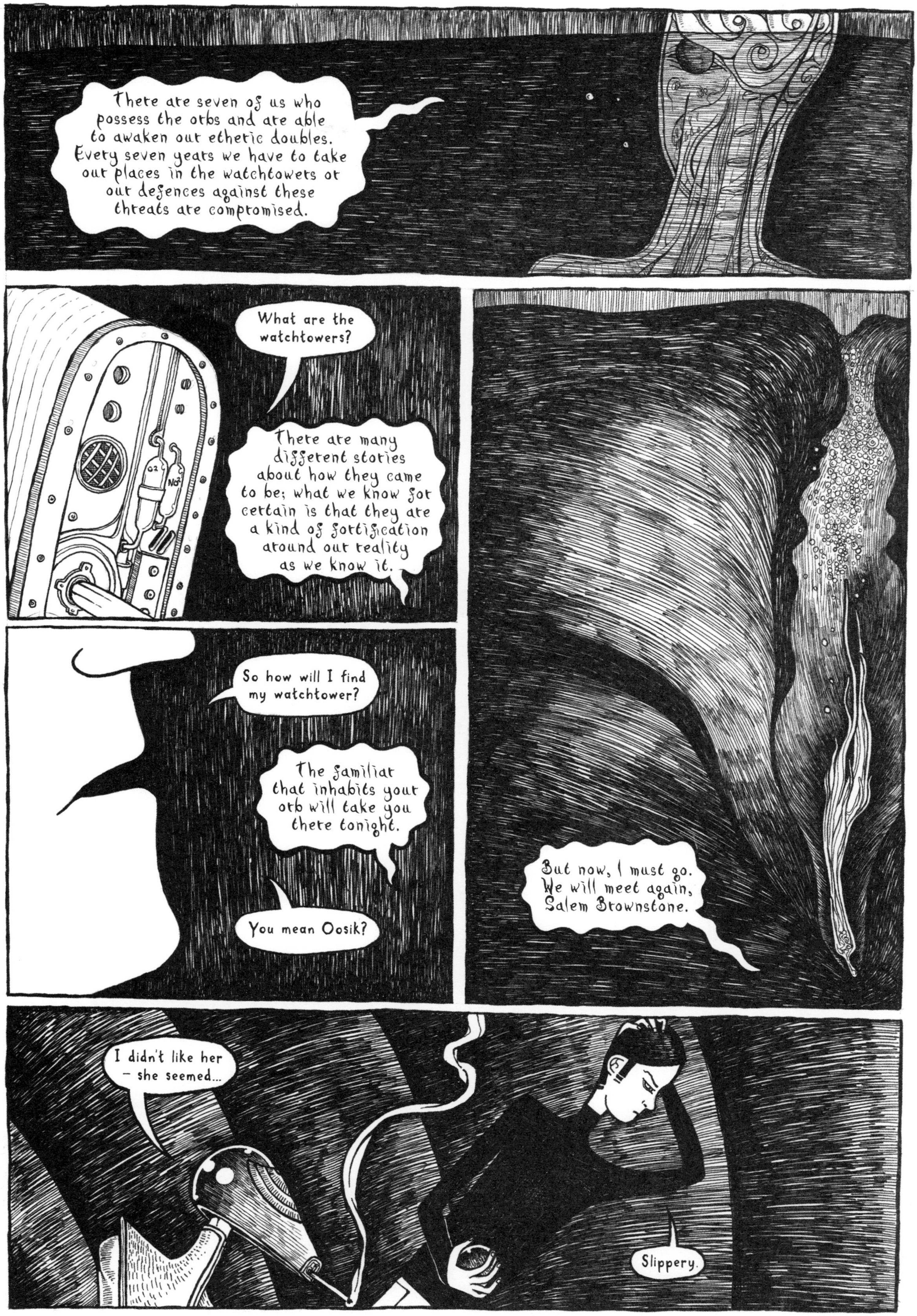
There are seven of us who possess the orbs and are able to awaken our etheric doubles. Every seven years we have to take our places in the watchtowers or our defences against these threats are compromised.
What are the watchtowers?
There are many different stories about how they came to be; what we know for certain is that they are a kind of fortification around our reality as we know it.
So how will I find my watchtower?
The familiar that inhabits your orb will take you there tonight.
You mean Oosik?
But now, I must go. We will meet again, Salem Brownstone.
I didn't like her – she seemed...
Slippery.

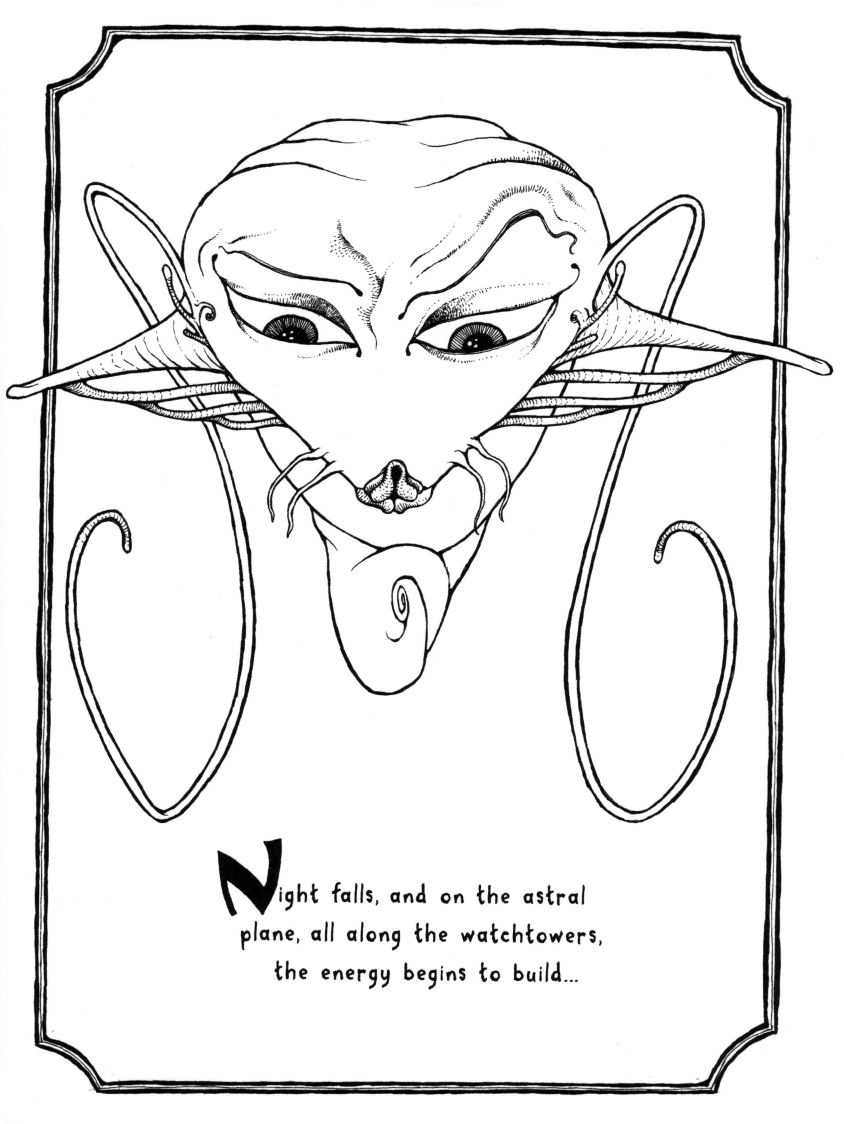

Night falls, and on the astral plane, all along the watchtowers, the energy begins to build...

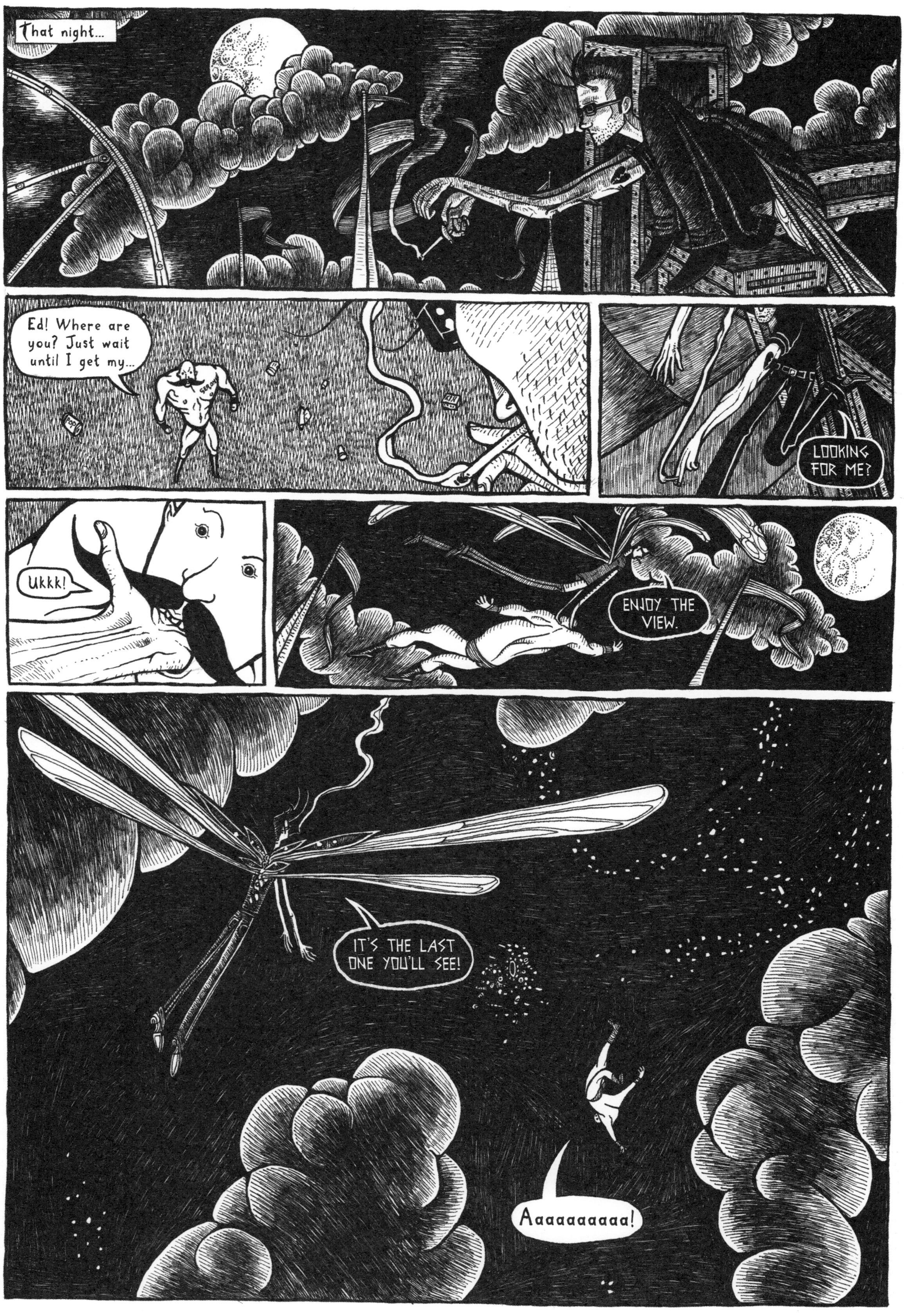
That night...
Ed! Where are you? Just wait until I get my...
LOOKING FOR ME?
Ukkk!
ENJOY THE VIEW.
IT'S THE LAST ONE YOU'LL SEE!
Aaaaaaaaaa!

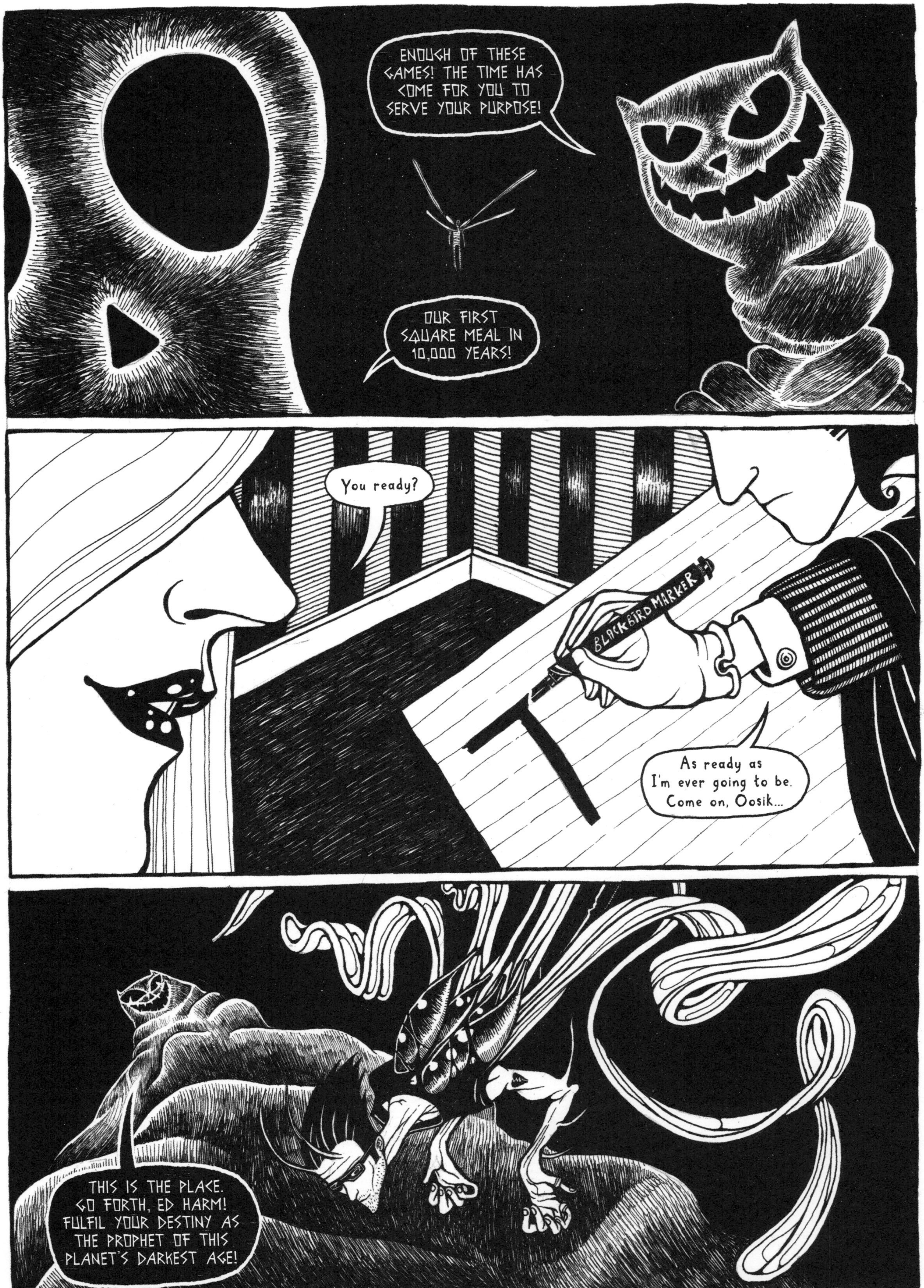
ENOUGH OF THESE GAMES! THE TIME HAS COME FOR YOU TO SERVE YOUR PURPOSE!
OUR FIRST SQUARE MEAL IN 10,000 YEARS!
You ready?
BLACKBIRD MARKER
As ready as I'm ever going to be. Come on, Oosik...
THIS IS THE PLACE. GO FORTH, ED HARM! FULFIL YOUR DESTINY AS THE PROPHET OF THIS PLANET'S DARKEST AGE!

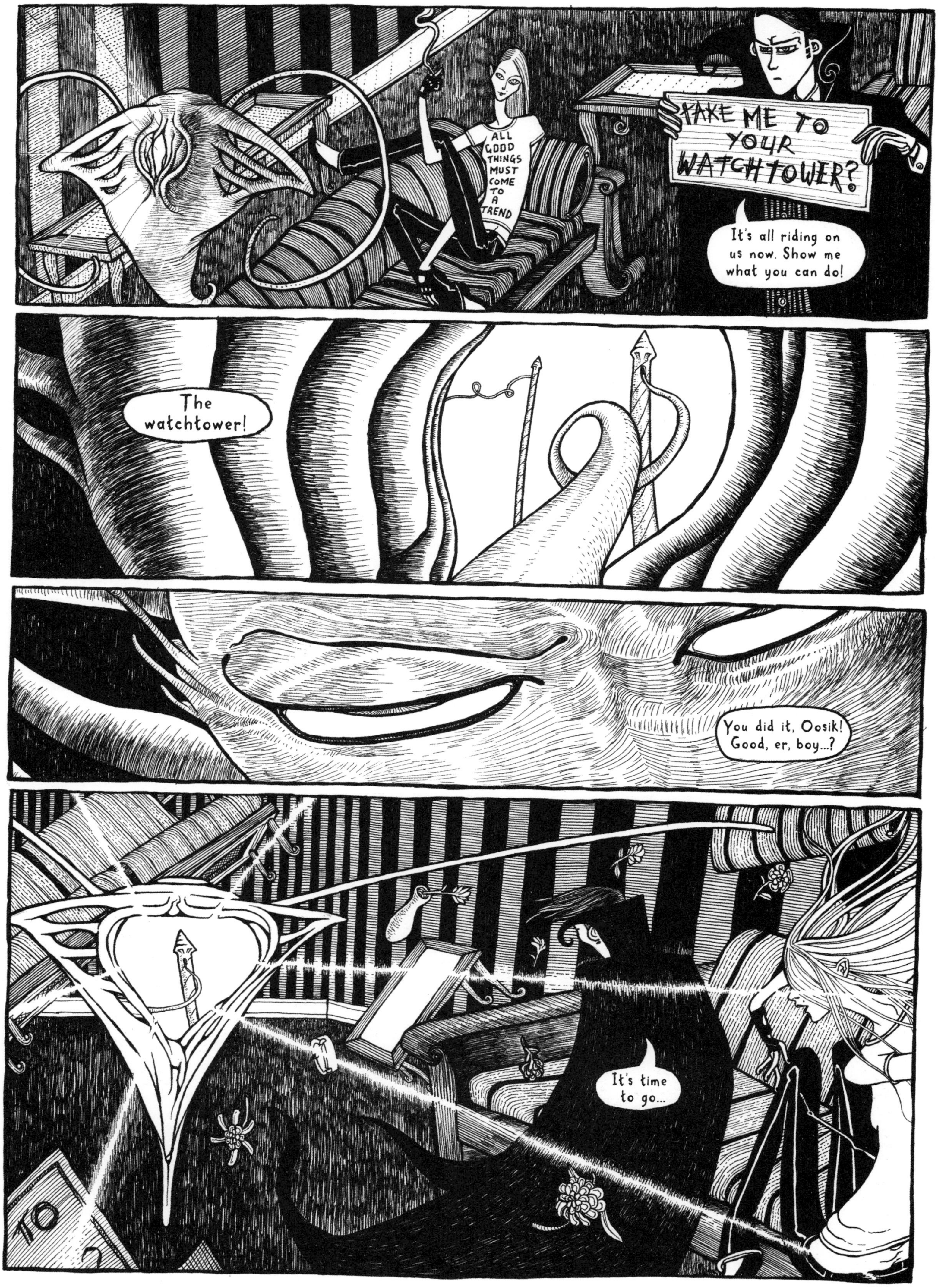
ALL GOOD THINGS MUST COME TO A TREND
TAKE ME TO YOUR WATCHTOWER?
It's all riding on us now. Show me what you can do!
The watchtower!
You did it, Oosik! Good, er, boy...?
It's time to go...

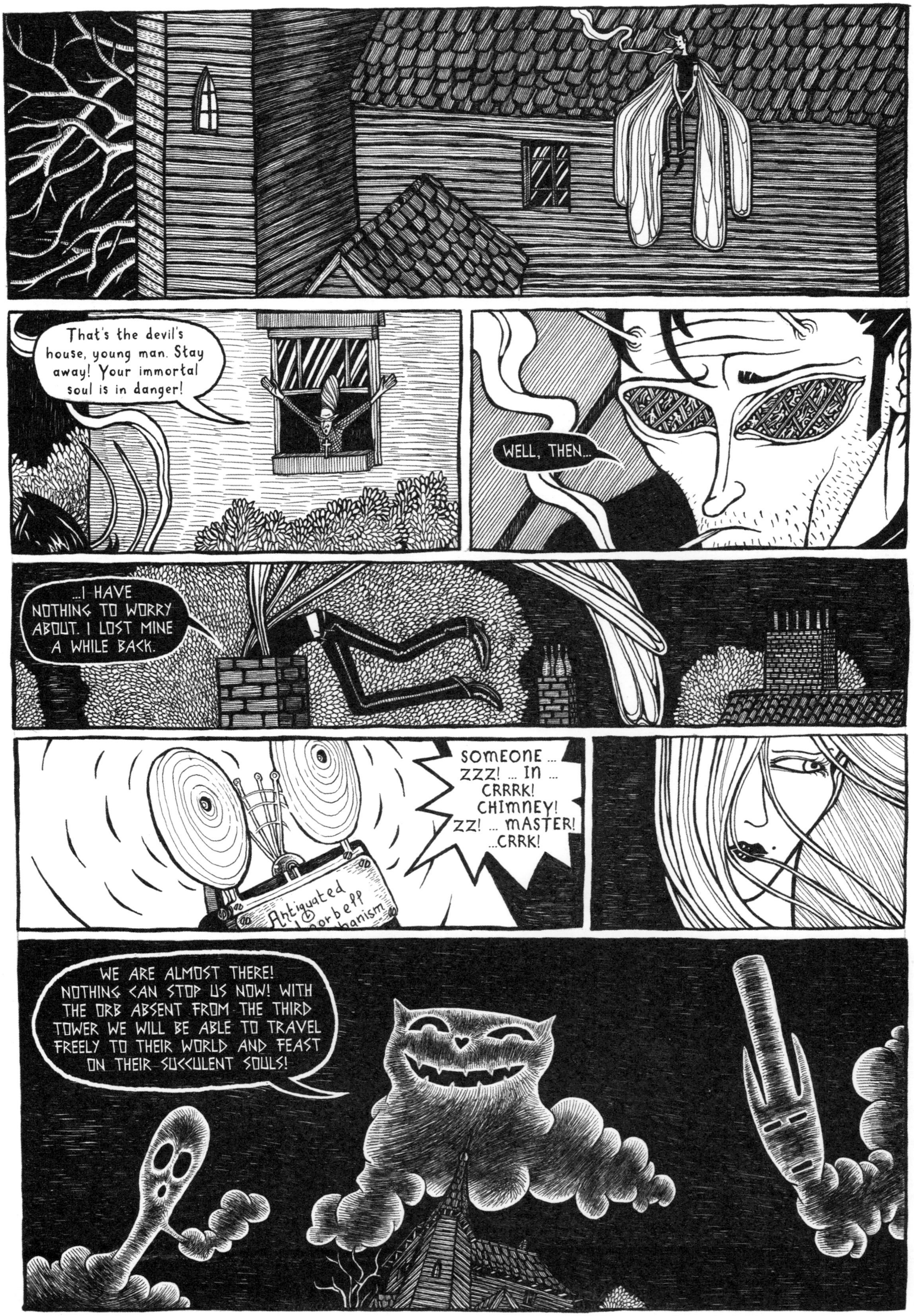
That's the devil's house, young man. Stay away! Your immortal soul is in danger!
WELL, THEN...
...I HAVE NOTHING TO WORRY ABOUT. I LOST MINE A WHILE BACK.
SOMEONE ... ZZZ! ... IN ... CRRRK! CHIMNEY! ZZ! ... MASTER! ...CRRK!
Antiquated
WE ARE ALMOST THERE! NOTHING CAN STOP US NOW! WITH THE ORB ABSENT FROM THE THIRD TOWER WE WILL BE ABLE TO TRAVEL FREELY TO THEIR WORLD AND FEAST ON THEIR SUCCULENT SOULS!

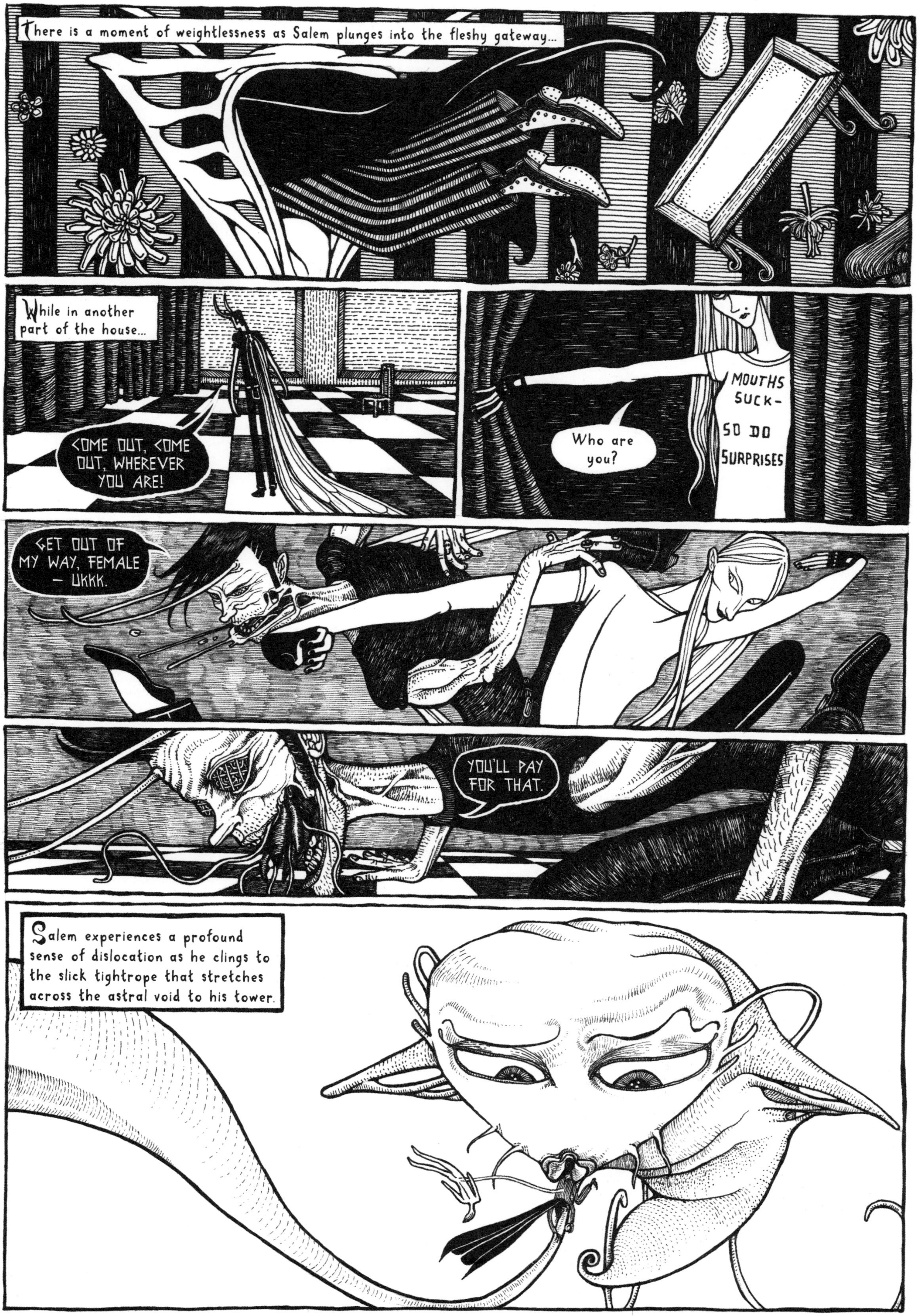
There is a moment of weightlessness as Salem plunges into the fleshy gateway...
While in another part of the house...
COME OUT, COME OUT, WHEREVER YOU ARE!
Who are you?
MOUTHS SUCK- SO DO SURPRISES
GET OUT OF MY WAY, FEMALE — UKKK.
YOU'LL PAY FOR THAT.
Salem experiences a profound sense of dislocation as he clings to the slick tightrope that stretches across the astral void to his tower.

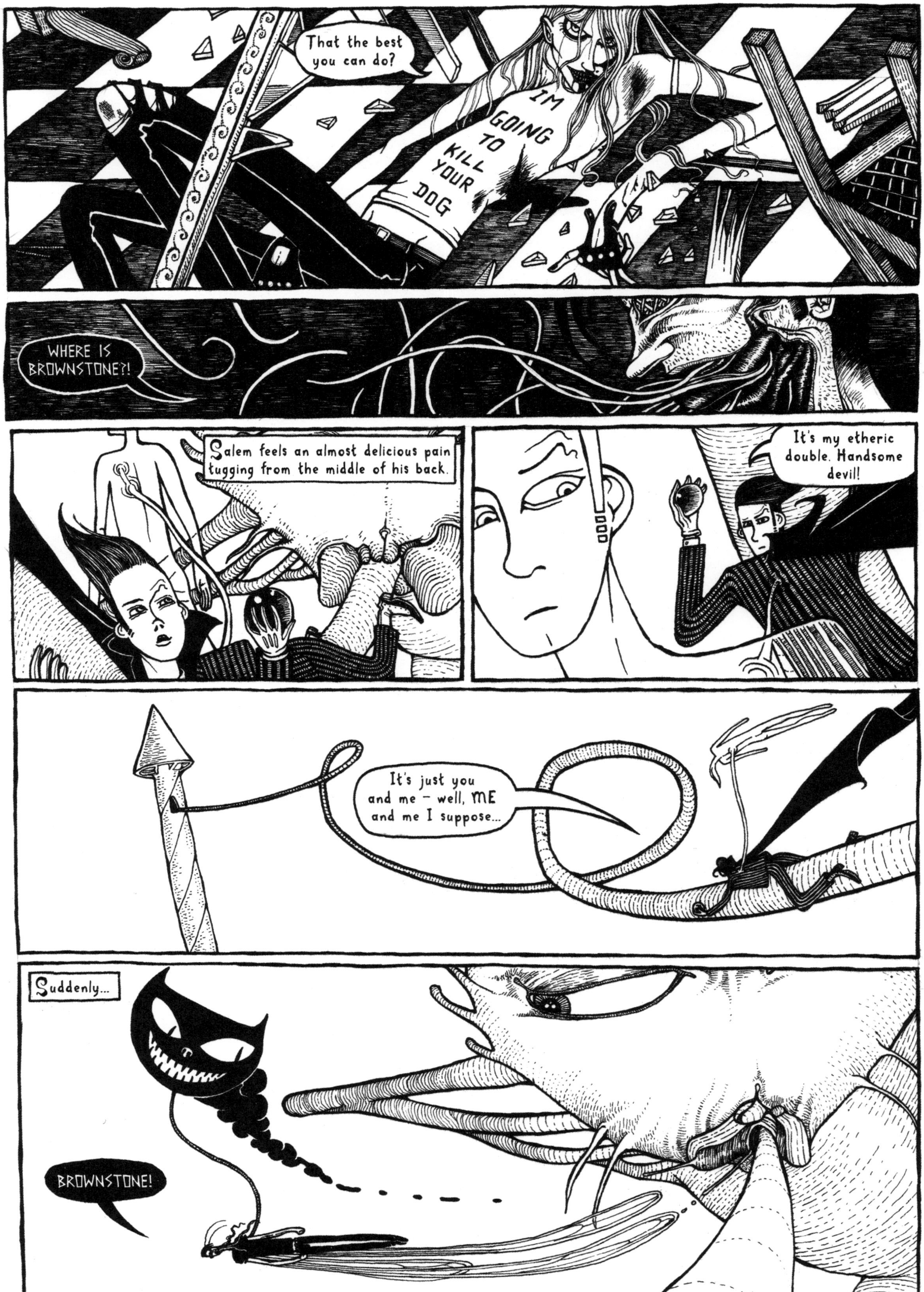
That the best you can do?
I'M GOING TO KILL YOUR DOG
WHERE IS BROWNSTONE?!
Salem feels an almost delicious pain tugging from the middle of his back.
It's my etheric double. Handsome devil!
It's just you and me – well, ME and me I suppose...
Suddenly...
BROWNSTONE!

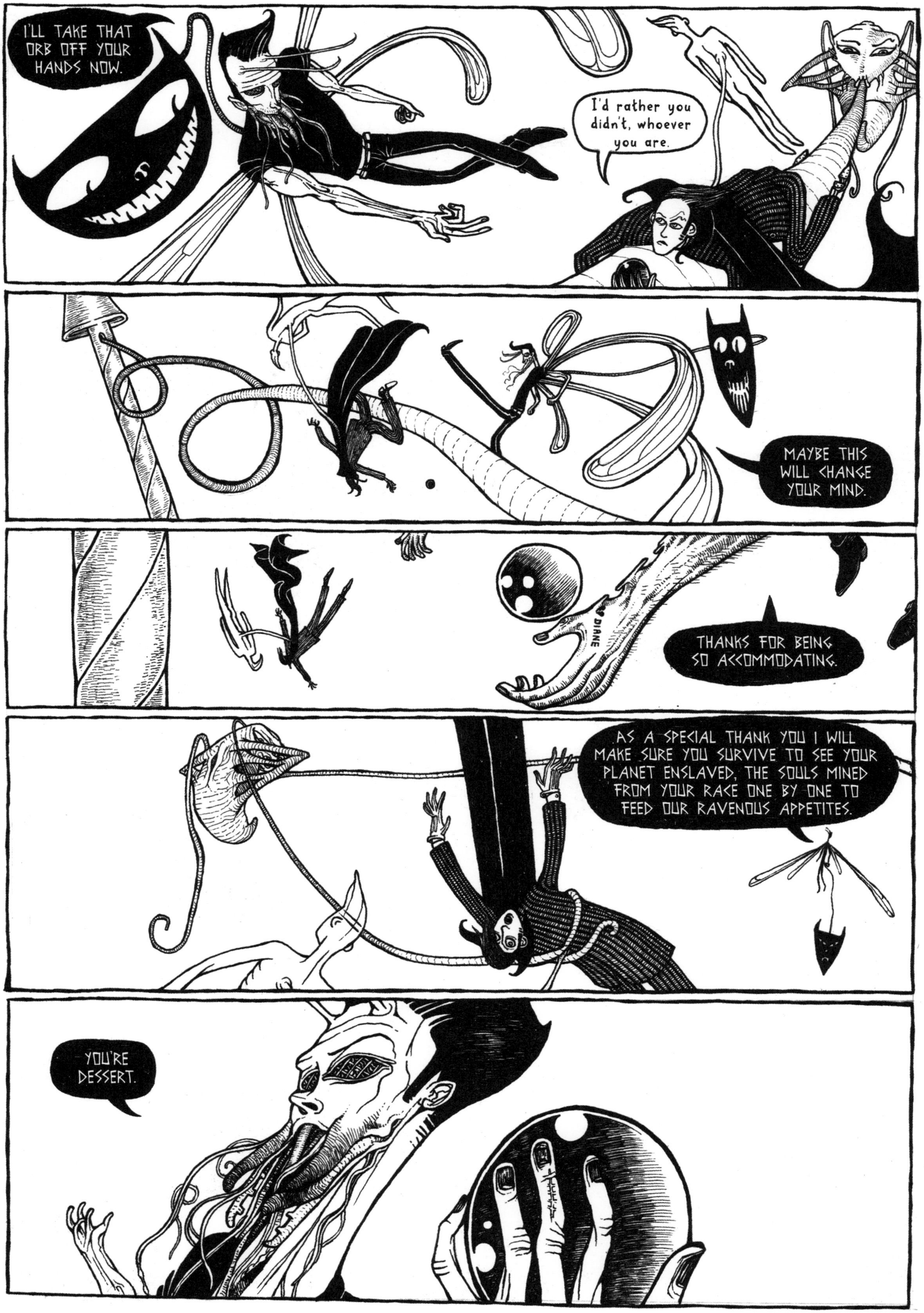
I'LL TAKE THAT ORB OFF YOUR HANDS NOW.
I'd rather you didn't, whoever you are.
MAYBE THIS WILL CHANGE YOUR MIND.
DIANE
THANKS FOR BEING SO ACCOMMODATING.
AS A SPECIAL THANK YOU I WILL MAKE SURE YOU SURVIVE TO SEE YOUR PLANET ENSLAVED, THE SOULS MINED FROM YOUR RACE ONE BY ONE TO FEED OUR RAVENOUS APPETITES.
YOU'RE DESSERT.

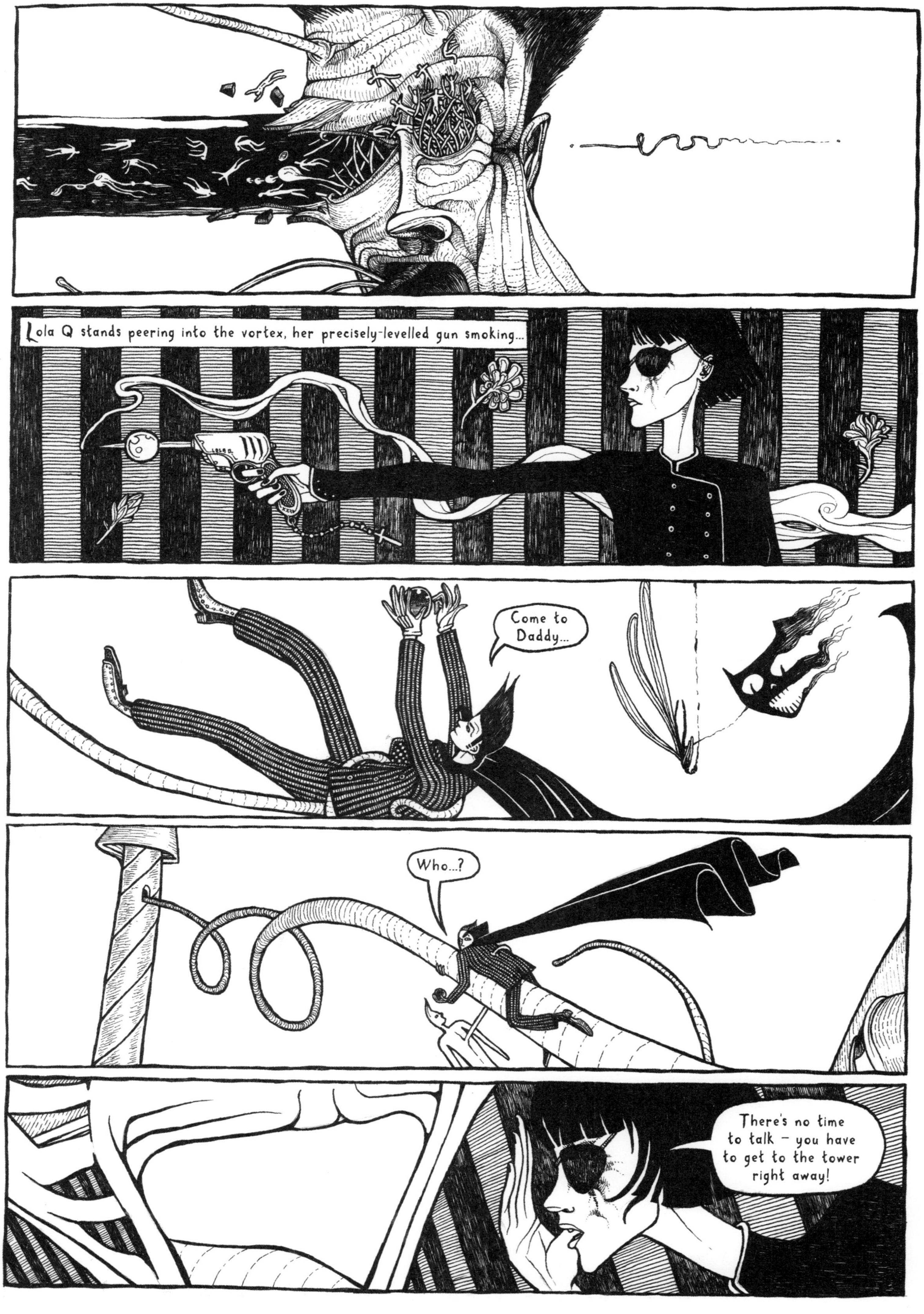
Lola Q stands peering into the vortex, her precisely-levelled gun smoking...
Come to Daddy...
Who...?
There's no time to talk - you have to get to the tower right away!

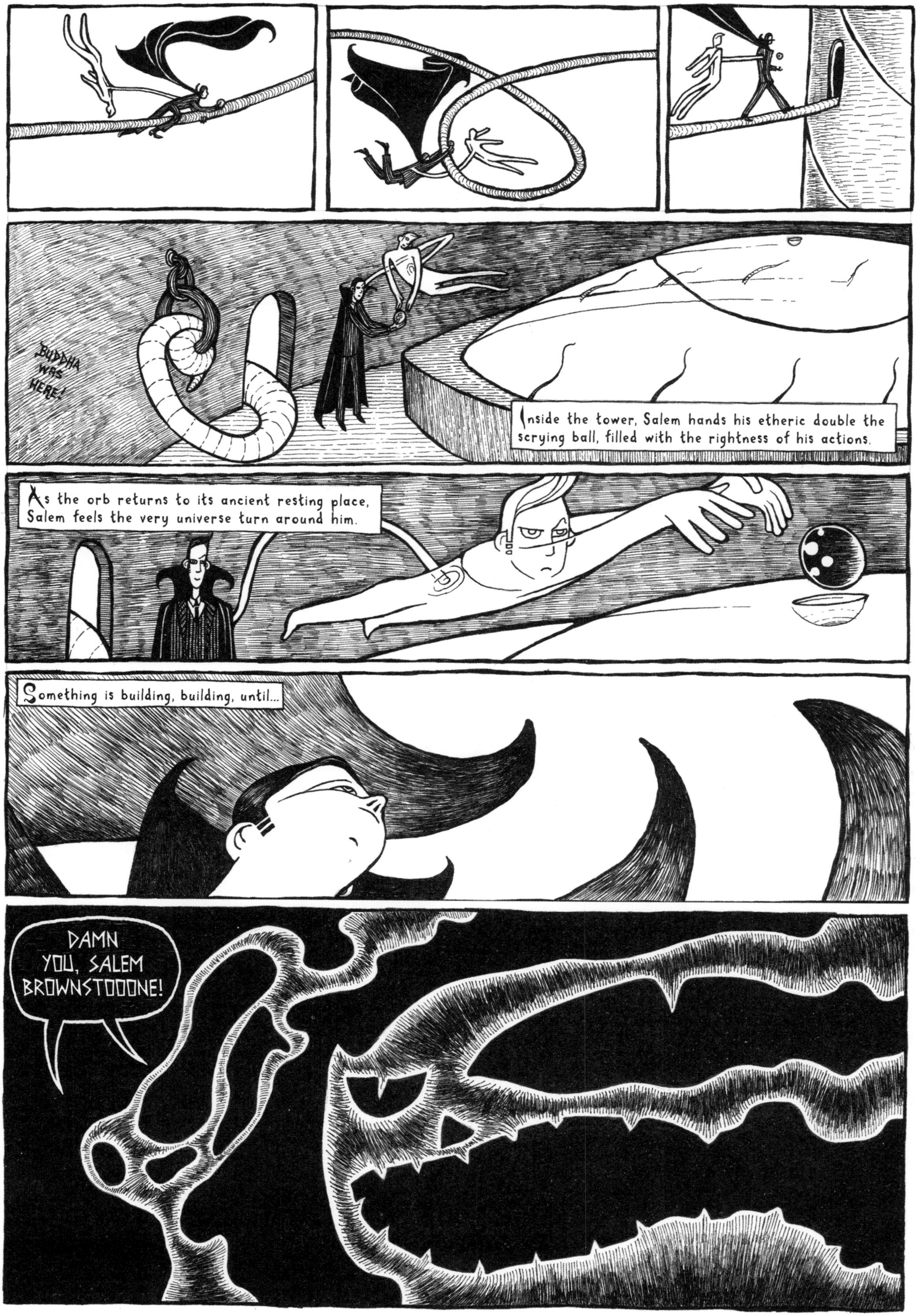
BUDDHA WAS HERE!
Inside the tower, Salem hands his etheric double the scrying ball, filled with the rightness of his actions.
As the orb returns to its ancient resting place, Salem feels the very universe turn around him.
Something is building, building, until...
DAMN YOU, SALEM BROWNSTOOONE!

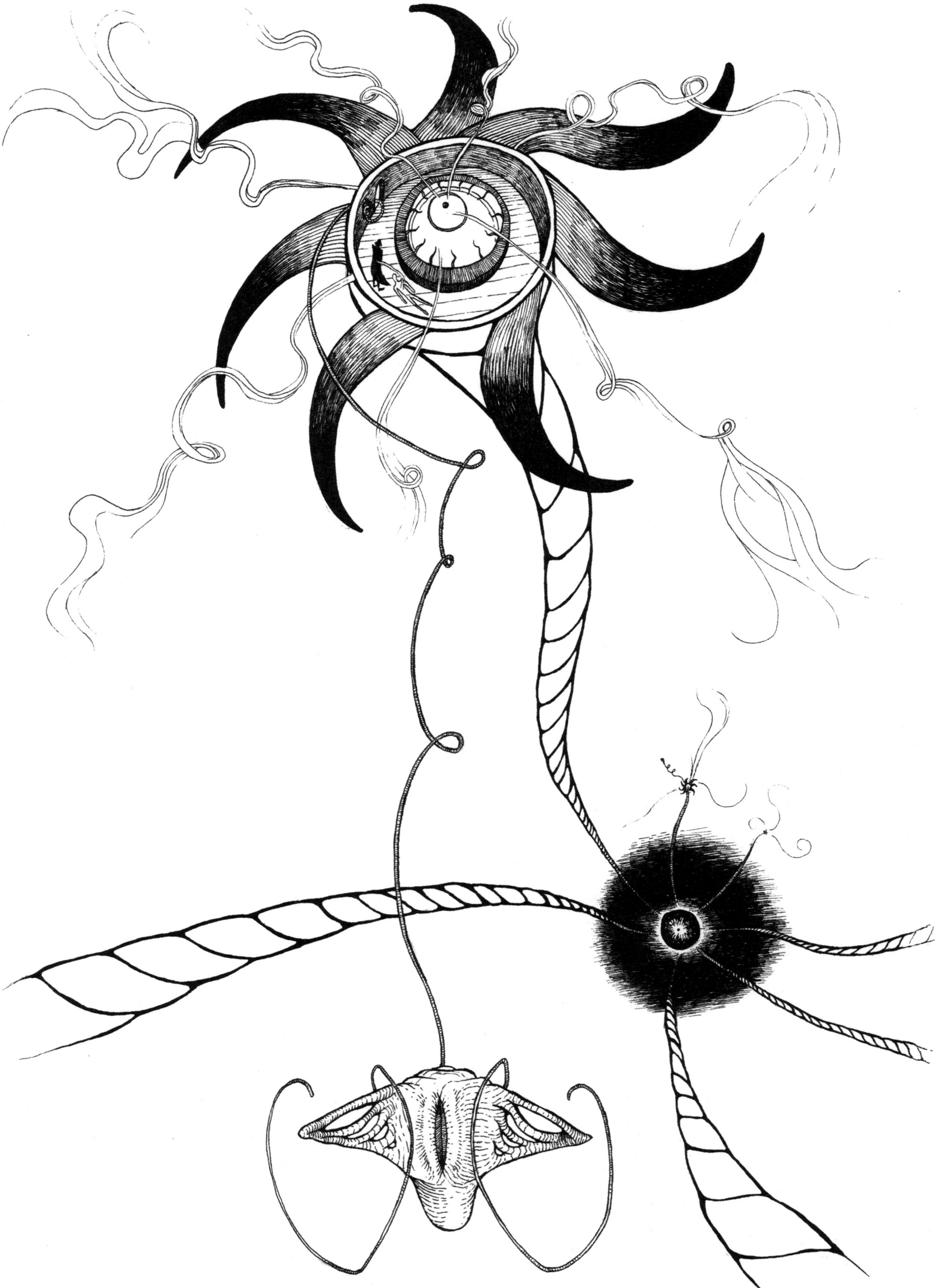

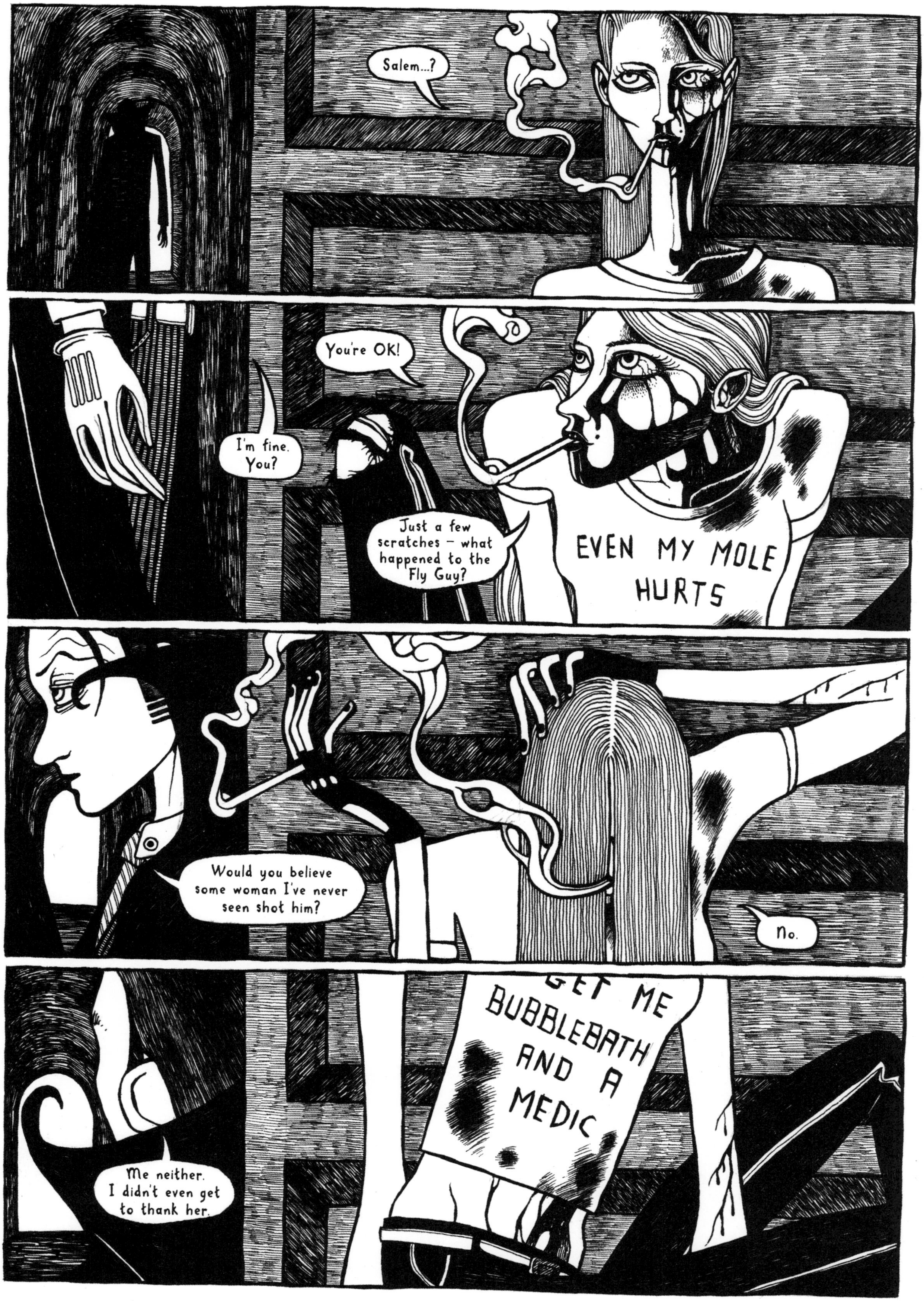
Salem...?
You're OK!
I'm fine. You?
Just a few scratches – what happened to the Fly Guy?
EVEN MY MOLE HURTS
Would you believe some woman I've never seen shot him?
No.
GET ME BUBBLEBATH AND A MEDIC
Me neither. I didn't even get to thank her.

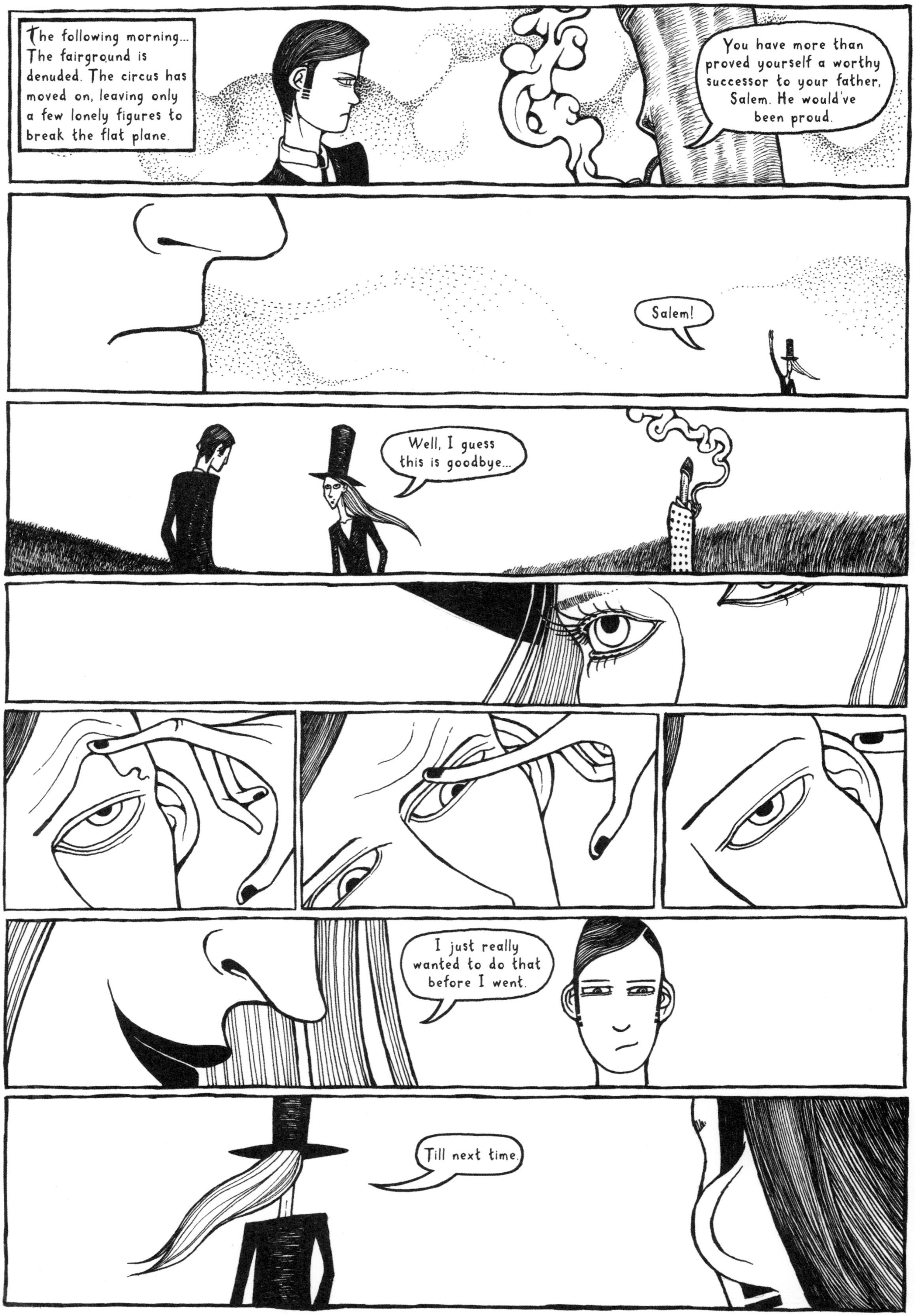
The following morning... The fairground is denuded. The circus has moved on, leaving only a few lonely figures to break the flat plane.
You have more than proved yourself a worthy successor to your father, Salem. He would've been proud.
Salem!
Well, I guess this is goodbye...
I just really wanted to do that before I went.
Till next time.

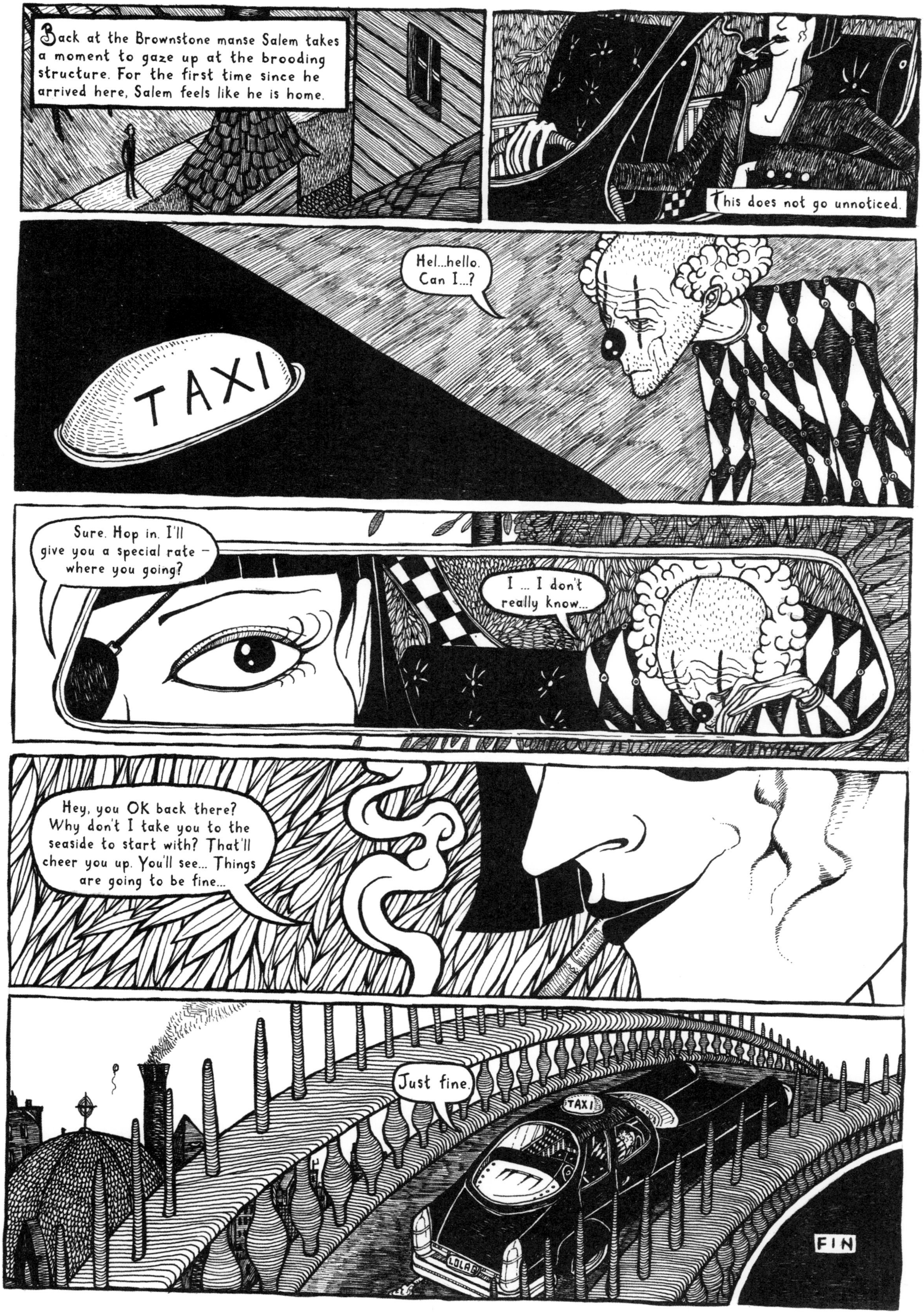
Back at the Brownstone manse Salem takes a moment to gaze up at the brooding structure. For the first time since he arrived here, Salem feels like he is home.
This does not go unnoticed.
TAXI
Hel...hello. Can I...?
Sure. Hop in. I'll give you a special rate – where you going?
I ... I don't really know...
Hey, you OK back there? Why don't I take you to the seaside to start with? That'll cheer you up. You'll see... Things are going to be fine...
Just fine.
TAXI
FIN

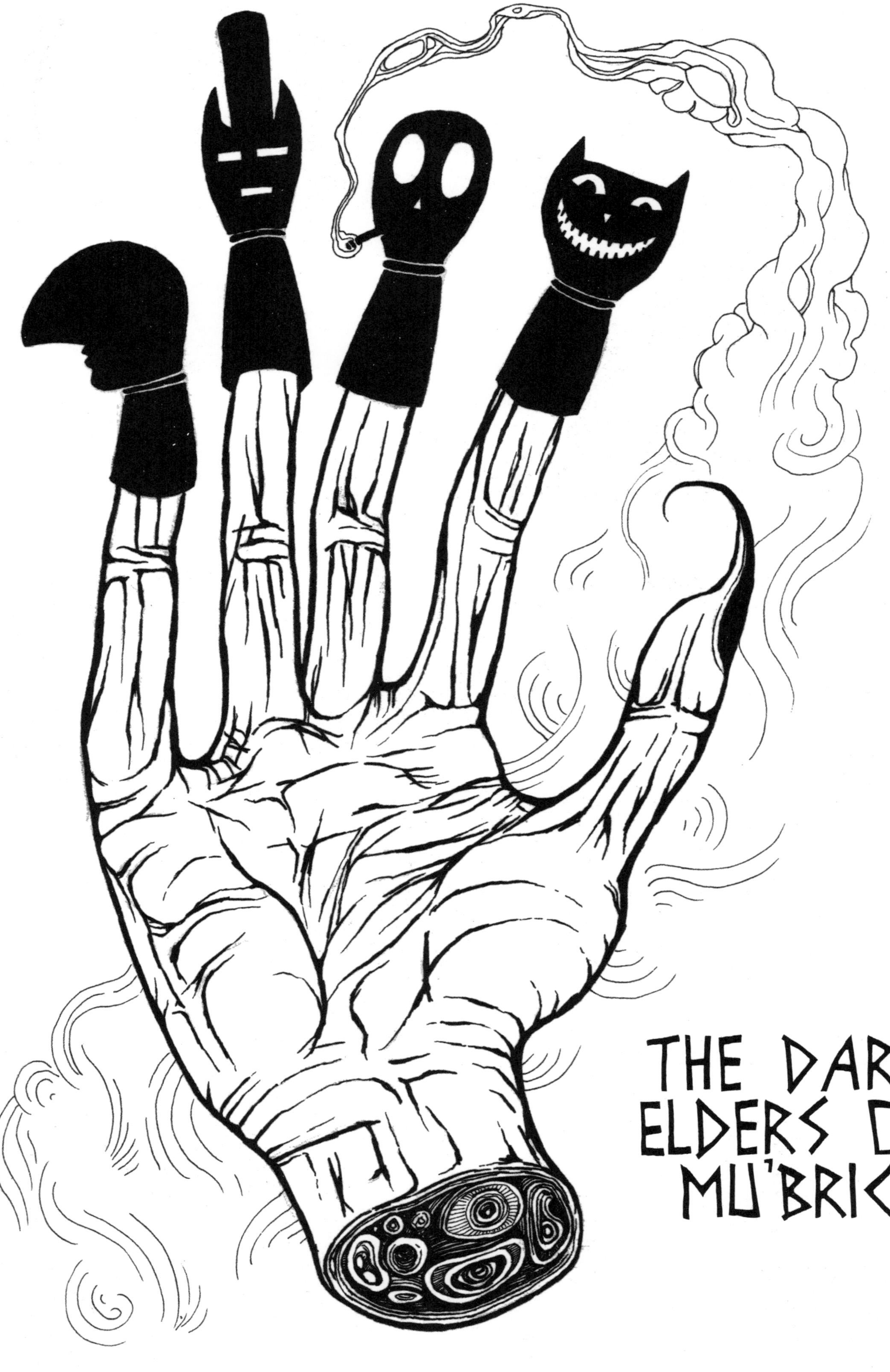

THE DARK ELDERS OF MU'BRIC

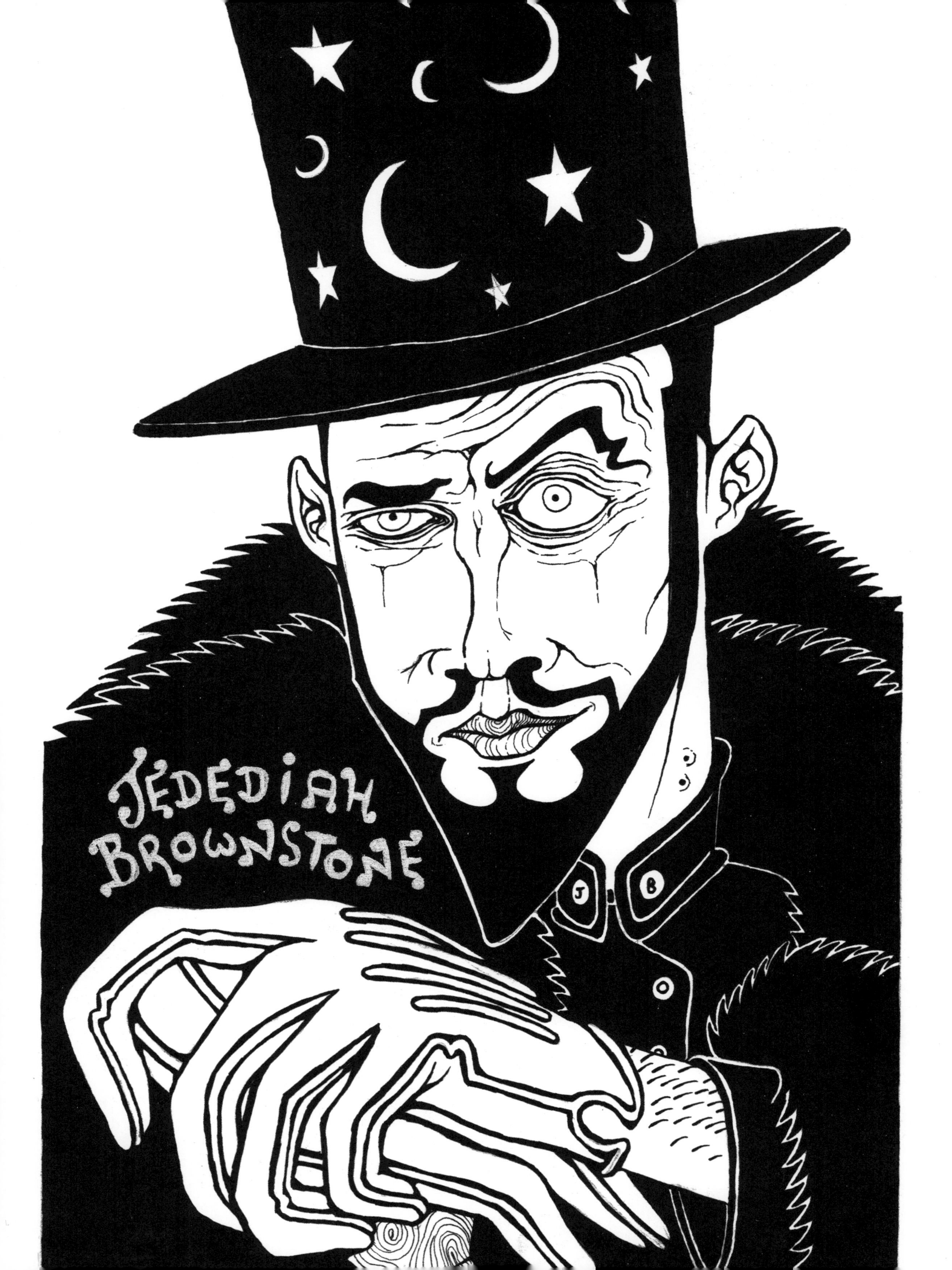
JEDEDIAH
BROWNSTONE
J
B

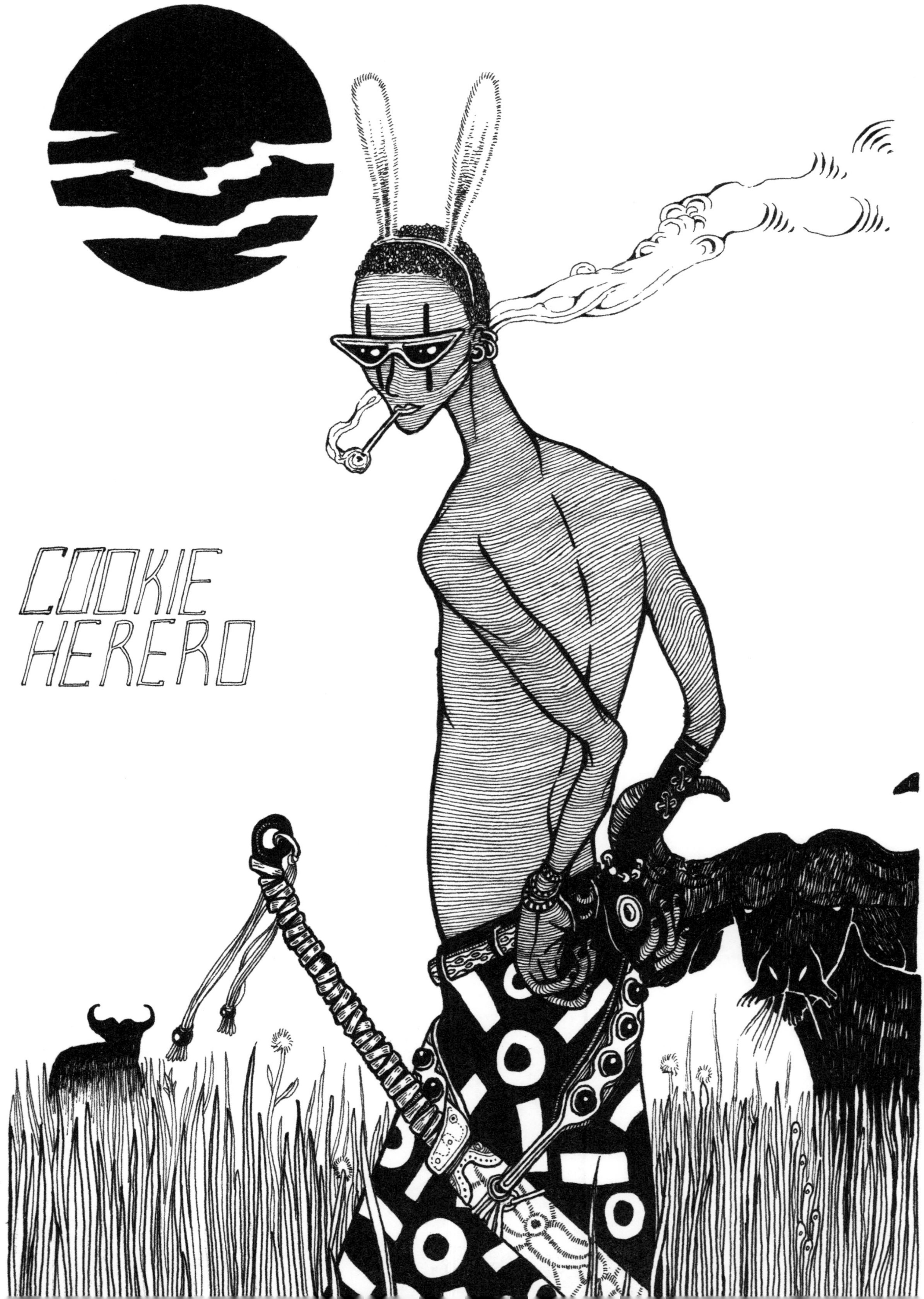
COOKIE
HERERO

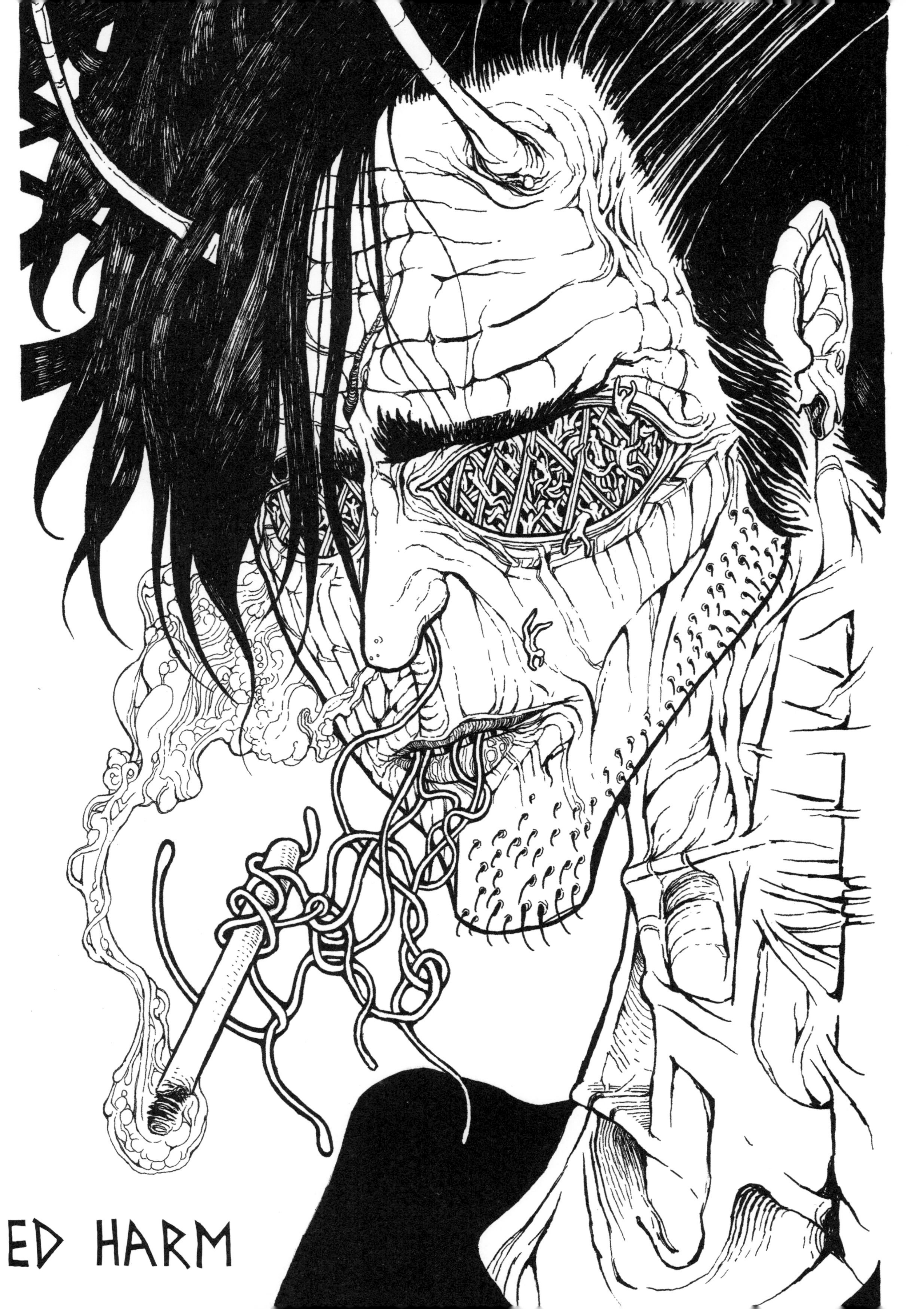
ED HARM

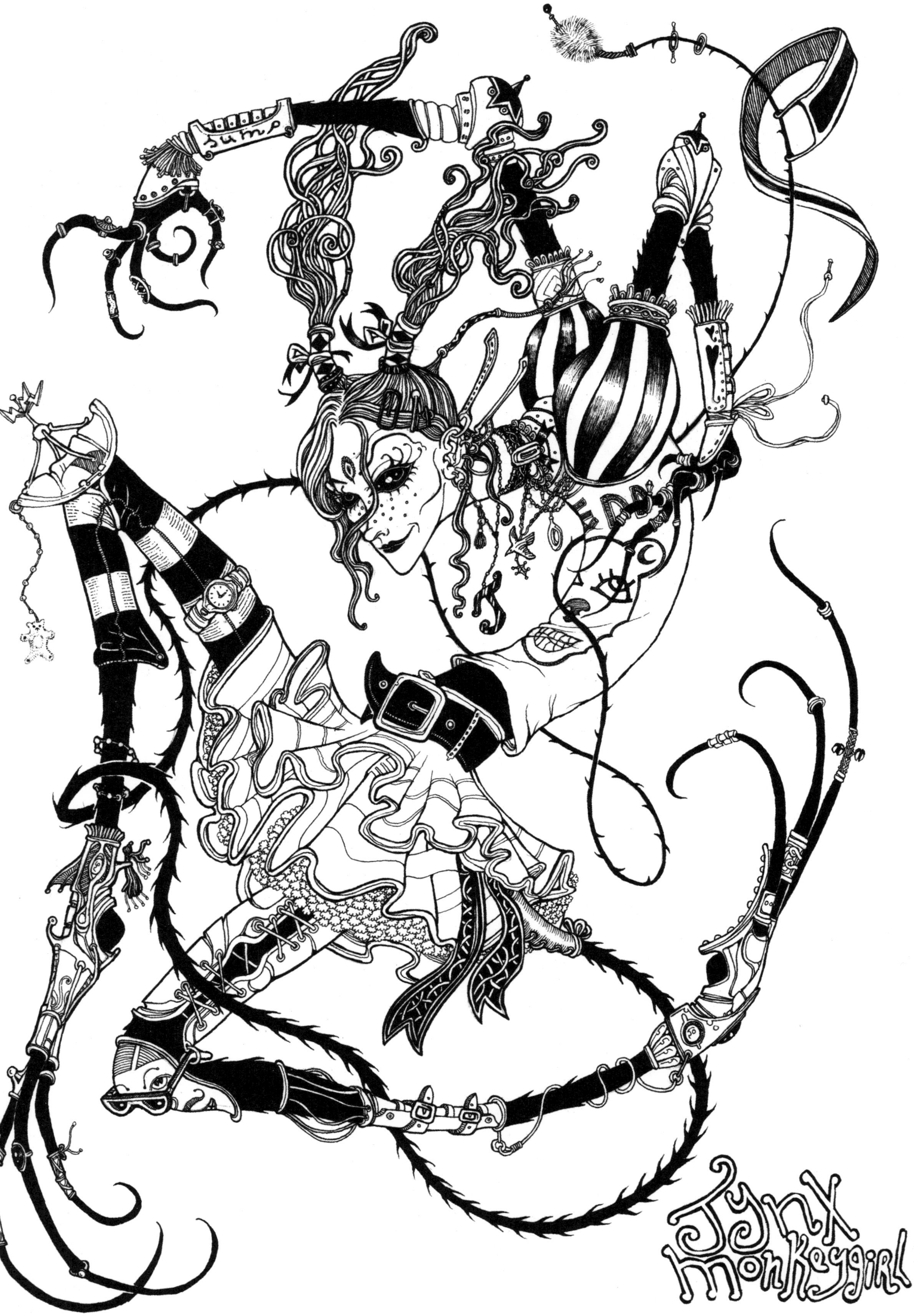
Jynx
monkeygirl

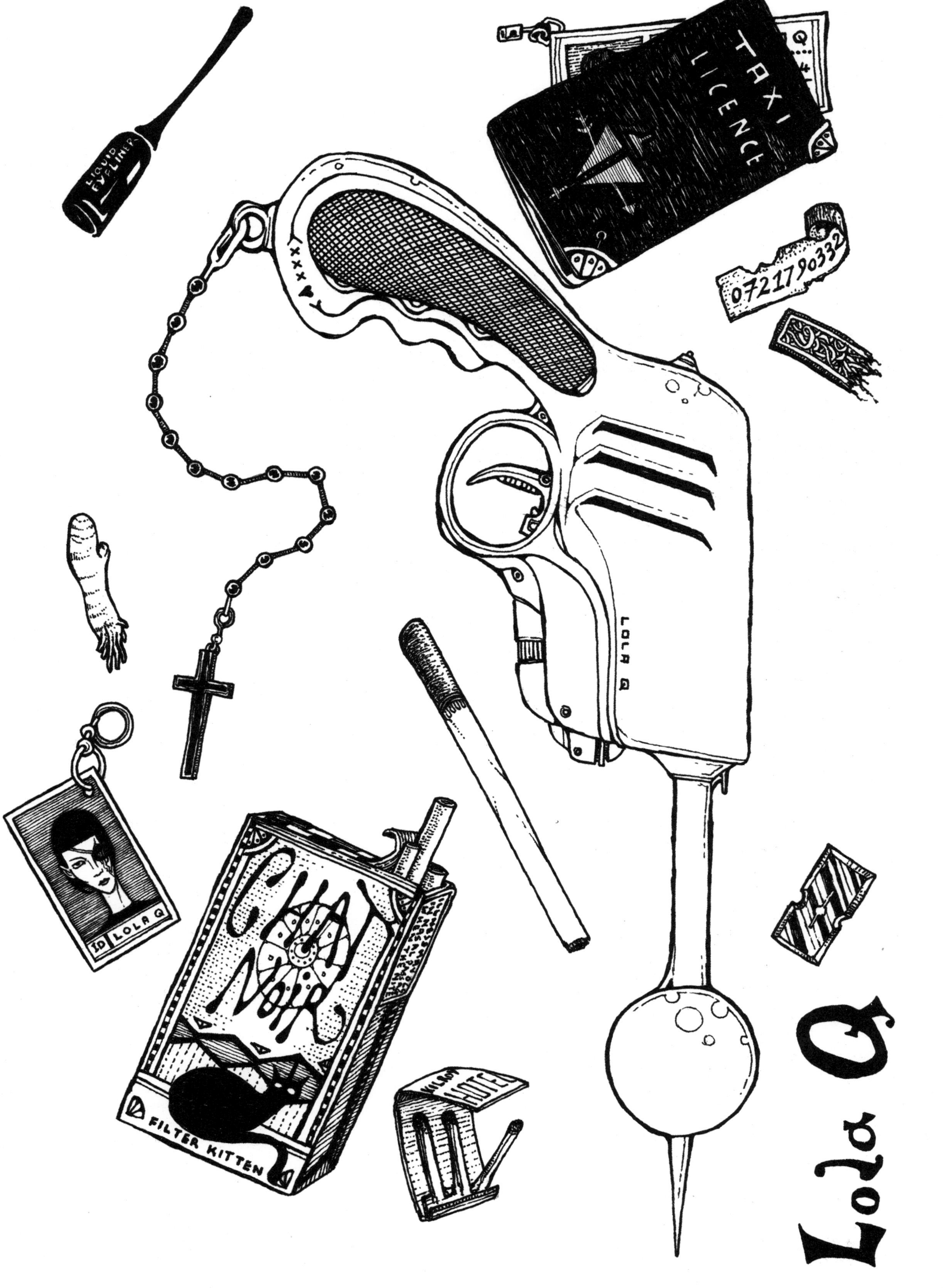

LIQUID EYELINER
TAXI LICENCE
0721790332
LOLA Q
ID LOLA Q
CHAT NOIR
FILTER KITTEN
Lola Q

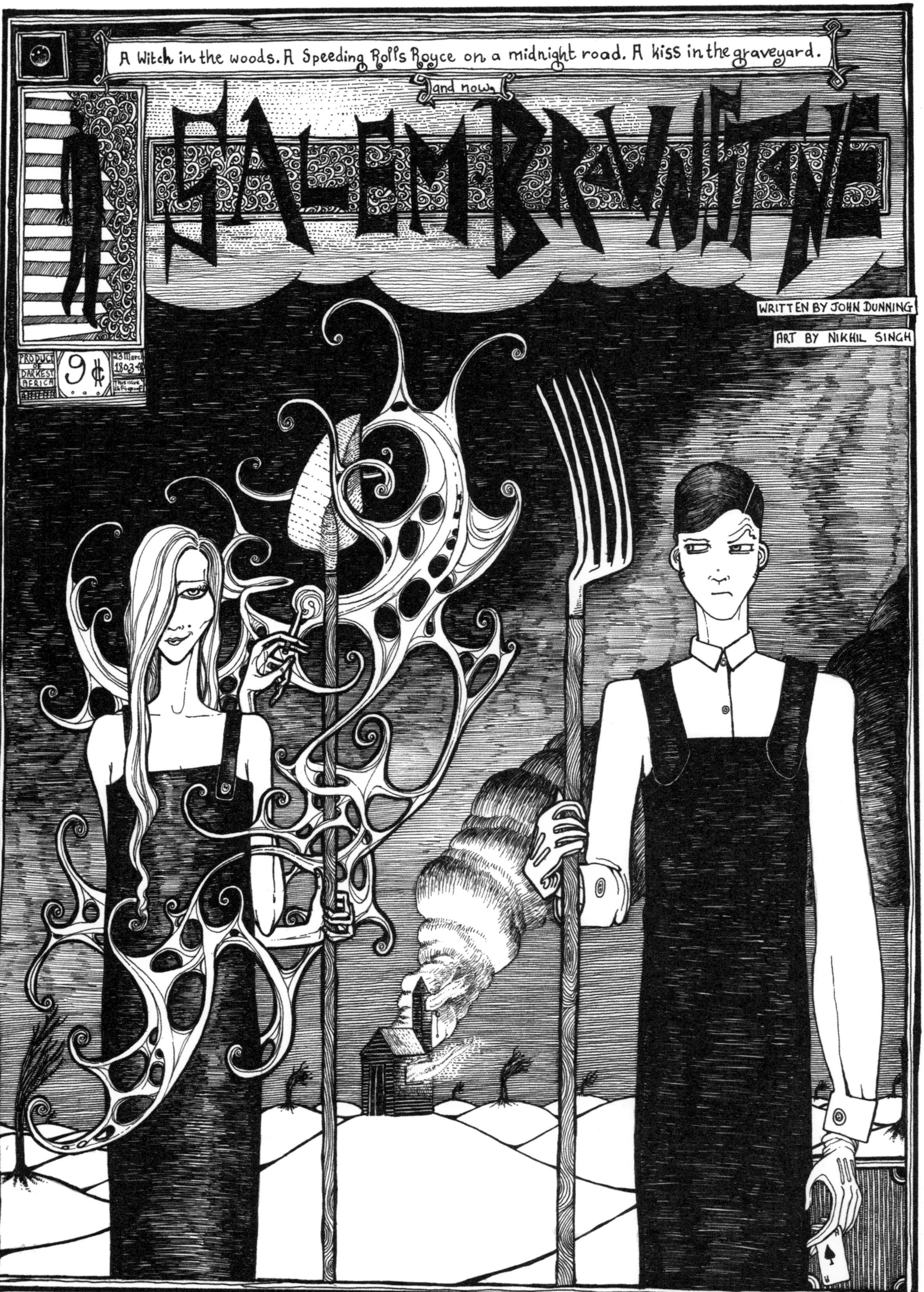

A Witch in the woods. A Speeding Rolls Royce on a midnight road. A kiss in the graveyard.
and now
SALEM BROWNSTONE
WRITTEN BY JOHN DUNNING
ART BY NIKHIL SINGH
PRODUCT OF DARKEST AFRICA
9¢
23 March
This issue is Fireproof

salem brownstone

would like to thank his uncle Paul Gravett; his godparents, Simon Davis and Sylvia Farago; Jefferson Hack; Patrick Insole; Harmony Korine; Fiona McMorrough; Anthony Minghella; Jon Morgan; Mark Sinclair; Lizzie Spratt; and Sarah Such.
Abracadabra!

★ ★ ★

Photo by Matt Hass

john harris dunning

This book is dedicated to Peter Watson, for all your love and support.

I'd like to thank my parents, Carol and Simon Dunning; my sister, Georgia Morris; and the rest of my family. The encouragement of my friends has been invaluable, especially that of Craig Bregman, Alex De Campi, Christian De Sousa, Lisa Cohn, Roland Erasmus, Jo Hebouche, Richard James, Lara Lombaard, Sacha Mardou, Mark Pool, and Rory Stead.

Big up to the Midwich Cuckoos: Dylan, Imogen, and Abigail Morris; Esmé and Milo Davis; Lucas and Max Abelson; Silva De Sousa; Alexander, Daniel, and Thomas Fives; Saffron, Hannah, and Amina Hebouche; Fynn Oldreive; Milo and Hela Watson; and Harvey Yeomans.

★ ★ ★

John Harris Dunning was born in Zululand, South Africa. He now lives in Hampstead, London's most haunted suburb.

Photo by Carmen Williams

nikhil singh

Salem was drawn sporadically over a period of seven years. Consequently, I am obliged to thank a lot of people whose help and assistance were both vital and invaluable.

The first half was drawn at the Daily Deli, 13 Brownlow, Cape Town.
The second half was drawn at 10 Kidderpore Gardens, Hampstead.

CAPE TOWN

Thanks to Melanie for being a guiding light and for showing me how to build the pyramid. Thanks to Angelika for the fireside freakouts — they helped! Thanks to Sinead for keeping me on track. Thanks to Bona for being a sibling. Thanks to Cass for the psychic hotline. Thanks to Elise for the mermaids. Thanks to Gareth for finding the frequency. Thanks to Len for defending humanity. And thanks to Jemstone for always grounding me in the universe.

HAMPSTEAD

Thanks to Pekka for unimaginable support and unshakable faith in rock and roll. Thanks to Simon Psi, the all-seeing eye. Thanks to Alain for popping a cap in Satan's Nazi ass. Thanks to Juan-Erh for the plot on the Orient Express. Thanks to my mom for being a good friend. Thanks to Talitha for the dreams in the doll's house. And special thanks to Carmen, Empress of the two White Cats, for keeping me alive in deep space, guarding the gate to fairyland, and riding the wild white unicorns.

★ ★ ★

Witchboy, were-cat, high-ranking member of the Venusian Secret Service, Nikhil left school at sixteen and has undergone no formal draining at any institutes of higher burning. He currently lives in an ivory tower and is never coming back to your planet EVER AGAIN.

Text copyright © 2010 by John Harris Dunning
Illustrations copyright © 2010 by Nikhil Singh

First U.S. edition 2010

Library of Congress Cataloging-in-Publication Data
Dunning, John Harris.
Salem Brownstone : all along the watchtowers / John Harris Dunning and Nikhil Singh. —1st U.S. ed.
p. cm.
Summary: Upon his father's death, Salem inherits a mansion as well as an unfinished battle
with creatures from another world, which requires him to seek the help of his guardian
familiar and the colorful performers of Dr. Kinoshita's Circus of Unearthly Delights.
ISBN 978-0-7636-4735-3
1. Graphic novels. [1. Graphic novels. 2. Fantasy. 3. Good and evil—Fiction.
4. Magicians—Fiction. 5. Circus performers—Fiction.] I. Singh, Nikhil. II. Title.

PZ7.7.D88Sal 2010
[Fic]—dc22
2009047413

10 11 12 13 14 15 16 ALF 10 9 8 7 6 5 4 3 2 1

Printed in Beijing, China

This book was typeset in Little Grog.
The illustrations were done in pen and ink.

Candlewick Press
99 Dover Street
Somerville, Massachusetts 02144

visit us at www.candlewick.com

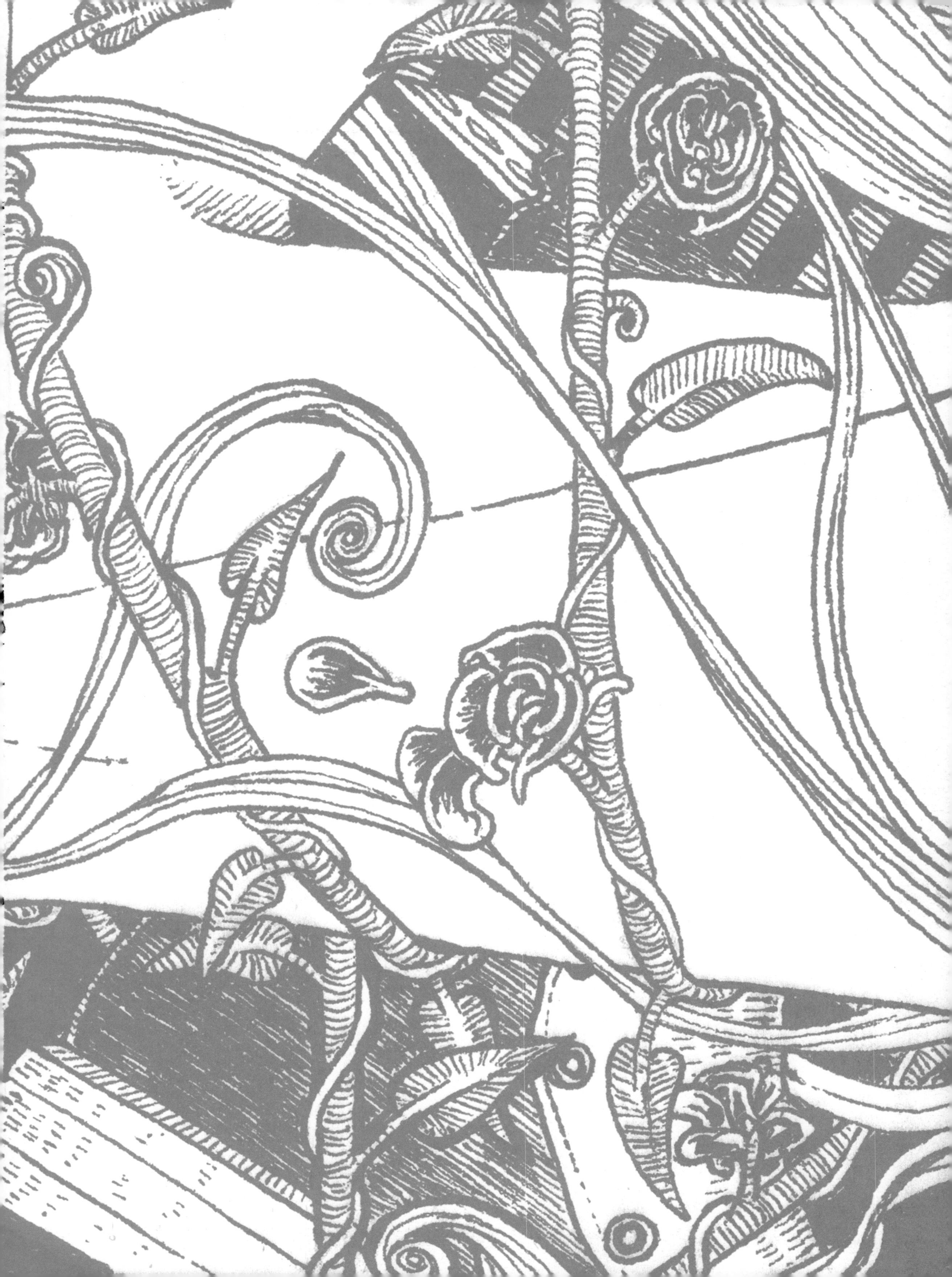

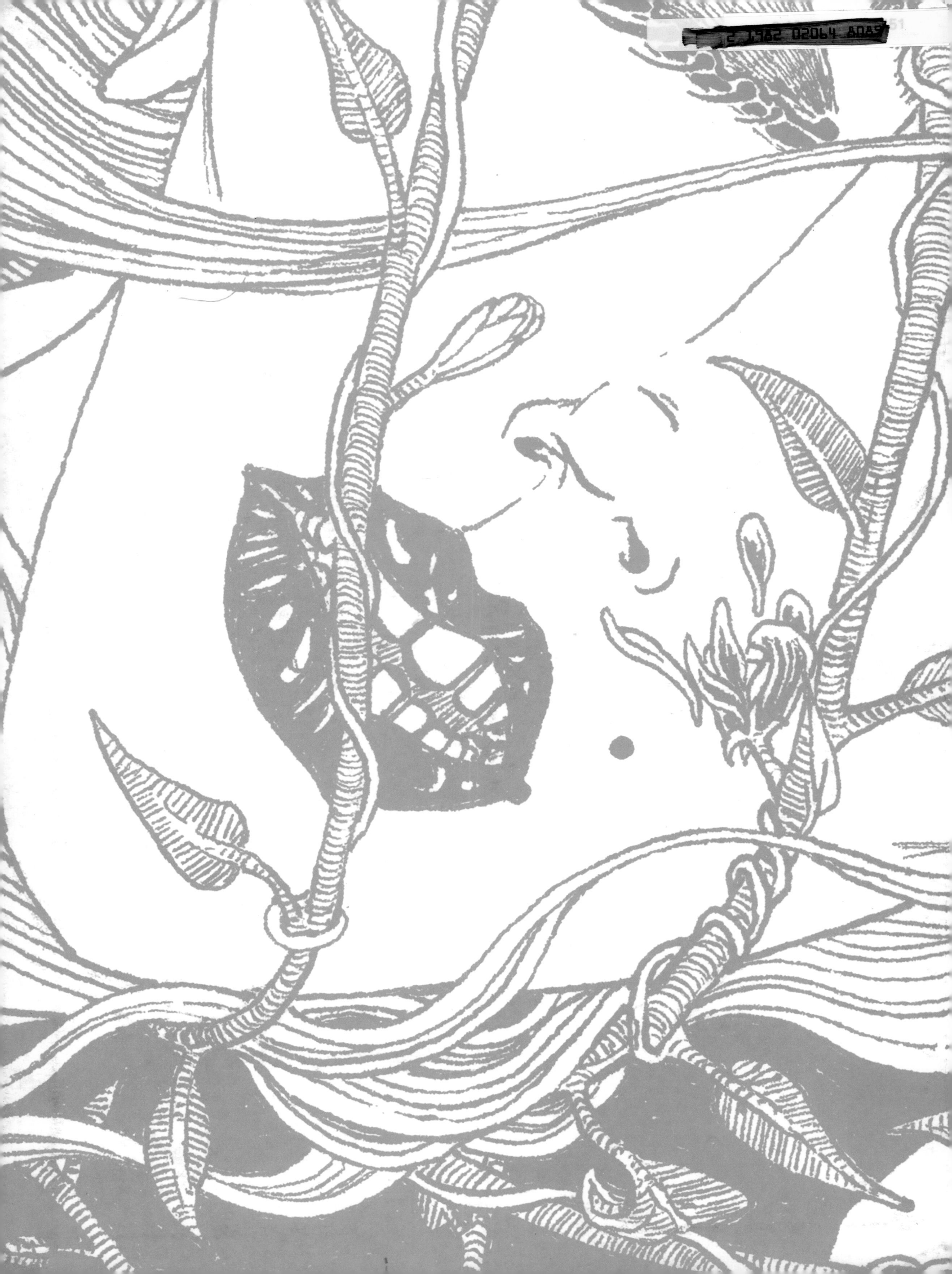